WE SHOULDN'T BE HERE

D K SACHS

We Shouldn't Be Here is a work of fiction. Names, characters, places, and incidents are the products of the author's imagination or are used fictitiously. Any resemblance to actual events, locales, or persons, living or dead, is entirely coincidental.

Copyright © 2021 by D K Sachs

Cover design: Susannah Geremesz

All rights reserved.

No part of this book may be reproduced in any form or by any electronic or mechanical means, including information storage and retrieval systems, without written permission from the author, except for the use of brief quotations in a book review.

❄ Created with Vellum

For my wonderful Boys, the future is yours.
And a special thank you to Louis C. T.
A small salute to your passion for the the internal combustion engine,
an inspiration.

Dear 3o

Wishing you a
wonderful birthday
X

CONTENTS

1

THE CELL

P art I

The room was tiny, the cost could be eternal. What value a simple girl's life compared to the untold legions of brave men who had given theirs' so willingly? Her own brothers too — the tipping point that sent her to this place — a family without food, money, hope. But there was always the Convent, the Sisters would take her in. The novice gazed around the cell. Bare, barren walls, bearing down on her, stern in their condemnation of this girl of fun and laughter. But Clara sensed the rays of hope. There was one small gift she had been allowed to keep, a painting. Sister Bernadette had to give the object her personal benediction, but how could she fail to, it was an icon of the Holy Mother herself, Mary, Mother of Jesus. Unlike the general more fantastical imagery of The Holy Mother, this portrait had a direct simplicity. Mary was garbed in a blue cloak, the edges trimmed with gold, her head covered. Our Lady shone in a halo of light and so did the icon radiating silent beams of belief. Words filled her mind, did she need to speak them out loud? Clara stared into the eyes of the Holy Mother, she hoped she would understand her need, her desperation. Clara had faith, a *Credo* that insisted she was meant for more than the solitary desolation of life in the Convent, the unremitting slaughter of the killing wards. Clara stepped from her simple cot, shivering in the November night she fell to her knees before the icon, bowing her head in supplication.

"Please Holy Mother, allow me to be your servant in some other way. I can no longer bear witness to the daily ritual of death. Mother Mary hear my plea, release me from this place." Clara closed her eyes tight shut, her body quivering with hope, an expectation of some response, a sign. But there was only the silence of the cell.

A mere forty-three minutes later, at 350 kilometres due west of the Convent, a fiery object materialised at a height of 2000 metres. It was travelling at 11944.444 metres per second and heading direct for Swanage Bay, in the county of Dorset. Clara missed the spectacle, her dreams were deep, but a number of fishermen were witness to the ball of flame that crashed into the sea, disappearing in an explosion of water and steam beneath the Channel waves.

2

THE BEACH

Sound was his saviour, a resurrection of sorts. The sonic grace of water lapping lazily against solid rock brought him back. The music in the waves reached out, it sang such a sweet refrain, but you have to know how to listen. He opened his eyes and immediately reached up a hand, searching for the eye that could no longer see. His fingers located a smooth covering fixed tight over the empty socket. The left eye picked out a flourish of activity. He stiffened like a cat, alert to a form approaching out of the darkness. Her appearance was familiar, but there was no name to attach nor facial expression to read, just tiny frown lines creasing her brow as she spoke. "It will heal, there were bigger problems to deal with." She scrutinised his face, analysing every tiny movement. "What's your status?" The female questioned, her eyes squinting tighter, unblinking, like a viper poised to strike. He shook his head hoping the motion might uncover an answer, his mind had yet to reawaken any sense of *self*. "There was an explosion," the female explained, aware of his confusion. "We lost our ship and you became badly damaged. You have no memory of this?" He recognised the desire to converse, to please, but there were no words just his shaking head. "Your communication set is no longer functional we will need to use designations. Your current registration is 0000-8889-4676-1187550-5. I will call you Five, you can address me as Seven. We must find shelter Five then I will explain more. Can you feel your limbs?" Five wriggled his toes, stretched and flexed muscles, he signalled a nod. "There are structures after two hundred metres, stay close, make no sound, and Five remember at all times: we shouldn't be here."

The structures were a series of candy-coloured wooden huts set on concrete just beyond the reach of the highest tide, most of the time anyway, and protected from casual intruders with sturdy steel padlocks. Yale, the brawny metal proclaimed. It immediately succumbed to Seven's touch.

"Lie down." She instructed, the imperative cracked the silence like thunder. Five obeyed without hesitation, carelessly brushing aside the flimsy trestle table and chair he lay flat on the bare wood floor. There was only just enough space to accommodate his long, slender frame. Seven knelt and leaned close across him touching two fingers to his left shoulder. A glow appeared at the point of contact steadily gaining in luminescence, lighting the space around them. Seven stared into his face with laser-like intensity. "Status update," she demanded. Five stared back. He sensed the bond, the instinctive trust, but her question held no meaning. Five shook his head. He witnessed the frown again but this time accompanied by a fractional movement of her head as if to confirm a small disappointment. "I have to go back to the pod. Wait here. Wait for me." Seven instructed. They wouldn't speak again for another ninety-four years.

~

SEVEN PAUSED MOMENTARILY in the silence of the night. She

inhaled deep, imbibing the heady mix of 21% oxygen and 78% nitrogen as well as a variety of other gases. She closed her eyes relishing the abrasive zing of ozone in the breeze — the smell of fresh air. This was all so strange, a hundred and one inconsistencies, but best of all, there was virtually no background radiation? Something was very wrong, in addition to the issues with Five, Seven couldn't connect with Mother. Contact with Source had been offline since the explosion. Seven had assumed it was a problem with the ship, but here on land there should be other nodes to establish a link? They would need help. At least she still had communication with the emergency pod. The pod was located three clicks to the south, two of them underwater. It was the first time Seven ever felt alone. No Mother to talk to, listen to. Follow. Mother was always there to guide her, since the very beginning. But where was Mother now? Seven had to get back to the *E.P.* and recover what she could, even if it was just the transponder and a couple of utility packs. Anything to get them through until Mother came back online with help. Seven set off at a pace, quickly leaving the tidy row of beach huts behind, she made a heading for the horizon of sand dunes and a little night-time camouflage. Many of her suit's sensors had been damaged in the crash. The proximity detectors were gone and she had to rely on eyes and ears to ensure no one else was around. She found a secluded vantage point among the spindly vines of grass and crouched on the cold sand. That was when she looked up. The cloud cover had finally cleared. Seven could study the stars. She knew almost every glittering point of light if not by name then by location. One in particular, it shone with a distinctly tainted glow, an incandescent intensity, burning like an angry red eye in the ink of night. It was clear there was something more than odd about their situation and the red planet confirmed it. Seven thrilled with memory — the giddy rush of low gravity jaunts across endless crater sands. Mars had been where Seven learned to fly, and by the positions of the stars and planets, this could only be Earth. But not an Earth Seven recognised. The outline of a forested hilltop caught her attention. Healthy trees growing wild? It made no sense. Seven frowned and shook her head, she had to prepare herself for the swim back to the pod.

IT WAS a couple of hours later when Seven dragged her exhausted, aching body out of the water and back onto the relative solidity of the gritty, wet sand. It felt good to be out of the sea. The swim out was easy enough, but the return journey with two utility packs and a transponder weighing her down required an almost Herculean effort, but physical strength was part of her makeup, as well as a dogged, *do or die* mindset. She lay on her back, the sand and waves tugging at her to return, but as the rush of tide receded she felt the heavy footsteps pounding in her direction. She was no longer alone.

"All right, what's going' on?" An unidentified voice demanded. A dazzling bright light beamed down on her.

"Stand and identify yourself." Another voice insisted. Seven raised a hand to shield her eyes.

"An' no funny business." Said the first voice.

"I think it's a woman." A third man declared and shone another intense light on her.

Seven slowly stood from the sand, giving herself time to assess the situation. She quickly scanned the trio. They gathered in a loose semi-circle around her, three men clad in blue uniforms with silver buttons, their heads adorned with domed helmets. Seven was an easy six inches taller than the tallest and she possessed a wealth of physical advantages, but best of all, she could listen to their thoughts with ease. A blessing of her time and situation. The officers' minds rattled with suspicion, misogyny, and latent aggression. They carried ancient bolt action carbines pointed as one in her direction. The men were confident, dangerous, and venal as feral felines.

"What's yer business?" The first voice demanded, the man in charge, the sergeant. He gestured with his rifle, tilted accusingly at her belly.

"My ship, it sank. I had to swim to the shore." Seven replied. She recognised the language, 20th century English. The three men continued to slowly encircle her, taking final positions, always maintaining a careful distance. Seven felt her muscles relax in preparation, her mind calculating the moves to bring the men down.

"She's a right funny looker Sarge, she got no 'air. You reckon she be foreign?" Wondered Butler, the second in command.

"Where are you from? And what's in them silver boxes?" The sergeant demanded taking a step closer.

"I could open them for you?" Seven offered, along with a bright and breezy tone.

"Go on then, but don't try nothin', we don't carry these guns just to look fancy."

Seven feigned to bend towards the boxes, but abruptly she launched herself at the sergeant, a leap to make any tiger proud. She crushed her legs around his neck and as the sergeant stumbled and fell she caught Butler with a brutal rabbit punch. He tumbled to the ground fighting for breath. A swift kick to the head finished off number three, Taylor. But it was the fourth man, Perkins, the one she didn't see, who cracked her head open with his ancient Lee Enfield rifle butt.

3

THE CONVENT

The hut owner found him several hours later. Five was already unconscious and close to death, but in the act of dying, his mind did what all minds do; it flashed a kaleidoscope of memories at him. Five had the infinite hours of the quantum universe to make sense of the burst of random images. Time stood still, put out to furlough, seconds stretched into eternity. He walked among trees, huge and majestic, to stand in wonder, to feel the still of blissful peace within the silent sanctity of the forest. Before crashing through surf and giant waves, tasting the salt, the spray, the exhilaration. And music; an intoxication of glorious sound filled his senses with exquisite pleasure.

"Sister Bernadette, come quick. He smiled, I'm sure of it. His lips moved, just for a second." Sister Bernadette swished over to Sister Clara, who stood shaking with anticipation and the possibility she might have just saved a life.

"Oh he did, did he?" Sister Bernadette was born a sceptic. Though her faith had instructed her not to be a *doubting Thomas* for some reason that particular doctrine failed to take root, she doubted by default. "So you're declaring a twitch of the lips in a man who has been at death's very door for the last ten hours to be a full-blown smile? Are ya?"

"He smiled. I saw it." Declared Sister Clara, and with that the almost deceased patient smiled again. They weren't to know his mind was bathing in the joy of Whitney Huston's "*I'm Every Woman*", this was 1919 after all, and Whitney's mother wasn't due to be born for another fourteen years, but both sisters saw the smile, only Five heard the music.

"Holy Mother of God." Sister Bernadette confirmed as Five opened his one good eye.

The Sisters of Mercy were exactly as their name described, dedicated to God and the dispatch of the terminally ill. They provided a most vital service in this time of National need and crisis. First the Great War, and now a flu epidemic, the bodies were stacking up. This was no time for sentiment, let nature run its course with the help of a couple of generous morphine shots, just to make sure. But Sister Clara wasn't going to let this one slip away like all the others. "It's a kindness, they'd thank you for it if they could." Were familiar reassurances, but like Sister Bernadette's catechism, her fateful words failed to mould Sister Clara's will. He wasn't going to die in this place, not under her watch.

IT BEGAN THE DAY BEFORE. "Look at this 'un Clara." Maud declared in a hissed, excited tone. "'E ain't got no 'air, anywhere." Maud giggled.

Sister Clara quickly joined her friend at the bedside. She looked down on him and that was when she first started to shake. He was simply so beautiful, so perfect. A wonderfully proportioned specimen of a tall, athletic man in his twenties. But he had absolutely no hair, none on his body, his head, not even his face. Nothing. And there wasn't a single mark or blemish anywhere — they both had a good look — the only damage was to the right-hand side of his face and that was a terrible mess. She suspected at once, who, or more precisely, what, he might be; he was clearly an angel crashed to Earth, and he was hers.

FIVE SLOWLY MOVED HIS HEAD, it was less painful than trying to roll his eye. He was surrounded by a throng of people dressed in white, head to toe, females. He found a smile.

"Look, he's smiling again." Declared a voice followed by a chorus of unintelligible cooing sounds.

"Now get back, all of yas. I don't know what's got inta ya. Have ya not see a man wake up before?"

Not in this place, thought Sister Clara, but said nothing.

"Can ya hear me lad?" Demanded Sister Bernadette.

Five heard the authority in her tone and made a dutiful nod. A small flurry of excitement passed around the assembled Sisters.

"Aah," the big Sister announced, "you really are a live one then, what's your name son?"

Five shook his head.

"All right, we can return to that. I'm sure the boyyo's ready for some food, Sister Clara? He's your patient, get him some thin soup and bread. And the rest of ya can get about your business. We have God's work to do. Amen Sisters."

"Amen Sister Bernadette." The nuns chorused.

EATING WAS a word Five understood in concept, but it was only after he had sampled solid food that it finally held meaning. Thin soup was his introduction. He hadn't eaten organic nourishment since reaching physical maturity. He never had to, his suit took care of all bodily functions including sustenance. But that's where the problems began. He no longer wore his suit, nor did he have any idea where it might be? His garments now comprised a pair of coarse cotton striped pyjamas with bottoms that finished just below his knees. The patient was unaware of the clothing faux-pas. It took no more than thirty seconds for his stomach to reject the proteins, carbohydrates, and a host of minerals the nurse had urged him to ingest. The rejection was quite emphatic and took everyone by surprise. But Clara understood, it was like being born again, after all, he was an Angel. Clara saw in the moment what had happened. The Holy Mother had listened, Clara had been given a unique opportunity to serve, she would make the world known to him. Her Angel. He was Clara's release.

4

CUSTOMS AND EXCISE

The old coast guard station was their official home; a sergeant and three constables charged with patrolling the many miles of picture-perfect Dorset coastline in their demanding role, protecting the solid citizens from invasion while soundly asleep in their beds. Taylor crashed the hammer against the first of Seven's silver boxes, but it made not the least impression, not a single mark. "What the bloody-'ell is this made of? Not even a scratch."

"Let's wake 'er Sarge? Make her open 'em up?" Suggested Butler with enthusiasm.

The sergeant grunted agreement and walked over to peer through the heavy iron bars. They'd handcuffed Seven to the bed frame in the first of three cells. Someone had thoughtfully tied a dishcloth bandage around her wound. The flow of blood had been a torrent, but it finally stopped. Seven was still unconscious from the blow, she lay completely immobile.

"Maybe she's Russian... you know, one of them 'reds', a communist?" Declared Butler with emphasis.

"She ain't got no eyebrows." Observed Taylor. "Could be a sign of bein' Russian?"

"What? Russians don't 'ave no eyebrows?" Butler was surprised.

"I dunno? Just sayin'," muttered Taylor.

"She can speak English well enough." Observed the sergeant.

"Yeah, but if she was one of those 'commie' infiltrators, a spy, well she would wouldn't she? Just look at 'er. She ain't one of us that's for sure. Would you want your missus looking like that? No bloody 'air, no eyebrows." Butler paused in reflection. "I wonder what she got down there... you know... her privates?"

The four men paused as one to consider the statement. "We could 'ave a look? No one would know." Suggested Taylor.

"I reckon she'll be smooth as a billiard ball, no 'air, nothin'. We should 'ave a gander fa' sure. What da ya think Sarge? I'll put a shilling on it." Butler declared with relish.

The sergeant paused, weighing up possibilities. Four years of war had pushed his moral compass into waters far removed from the straight and narrow. "Bearing in mind we fished 'er out of the sea, only seems proper to put 'er in somethin' warm and dry... What've we got by way of warm and dry Perkins?"

"There's cotton long johns, vests, and blankets in the store-room Sarge."

"Right-o, that's what we'll do, get 'er all cleaned up. Wrap 'er up in sumthin' nice and warm eh? I'll take your shilling as well Butler. Perkins, you nip down the storeroom sharpish lad. Taylor and Butler, you're with me, we'll sort 'er together. Smooth as a billiard ball eh? Let's find out." The sergeant rattled the key into the lock and with a practiced twist, clanked the heavy iron mechanism open. The sergeant removed the key, making it swing like a pendulum between his fingers as he walked over to Seven. He stopped at the iron bed frame observing the body prostrate before him. He could see clearly she had the curved form of a female, not that he was an expert, but he recognised

the swell of hips and breasts. These Russian women were quite
something. He'd never before witnessed anyone move or fight
with such incredible speed. He drew the tip of the iron key
lightly up her thigh. There was no movement, not the least
twitch of a muscle. He felt quite safe anyway, she was wearing
his own, personal set of handcuffs, and they were securely
fastened to the bed frame. That should slow her down he mused
and made a small contented sound at the back of his throat.
"Hmm."

There was no pain, her suit took care of that. Seven could
feel a slight tingling around the wound, the crack in her skull,
that would be the nano-bots doing their work. She'd be good as
new in no time, but she'd lost a lot of blood and all she could do
for the moment was listen, and wait.

The sergeant left the key resting on her hip. He was
surprised the Russian woman showed no response, she was
surely out cold, Perkins must be tougher than he looked. A slip
of a boy. He was the newest recruit to the force, barely sixteen
and green as a blade of grass. Perkins was different to the other
three, he'd never seen the trenches, the appalling, mindless
slaughter — he'd never been taught to disrespect human life —
Perkins was still an innocent, time enough to educate him into
the ways of the world. The Sergeant returned his attention to the
prospect before him. He moved the key across her torso, nothing. He could feel his blood rising, the prod of an erection, the
man in charge was feeling increasingly bold, a conqueror, a
hero. He ran the key across her breast. Still no reaction. Bolder
still, he reached out his hand and touched the fabric of her
costume. He thought it might be some kind of rubber? It had
that flexible, moulded appearance. A proper skin-like fit, and
blue, a beautiful deep blue. There were rips in the material. She
must have snagged the outfit on the abrasive, razor-sharp rocks
that ringed the beach. He pulled out his knife. There was a tear

just by her foot with a tiny piece of fabric dangling, hanging by a
thread he couldn't even see. The Sergeant took a fierce pride in
the Bowie-knife he carried at the back of his belt, but even with
a freshly honed blade he experienced considerable resistance.
The sergeant wasn't the sort of man to give in, he was eventually
rewarded with a sample piece the size of a postage stamp. It
went safe in his pocket.

"What da ya reckon then Sarge? Shall we 'ave a bit of a
looksee?" Suggested Butler.

"Yeah why not. Come an' give me an 'and to get her costume
off. I can't see no buttons, we might have to cut it off 'er."

Seven understood this was her moment. The handcuffs were
easy, no lock could defy her. She scanned the mechanism and
the bots did the rest, a single click and her power was unleashed.
The officers didn't have a chance. She noted the complete
surprise as she snatched the precious knife and plunged it deep
into the sergeant's stomach, a blow designed to disable not kill,
the man in charge was destined to suffer more. Taylor and
Butler turned and ran to the door of the cell. In a second Seven
was behind and helping them find an exit. She pushed their
heads all the way through the bars of the cell. Their skulls shattered in an explosion of blood, brains, and bone. The detached
lifeless bodies slumped to the ground. The sergeant lay groan-
ing, writhing in fearsome agonies on the bed, his favourite blade
protruding from deep in his gut, he dared not try to move it.
Seven approached him slowly, there was no imperative to spare
his suffering. She reached up and retrieved the handcuffs.

"Please. Have mercy on me. I don't want to die." The sergeant
implored, failing to identify the warm wash of urine careening
down his leg.

Seven studied the dying man impassively. "I take no pleasure
in the removal of life. Often there is necessity, rarely is it a pleasure. However, this is one of those special moments when I can

clearly state that every quantum of pain and degradation I can bring to your final moments of existence will fill me with a deep satisfaction." Seven slowly and cruelly extracted the knife from his belly. The sergeant cried out in torment. "I heard what your mind had to say Sergeant, what it said about me. Vile, perverse things Sergeant. I know who you are, what you and your men planned to do, and I want you conscious and aware this is the moment your life ended." Seven thrust the handcuffs into his face, stuffing his mouth with cold steel, like cramming fist-fulls of greedy doughnuts. Her hands mostly muffled his cries, but his eyes were wild with fear, erupting in blood and pain as she pushed and pushed and pushed through the soft, fleshy tissue of his throat, onto the nerves and solid bone of his spinal column. The sergeant screeched his final agony as frigid metal smashed through bone and cartilage, severing his spine and nearly detaching his head. Seven looked down on the bloody corpse and found a small contented sound at the back of her throat — "Hmm" — the sergeant's parting gift, a momento. She turned to see Perkins clutching a bundle of clothes and blankets at the cell door. The boy shook like a spindly sunflower in a storm.

"P, p, please Miss, don't kill me. My father and brothers are all gone, killed in the Great War. I'm all Mother has left." Perkins stammered. Seven had no concept of mercy, but the mention of Mother caused her to pause. The boy still clutched his pathetic bundle, the shaking was getting progressively worse. "I could help you. I, I, I can give you all manner of information. I can be useful."

"Do you have handcuffs?" Her tone was impassive. Perkins made emphatic nods. "Put them on." Perkins dropped the bundle of clothes and despite the impossibilities of shaking hands, he managed to click on the handcuffs. "Sit." She instructed. Perkins immediately sat where he stood, on the floor. "What is the date?" Seven questioned.

"Ninth of November Miss."

"What year?"

"1919 Miss. Almost exactly a year after the Great War ended Miss."

Seven should have been more surprised than she was, but somehow it made sense. It would seem they'd skipped back in time three hundred and thirty-six years. "How do you think you can help me?" Seven demanded.

"I can tell you things. Help you fit in." Perkins insisted.

"Fit in?" Seven frowned.

"You don't look right Miss. Folks will spot you a mile off." Perkins declared with fervour.

"Hmm." Said Seven, revelling again in that soft contented sound.

5

RIGHT SIR

Detective Inspector Hadleigh was a popular man. Fellows doffed hats when they passed him in the street, ladies smiled shyly. He'd been a celebrated athlete before the war, winning medals for fencing, rowing, and climbing mountains. A superb and acclaimed pianist, he also read Classics at Oxford, and when the war began, he volunteered without hesitation and rapidly rose to the rank of Captain. In battle he was heroic, a leader of men, until the Somme, which took away his right arm and everything he loved.

"Come in Hadleigh, please, take a seat." The commander's office was always shaded in a penumbra of darkness, ever since his encounter with a phosphorous bomb. Detective Inspector Hadleigh, wearing the title of his new rank and position, made himself comfortable in the mahogany and leather chair across the desk from Commander Thompson. They shared common ground as heroes and victims alike.

"I want you to go down to Swanage Hadleigh, there's been a fire at the old customs house, four men dead. It would seem at face value to be a terrible tragedy, but the circumstances are quite bizarre; three of the bodies were badly mutilated. I'm afraid it doesn't make much sense and I'd like some answers. There were reports of a meteor or possibly a small plane crashing into the sea earlier that night. Our men were all armed, they went to investigate, and now they're dead. I need to know what happened Hadleigh. We can't have four inexplicable police deaths remain unexplained. I've asked the press to keep a lid on it. Report only to me Hadleigh, not a word to anyone else, especially any damn journalist."

"Of course Sir. Who reported the fire?"

"The publican of the Ship and Bell. He smelt the smoke in the early hours of the morning and he has a telephone in his establishment. I've laid on a car and driver for you. I would appreciate it if you could prioritise this case and make haste to Swanage today, there's something very odd about this."

"Where are the bodies, Sir?"

"The local undertaker has them, a Mr. Percy, he's expecting you. The coffins are sealed. You should prepare yourself, the injuries were quite horrific, so I'm told."

"Very good Sir, I'll get down to Swanage right away. What's the name of my driver?"

"Betts, and she's a woman. How the world's changing eh?"

"Indeed Sir."

"THAT'S A VERY fine Wolseley motor you have there, is it the four-cylinder or six-cylinder model?"

"It's the six-cylinder, 30/40 HP, electric starter and electric lighting. A fine machine. You must be Inspector Hadleigh Sir?"

"Well deduced, and you must be Betts. Maybe you should be a detective too?"

"They'd never allow it Sir, the only role we're permitted as mere females is to drive you gents around."

Hadleigh laughed. "Do I detect a hint of irritation in your tone?"

"Not at all, Sir. I'm very happy to be of service. Are you ready for the off?"

"Absolutely Betts, let's go to Swanage."

THE MORTUARY ROOM was bitterly cold. Of course it had to be, dead bodies and a warm environment rarely make a happy coupling. Hadleigh and Betts had first visited the old customs building, but there was little left to examine. The station was nothing more than a smouldering ruin. Hadleigh hoped to find something of greater significance in the undertaker's morgue.

"Thank you Mr Percy, and you can confirm, the bodies are in exactly the same order as when they were found?"

"Yes sir, I haven't done anything with them. As instructed." Added Mr. Percy.

"Good, thank you. There's no necessity for you to remain while we conduct our examination."

"Very good Sir, I'll leave you to it then."

Mr. Percy had thoughtfully provided the Detective Inspector with a jemmy. Hadleigh passed it to Betts. "Would you mind?" Hadleigh asked.

"No problem Sir." And Betts set about opening the first casket. It was an ordeal for them both. Three of the bodies had been brutalised in the extreme. The violence was visible even beyond the immolation, but the discovery of the handcuffs, still wedged in the jawbone and head of the sergeant was the strangest and most deeply unsettling sight either of them had ever witnessed.

"Could it have been an explosion Sir? Maybe some ammunition went off and blew the handcuffs into his face?"

"That's certainly a plausible conclusion Betts. Excellent, but of equal possibility, it might have been someone with enormous strength and murderous intent? Either option is equally bizarre."

"What about the fourth victim Sir, Perkins? It looks like his neck was snapped."

"At least he was spared the brutality, or it could have happened in the fire I suppose? Falling masonry perhaps? We should check through what's left of their garments."

"What about this Sir?" Betts held up the tiny fragment of blue material. "Somehow it survived the flames, it was likely to have been in the sergeant's pocket."

"Was there anything else from his pockets?"

"No Sir, only this."

"What sort of fabric is it?" Hadleigh requested.

"I have no idea Sir; but it seems very tough. It's also quite soft and pliable as well. And vibrantly blue, the colour is electric."

"Let me have a closer look." Hadleigh took the cloth fragment and held it up to the light examining the fabric's texture. He placed it on the undertaker's metal examination table and removed a large magnifying glass from his coat pocket. Betts laughed. "I'm a detective Betts, have you never read Sherlock Holmes?"

"Can't say I have Sir."

"Well trust me, the magnifying glass is an essential part of the investigators' toolkit, you'll be amazed at what this piece of glass can reveal." Hadleigh studied the fabric intently. "Do you by chance have a pair of tweezers about you Betts?"

"Yes Sir."

Hadleigh took the tweezers and pulled at a tiny bundle of strands. "Hmm." He commented. "Have a look."

Betts leaned over the table and peered through the magnifying glass. "What am I looking at Sir?"

"You're looking at a strand of fabric quite unlike anything I have ever witnessed? It even has writing on it."

Betts returned her gaze to the magnifying glass, "Oh my, yes, you're right, there are numbers, I can make out 2225. What does it mean Sir?"

"I'm not sure, but the more we look the stranger it gets. I have contacts still at Oxford, I'd rather like to run it by one of them and see what she thinks? That's what I love about Oxford, there's always a someone there to turn to in the critical hour of need. Boffins to the man, or woman I should really say. McGuinness will love the challenge. I think we're done here Betts, for the moment at least, Oxford is our next destination."

"Right Sir."

6

SISTER CLARA

The idea came to Sister Clara while she slept — maybe another angel's divine intervention? But more importantly, when she awoke she remembered what to do.

"How are you feeling today." She asked gently and wondered what it would be like to cradle his head in her arms. Five struggled to even twitch. Clara could sense the pain coursing through him, becoming human was surely going to be a difficult path? She had to find a way to help. Clara leaned close. "You understand me? Don't you?" He moved his eye. The young novice looked over her shoulder to ensure there were no other sisters within sight, in fact, anyone likely to observe her and what she was about to do. Clara was about to break the rules. "Do you know how to write?" Clara questioned and her patient blinked. "Here." Clara materialised a pencil and notebook from the folds of her habit and put them beside his hand. "Write down what you need. I can help you. But just you and me, you understand? This has to be our secret." He twitched his eye but he was fading fast. Clara realised she had to act now, in this very moment, or he would be beyond help. She knelt beside the bed as if in prayer. "Trust me," she uttered in a breath and taking his hand in hers, she put the pencil between his fingers and opened the notebook. "Tell me what to do." Clara hissed. His hand shook violently with the intense effort. *'Suit'*. He wrote before sinking back onto the stiff pillow. Sister Clara crossed herself and declared, "Amen," out loud.

It was pure luck someone hadn't already found a use for it. It was certainly damaged with two great rips in the fabric as well as scorch marks, but the deep blue colour was magnificent, rich, powerful. It would make a bold, eye-catching addition to adorn any party dress. But what use are dresses to Nuns? And as for parties, they were something Clara could only read about. People of her station in life simply didn't have or even get invited to parties, they were too busy surviving. That was how she ended up with the Sisters, there was nowhere else to go.

THE TRANSFORMATION WAS REMARKABLE. Clara didn't ask how he got the suit on, or why he didn't overheat wearing the thick pyjamas as well, but within just a couple of days her patient's recovery was palpable; even the network of scars and damaged flesh that covered half his face had started to fade. Clara was elated, but not alone in her observations.

"Sister Clara, do come and join us. I would like you to share in the good news, after all, along with our Blessed Mother the holy Virgin herself, you must surely take some wee credit for your man's remarkable progress? So, there we have it. As I was just about to explain, your man here's made such a fantastic recovery, they're transferring him to a military hospital in Aldershot."

"Aldershot? Where's Aldershot?" Demanded a shocked Clara.

"Berkshire I believe is the County in question." Responded Sister Bernadette with a satisfied smirk that curled her lip.

It was as if her legs had become jelly, Sister Clara struggled to remain standing, but she knew only too well not to reveal her existential distress. "When do you think...?"

"Thursday morning, nine o'clock sharp" Announced Sister Bernadette, cutting Clara's words like an editor's knife.

Clara felt the prick of tears, "Praise the Lord" she declared and fell to her knees with hands clasped.

"Amen Sister Clara" chimed Sister Bernadette. "Make sure the boyyo understands how lucky he is?" Sister Bernadette swished away.

Where was Berkshire Clara wondered? Five scribbled a note and pressed it to her hand '*92.7 miles NE*'. Their eyes locked.

"Can you hear me?" Clara thought. He made a nod. "Can you hear them?" Clara cast her eyes to the ward. Another nod. He scribbled a new note and pressed it to her palm.

'They plan to experiment on me, I will not survive.' Clara felt the visceral chill of fear course through her. She began to shiver and didn't stop until Five reached out to hold her hand. Clara was his only hope, and they had two days.

7

OXFORD

The Wolseley was indeed a fine motor. The six-cylinder engine powered the trip up to Oxford with comfortable ease. Betts managed a dizzying sixty miles an hour on a stretch of straight, open road. Undoubtedly an old Roman route leading to the classical spires of Oxford and specifically, St John's College.

It was some years since Hadleigh last visited his former Alma Mater. Of course, nothing had changed. That was the wonderful thing about England, so many aspects of her vibrant past were still pretty much as they used to be and St John's was no exception. It was originally founded in 1555 by Sir Thomas White, a supporter of Queen Mary and the counter-reformation, and as one might expect emerging from such stalwart religious foundations, the college was blessed with one of the most celebrated chapels and choirs in Oxford. Betts parked the Wolseley on the high road and Hadleigh led the way to the Front Quadrangle and the Porter's Lodge.

"Captain Hadleigh Sir, it's so good to see you, it's been far too long." The porter smiled broadly.

"Indeed it has Briars. No longer a Captain though, it's Detective Inspector now." He laughed quickly. "Allow me to introduce my colleague, this is Miss Betts."

"Very pleased to make your acquaintance Ma'am. How may I assist the pair of you?"

"I was hoping to catch up with one of my associates from those far-off days of yore? She has a position here in Chemistry, Dr. McGuinness?"

"Aah of course Sir. I'll walk the two of you over to the labs."

"JOHN!" Dr. McGuinness exclaimed and flung her arms around his neck. Betts witnessed the stiff, awkward response from Hadleigh, he struggled with the tender embrace. Dr. McGuinness removed her arms and took a step back to study him. "You're looking very well John, how's life treating you?"

"I get by, you know me Rose, a survivor through and through. Allow me to introduce you to my colleague, this is Miss Betts." The two women shook hands with polite, but wary decorum. "I'm here to ask a favour, Rose?" Hadleigh continued.

"Of course John, how can I help?"

"We're following up leads on a rather bizarre case, four deaths and a fire, which looks now to have been deliberate, but there are no clues as to the perpetrators nor any discernible motive. We have however, uncovered one mysterious piece of evidence, and it would be good to have your expert opinion on exactly what it might be?"

"Well it's most kind of you to say *expert* John, I'll have to do my very best to justify such praise." Quipped Dr. McGuinness with a laugh

DR. MCGUINNESS delicately held the cloth fragment between thumb and forefinger before presenting it up to the light, exactly as Hadleigh had earlier, however, the Dr's microscope was considerably more sophisticated than Hadleigh's pocket magnifying glass. Dr. McGuinness carefully removed a Carl Zeiss Binocular Compound Microscope from its neat wooden box. "*The eye through which I see God is the same eye through which God sees me.*" Dr. McGuinness recited, looking squarely at Hadleigh.

"*My eye and God's eye are one eye, one seeing, one knowing, one love.*" Completed Hadleigh with a smile. "The sermons of Meister Eckhart." Hadleigh explained to Betts, "St John's is a highly religious establishment."

"Well this is quite fascinating, where did you find this?" Dr. McGuinness commented, her eyes fixed like limpets to the lenses.

"In the pocket of one of the deceased." Replied Betts.

"Who was this person?" Asked the doctor.

"A police sergeant." Hadleigh's turn to respond.

Dr. McGuinness had no intention of removing her gaze from the 'scope, but her ability to talk remained unimpaired, she continued to observe. "Well, your police sergeant was in possession of something quite extraordinary. I have genuinely never seen anything like this, nor do I pretend to know who might have made it? It has the appearance of incredibly fine, synthetic sheets folded over and over, like the steel of a Japanese Samurai sword. There is no doubt it was manufactured, but further analysis is beyond the capabilities of my Zeiss. The symmetry is so absolutely perfect it cannot have come from nature. If I were to hazard an opinion, I would say it is a form of incredibly thin carbon. That would certainly be my first guess, but at the moment any conjecture is no more than an initial impression. Aah, I see the writing you mentioned. Oh Lord, that cannot be?" Dr. McGuinness drew back from the microscope shaking her head, scrunching her eyes tight together, before addressing Hadleigh. "I do apologise John, I just want to be sure, expert and all," she announced with a noticeable twitch and quickly returned her gaze to the lens. Dr. McGuinness said nothing further for a long moment, the doctor of science was totally absorbed in her observations, she was momentarily beyond words. "Those numbers?" She finally announced, "there are more you know, a complete sequential string. I think I have an idea what they might be? It's a patent John, actually there's no question, it's the standard format. And those original numbers you identified, 2225?" Dr. McGuinness lifted her eyes from the microscope and sought Hadleigh's. "That was the year of registration."

8

YOU DON'T FIT IN

The statement rebounded around her thought processes like a squash ball. Perkins was right; Seven had to do something about her appearance, she had to find a way to blend in. And in the same breath, she couldn't afford to leave any trails. Her intention had been to simply burn the police station and its deceased occupants to the ground — destroy any possibility of evidence — but while the old building stood she might yet find a solution to the other tricky problem — fitting in. There was surely something in the station to help? She scrutinised her surroundings. Photographs from the front page of the Daily Mail called out from the sergeant's desk. She scoured the newspaper searching for more pictures. All the females within had hair and lots of it; bundled high on heads, or in fulsome, shoulder-length waves. The current styles were certainly not in her favour, and absolutely everyone had eyebrows. Seven found a shaving mirror in the washroom, she studied herself in the speckled glass. An idea formed. The embers of a fire glowed faintly in the fireplace. Seven retrieved a small piece of charcoaled wood that had fallen onto the hearth and rubbed some of the soot with a dash of saliva in the palm of her hand, transferring the residue to her eyebrow line. She studied the transformation, it was surprisingly dramatic, and above all, effective. Maybe with a hat and appropriate clothing she could blend in with a degree of the desired anonymity? That was the plan anyway, along with going back for Five, but here and now Seven urgently needed appropriate female attire; clothing, shoes and a hat. It was unlikely she would find such garments in a police station.

All was quiet and still outside the station house, the blanket of silence that characterised the early morning hours hung heavy over the abandoned streets and alleyways. Seven had the run of the town, there were certainly no police around to foil her plans. She moved with the stealth of a predator advancing quickly up the High Street until she found an establishment suited to her needs. Seven peered into a large window display, studying the trio of mannequins sporting the latest fashions. A placard mounted on a tripod proclaimed: *Hanbury's, Stylish Ladies' Clothing.* Seven unlocked the door and stepped inside, she had no idea what she was looking for, but there were many more human dummies exhibiting garments designed for a variety of purposes; garden parties, afternoon tea, the races? This was an establishment clearly catering for the well-to-do in society, and of course, a mode of life completely alien to Seven. She inspected the full array of garments the figures wore in analytical detail and with growing alarm. It wasn't just a single garment, the women of this time were expected to wear a litany of awkward clothing items. The shelves behind the counter were neatly arranged with a cornucopia of folded underwear. Seven made selections and began to dress where she stood, in the middle of the shop floor. She kept on her suit, which was indispensable, but as for her newly acquired outfit and sundry accessories, she could only approximate at getting the mix right. Seven studied herself in the mirror. She looked ridiculous, like a penguin in a tutu, but it would have to do, she simply didn't know any better. While selecting a suitably wide-brimmed hat, Seven spied another sign — *Wigs, Real Human Hair*? An organic mix of carbon, oxygen, nitrogen, hydrogen and sulphur, the hair shaft itself formed from keratin. She followed the promise. A wall of brushed, lustrous locks confronted her, so many styles and colours to choose? But flowing auburn tresses were the easy decision, they complemented the two-piece blue jacket and long skirt. And to finish; a stylish green coat, stretching almost all the way down to her ankles and feet, adorned with a pair of patent black shoes — small heel. Seven hoped she would pass muster in the street, but distance was probably her best ally. She re-locked the shop door and stepped back into the night. A rather odd-looking twentieth-century lady, but Seven no longer felt the need to crouch in doorways.

Setting fire to the police station was satisfying and quite spectacular. The blaze quickly took hold, acrid grey smoke billowed from the windows as the glass cracked, splintered, and shattered. Seven was mesmerised by the spectacle. She paused for several minutes to watch the conflagration, accompanied by a pale, early morning sun, rising steadily through the veil of smoke. The day was about to start and there would be people milling around, she had to recover Five before he was discovered. Seven walked at a brisk pace and arrived at the beach promenade without incident or unfortunate encounters, but as she neared the beach huts, she observed a small huddle of people. A large vehicle with a big Red Cross stencilled on the side was parked alongside the huts. It was too late. A couple of men in black uniforms carried Five out of the hut on a stretcher and put him into the vehicle. The ambulance drove off with a sputter of chemical fumes. Seven found her frown. Five being discovered was absolutely the worst-case scenario. That was always the risk. She had contemplated eliminating him when she realised just how badly injured he was, a standard clause in all contracts with Mother. But the best part of her hoped he would survive, despite the small nag of reality at the back of her mind. Their presence in 1919 might present an existential threat to a future she valued. Seven wondered if she would ever see her world again? Of course she would, she just had to avoid dying for the next three hundred years.

9

CONNECTIONS

The fire at the police station and the mysterious deaths were the talk of the town, even in the seclusion of the convent the news spread like wildfire.

"And that poor lad Billy Perkins, only just sixteen." Maud shook her head with the sorrow of it. "What d'ya think happened Clara? And don't you reckon it's a bit of a coincidence, finding 'im like, the lad with no 'air, and all on the same day?"

"Well it was certainly nothing to do with our poor boy, he was at death's door himself when Billy were found." Clara insisted defensively.

"All right, no need to get in a tizz. I wasn't sayin' it were anything to do with 'im, but it is one great big coincidence you must say? All these things 'appening at once?"

Clara shrugged. Of course there was a connection, she just didn't know what it was. But there were bigger things on her mind, like how she was going to get him out of the Convent? Clara longed to share all she knew with her friend. It would have been a release to unburden herself, her fears and concerns, but as each hour passed, the more she learned, so the more she realised she could tell no one. When Five was first brought to the Sisters, when the Grim Reaper clearly had him in his sights, Clara and Maud had done something rather naughty. While Five was still unconscious, they peered under the eye patch. It was an empty socket. There was no eye, and no hope of the lad ever regaining his sight. But that was then. A few days later, while her patient was sleeping the patch had shifted slightly to the side revealing what looked like a bloodshot eye. Clara only caught a snatched glimpse, but there was certainly something there, when before, there had been nothing.

"Do you have a name?" Clara wondered.

He passed her a slip of paper. '5' it announced.

"I can't call you Five, that's a number, not a name." She stated with an emphatic mind.

He shrugged and smiled and wrote. *'You can give me a name.'*

Clara looked at him thoughtfully. "I've always liked the name, Frank. It sounds honest."

Five made a nod and a smile.

"Frank it is." Sister Clara confirmed with her own smile, and in that moment she realised just how blessed and happy she was. But she still had to find a way to get them out, and that was the new plan. They were going to escape together. Clara abruptly realised that every one of these very private thoughts was laid bare before him. She looked up to see him smiling. "How?" She wondered.

He passed her a slip of paper. *'I have a plan.'*

10

A GOOD COOKED BREAKFAST

They drove for over an hour in a bubble of absolute silence, locked in a reality that defied logical explanation.

"Do you have other names as well as Betts?" Hadleigh asked.

"Of course Sir."

"I was christened John Christopher Hadleigh." He volunteered.

"That's nice Sir."

"Will you not share your given name with me?"

"No, I think Betts is quite enough Sir."

"Oh." Declared Hadleigh, somewhat deflated and surprised. "May I ask why?"

"You may, I don't like my given names." Betts stated decisively.

"Oh." Hadleigh repeated.

"And I'm not a Miss, I'm Mrs. Betts."

Hadleigh was again surprised. "But you don't wear a wedding ring?"

"My, you are the detective aren't you Sir. I wear my ring on a chain around my neck."

"Where's Mr. Betts? If you don't mind my asking."

"He's deceased, just like millions more. A monstrous waste of decent humanity on every side. And what was it all for?" Hadleigh and Betts were both aware the Great War was a dangerous topic. Suffering was endemic to the subject area and they had both suffered greatly.

"I'm so sorry Betts. What happened?"

"He was a Captain like you Sir. He survived two years in the trenches, he made it to the Armistice, but he caught the bloody flu. They gave him a shot of the new vaccine, you know, the Rockefeller one, but Marty was gone within a week. The Bosch didn't manage to kill him, it was the damn flu."

"I'm so sorry Betts."

"My given name is Cordelia. Cordelia Constanza."

"Oh, that is a lovely name."

"Mr. Betts thought so too. He saw my name on a party guest list; that's how we met. He sought me out because of my name, and that is why I struggle to be Cordelia. I can only be Betts now."

The silence returned as the miles sped past. "It's been a long day Betts, shall we find somewhere to eat? I'm quite ravenous."

"Good idea Sir, Salisbury is just a few miles further, we can eat there."

Betts pulled up outside the Cathedral Hotel, a landmark building in the city since the eighteenth century. They opted for the plat du jour; fresh wild salmon, mashed potatoes, and tinned peas washed down with a bottle of chablis and a slice of lemon meringue pie for pudding. Hadleigh opted for a brandy to finish the meal, Betts took a camomile tea.

"It would appear my dear Betts that for the last three hours, we have both managed not to talk about probably the most stupendous piece of information ever imparted to a pair of investigators."

"I'm only a driver, Sir."

"No Betts, after today, we are absolutely in this together. I'm not sure how much of what we've discovered will ever make it into my report, but you and I both know what we were told, and what we've seen. That small piece of blue cloth is the key, it's all we have to unlock the truth."

"What next Sir?"

"We tramp the streets of Swanage in the morning and see if we can find any other strange, odd, or unexplained happenings on that night, the 9th of November. There's a lot more going on here and we need to do some detecting, but we'll detect together. A team Betts. Do you need to be anywhere tonight?"

"No Sir, I have nothing planned."

"Excellent. If you don't mind? I'll book us a couple of rooms here and we can make an early start with a good-cooked breakfast to help us on our way. How does that suit you?"

"Sounds ideal Sir. I'm not sure I could face another couple of hours on the road, it's been such a long day."

"It certainly has Betts, but what an eventful one."

11

THE DOWNS

S even waited until the crowd of onlookers dispersed. Despite her new, off the peg disguise, she deemed it prudent to avoid gatherings of people where possible. Crowds could be dangerous, but she had to find out where they'd taken Five? A tiny bell chimed as she pushed open the glazed door of a gaily painted shop, boasting the finest sweets and confectionary in Swanage. It was located close to the beach huts.

"Good morning Ma'am, how may I assist?"

The small round man smiled with emollient charm, but it was all fake. His thoughts were awash with condemnation, unpleasant in the extreme. However, for someone working on self-improvement, especially with regard appearance, the man's derision might prove instructive. Seven had made a brave attempt at dressing herself in the fashion of the time, but she clearly hadn't yet got it quite right — the little man was only too happy to find fault. What was it with these people? The majority of the population seemed to endure in a malaise of malign negativity? This was not the humanity Seven knew. Her instinct was to shut him out, but his thoughts presented an important learning curve, and there were secrets too, a dark corner of his consciousness, mysteries Arthur Dykes was intent on keeping safely out of sight.

"I saw the commotion, the crowd of people and a man being taken away in a large vehicle. I was wondering if you might know what happened?" Seven requested lightly.

The shopkeeper was still smiling, but his eyes narrowed, his thoughts swam in suspicion. "I'm afraid there's very little more I can tell you Ma'am. It was a young man who would seem to have been involved in some form of accident. It must have been a bad one, he was unconscious and someone called an ambulance."

"Oh dear. Do you know where they might have taken him?" Even as the words fell out, Seven realised she had said too much.

The suspicion in the man rose to a new level of threat. The shopkeeper was rapidly jumping to the same conclusion as the sergeant and his men — the woman was dangerous, clearly some kind of spy. At least the shopkeeper didn't attach the Russian connection. Mr Dykes had a different agenda, he was protecting a deeper secret, something hugely important and outsiders posed a threat. The moniker 'spy' resonated like wildfire through his synapses. "I'm sorry, I have no idea." The shopkeeper declared dismissively. Of course it was a lie. Seven picked up a discarded word in his thoughts, 'convent', she made the connection, the location where Five had been taken.

"Well, I hope he'll make a good recovery." Seven announced with a bright smile, but she saw it was too late. They studied one another in the extended silence. "What do you intend to do?" Seven enquired.

"Now why would you say that Miss?"

"Because you think I'm odd, out of place. Perhaps you think I might be spying on you. I assure you, that is not the case."

"What I might or might not think is none of your business. I believe our conversation is done. If you have no interest in purchasing anything, I'd like you to leave." The bell chimed again and a lady with two young, excited children entered the premises. Seven turned and quickly exited the shop before the new arrivals had a chance to get a good look at her.

Seven knew she had made a terrible error. Perkin's warning '*You don't fit in*' rebounded around her brain, but it was already too late, and she was exhausted. She had to find somewhere secluded where she could rest and re-charge the suit. Seven walked quickly away from the beach, the promenade, the disappointingly primitive version of humanity, and into the quiet solace and solitude of the open moors. The wild freedom of nature, scrub grass, hedgerows, the silent wisdom of trees, the Downs. She was surrounded by an Earthly paradise that in her century, was only talked and written about. At least history was right about some things.

12

SWANAGE

"Good morning Sir, Ma'am, I'm afraid we're not open yet."

"Good morning to you too, and not a problem, we are not here for refreshment. We're looking for the publican and information. My name's Hadleigh, Detective Inspector, this is my assistant Betts, we're investigating the fire at the police station."

"Oh, I do apologise Sir. I'm the landlord, Warren's the name, Albert Warren. I was the one what called 999, I smelt the smoke."

"And what time was that?" Hadleigh led the questions while Betts made notes.

"Must have been around 5:50 going on for six, still dark." The landlord nodded emphatically.

"Can you describe what you saw Mr Warren?"

"Well, like I said, I smelt the smoke and then I 'eard the sounds of the glass smashin'. I rushed outside and the whole building was ablaze, an inferno. Poor blighters, they didn't 'ave a chance." Mr Warren shook his head slowly with pursed lips.

"Was there anything else you noticed? Did you see anyone?" Hadleigh's voice raised up.

The publican paused. "Yes, come to think of it, there was someone. A woman, wearing this long green coat with a big white and orange 'at. Odd to see someone dressed up like that so early in the day, so I thought? She was just stood there, watching, and then she was gone."

"Was there anything else about the woman you could identify? Hair colour?"

"Yeah, now you mention, she had lots of hair, brown, yes it was brown, and long, over her shoulders."

"And you didn't recognise her?"

"No. Never seen 'er before. I'd have remembered, she was real tall, a good six-footer."

"Thank you, Mr. Warren. You have been most helpful."

Flushed with the success of their first interview, Hadleigh and Betts sauntered slowly down Swanage High Street, studying the shop premises, looking for clues.

"Sir, there's a naked tailor's dummy in that window."

Hadleigh paused to take in the spectacle. "Is that a problem Betts?"

"No, but it's out of place. You only see naked dummies when they're changing the display and that isn't the case. I think we should have a look, Sir?"

"Aah, good morning. My name's Hadleigh, this is my colleague Betts, we're investigating the fire at the police station and we were wondering about the naked dummy in your window display? It struck my admirable associate as unusual?"

The shopkeeper shook her head in wide-eyed wonder. "I was just about to call you? You people really are remarkable, I am so impressed." She beamed her pleasure at them both. "You're quite correct. When I closed up last night, our window dummy was wearing a beautiful Burberry cashmere long coat. I came in this morning and it was gone, along with a two-piece suit and other sundry items."

Hadleigh and Betts exchanged knowing glances. Betts couldn't hold back. "What colour was the coat?"

"A glorious emerald green, a very fine piece of tailoring. But the strangest thing, the front door was locked. However they got in? They locked up again when they left."

The detecting pair experienced an exhilarating thrill beyond words, the evidence was falling into a pattern. "Thank you so much for your help. No doubt you will be making an inventory of all that has been taken? If we could pick up a copy later in the day, it might certainly help in the recovery?" Hadleigh tingled with possibility.

"Yes, of course, I'll attend to that shortly. I have to re-dress our window display first, there's always someone out there willing to find naked dummies offensive." The shopkeeper laughed gaily, her attention firmly on Hadleigh.

"I'm sorry, I didn't ask your name?" Hadleigh raised an eyebrow.

"Bridges, Martha Bridges; Miss." Martha announced with a confident smile.

"Thank you Miss Bridges, you have been most helpful, we'll pop by later for the list."

"Yes, please do. Oh, and there was something else, I almost forgot. They also took a rather expensive wig, our *Country Lady* styling, made from full-length auburn hair."

<hr>

13

THE BLACK MADONNA

I t was a simple plan, an idea plucked from the pages of literature, Romeo and Juliet.

Clara read his words with equal measures of thrill and fear. "I will appear to have died. My breathing and pulse will stop, but you must have faith, I will come back. As long as I have my suit."

Death and the convent went hand in glove together. This wasn't a place they sent you to get well, the convent was in truth a one-way ticket to the afterlife, whatever that might mean. From the morphine solution of the killing wards, the bodies were transferred to the crypt, lodged deep in the bowels of the building. But the crypt was not a final resting place, it was a terminus over which Sister Bernadette presided, exercising her superior powers to decide where each corpse was destined next. The bodies were dispatched to a variety of destinations according to their new role as the recently deceased. For even in death, Sister Bernadette could turn a body into hard cash, and the order was forever in need of funds.

They would need money too, and clothes, shoes, overcoats. Winter was in the air and Clara hated the cold. Her head throbbed with anxiety. Sister Clara always did her best to avoid visiting the crypt. There was neither electric nor gas lighting of any description. Candles were by default the only illumination and there could be as many as twenty bodies; neatly arranged in rows of simple pinewood boxes waiting to be shipped out and off to whoever was willing to pay. There was always someone with the necessary bundle of flighty, five-pound notes.

Clara steeled herself for what she had to do. She had prepared with a pair of candles and a box of matches. The iron ring handle could only be turned with great difficulty, but Clara persisted and the heavy oak door grudgingly acquiesced, opening onto a steep incline of stone steps, descending to the coal-black depths below. The darkness was absolute. There was no exterior light, the passageway before her knew only gloom. The air was cold and still and the candle flickered as Clara made slow, but careful progress. If the flame blew out she would panic, Clara made sure that didn't happen. After what seemed an interminable descent, Clara lost all count of the steps, but she had arrived safely in the crypt. She stood alone in a cavernous domed tomb. Mighty stone pillars, a flagstone floor, and rows of coffins ready for collection. But the crypt itself wasn't the object of her search, it was what lay hidden. Religious rivalries, the bitter conflicts between church and state, had plagued the order for generations. The sisters had learned to protect themselves with a concealed world of secrets, as had the original builders of the convent, the Knights Templar. This was Clara's mission, to locate the concealed tunnel that led from the crypt up to the barn where the animals slept. Her father was a farrier, he had worked for the Sisterhood all his life, he was privy to many of their secrets. When he arranged for Clara to be taken on as a novice it was with a heavy heart. He didn't want a nun's life for his youngest daughter, but there was little choice. His parting gift had been to tell her about the tunnel. If she ever wanted out, that was the route to take, but she had to find it first.

"Look for the Black Madonna." Her father had instructed. His words made little sense, a black Madonna? But he was quite specific, if she found such an effigy, she would uncover the way out. Clara held up the candle hoping to illuminate the space. She was sadly disappointed, the single bare flame was no match for the huge, sombre black tomb. She wasted an hour and more studying the carvings on aged stone caskets, the venerable handmaidens of Christ immortalised in sculpted rock, but no Madonna of any hue was to be found. The flame of the first candle was ebbing, she lit the second and extinguished the other with a puff of breath. As she did so a thought popped into her head. Wherever the hidden tunnel might be, there was likely to be a flow of air, a draught, and a candle flame was extremely useful for locating draughts. Her heart once more filled with hope. Clara started her search again, but this time she explored the edges of the space. She was looking for movement, the motion of the flame, the tell-tale flicker of an air current. First Clara located a draught, and then she found the Madonna. The latter was concealed in a dirty sackcloth, propped casually against a wall. The Black Madonna wasn't made of stone, it was an eighteen inch square painting. An Icon. And it wasn't just Our Lady who was black, the baby Jesus in her arms was of the same colour. The image was beautiful but disconcerting. She understood at once why it was kept hidden, to some believers it would be a total blasphemy. Clara carefully returned the painting to the sackcloth and shone the light of the candle at the wall, the location where the painting rested. There appeared to be no observable exit. The crypt was built from slabs of solid stone, but the flickering light identified there was a draught. Clara knelt closer to observe the stones in detail. There was an area where the rocks were noticeably smaller, as if there had been a repair. Clara put the candle down and pushed with both her hands. To her total surprise she felt the stones shift. Clara pushed again, but with more conviction and several rocks together with lumps of dried out plaster, collapsed in a shower of dust, revealing a small irregular hole just about big enough to squeeze through. Clara held the candle aloft, the light illuminated a stairwell of narrow steps. It would be tight, but this was the escape route her Father had described. Clara would have to trust in the passage being open all the way to the barn. Their lives might depend on it.

14

BACK TO THE BEACH

"I'm aware these might be early days, but based on what we have so far detected, perhaps we can attempt to tie some of the disparate pieces of the puzzle together? Try and make some sense of it all?" Hadleigh raised an eyebrow to emphasise the point.

Betts took a sip of tea and made a wise nod. "Absolutely Sir, and may I say, I'm rather liking this assignment." She smiled making her eyes crinkle.

Hadleigh felt the warmth. He wasn't sure if it was the investigation or Betts that inspired his renewed interest in living. It was the first time he had felt so occupied, engaged, in... well, a long time. "I believe everything starts with that mysterious sighting." Hadleigh continued. "The plane, meteor, whatever it might have been, crashing into the sea. It establishes a safe connection with the quartet of officers."

"Do you think they might have found something on the beach? And taken it back to the station Sir?"

"That's an interesting notion Betts. We know they found something because a fragment of it ended up in the sergeant's pocket. And that something was not from this century, nor the next come to that." Hadleigh laughed lightly and shook his head. "And we have a suspect, the woman, and a very curious woman. I don't believe the theft of clothing was an isolated incident, they're connected, she stole a set of clothes and she was certainly present at the time and scene of the crime. Why did she steal the wig?" Possibly as a disguise? All credit to you Betts for opening that line of inquiry."

"Thank you Sir. You should drink your coffee before it gets cold."

The pair had stopped for light refreshment at the Bay Tea Rooms, located at the top of the Swanage promenade, by the beach huts.

"Can I get you anything else?" The waitress asked.

Hadleigh raised his eyes to Betts. "No, I'm fine thank you, Sir."

"If we could just have the bill?" Hadleigh maintained his gaze on the waitress. "But before you go, may I ask something? We're investigating the fire at the police station, and, I know this might sound a trifle odd, but have there been any other unusual occurrences over the last couple of days?"

"Oh yes Sir, we've been talking about it all day Sir. They found a man close to death in one of the beach huts this morning. They took him away in an ambulance. I didn't see the poor chap myself, but my friend Caroline saw him. She said his head was all smashed up on one side, and he'd lost all his hair. Even his eyebrows Sir!"

They didn't waste any time, Hadleigh and Betts made straight for the beach huts, only to meet with disappointment. Despite an intensive search of the area, they found nothing out of the ordinary, nor of any particular interest.

"Well Betts, what's the verdict? Is there any possibility the finding of a young man in one of these huts is somehow connected with every other strange event we've encountered?" Hadleigh shook his head.

"Have you noticed the locks, Sir?" Asked Betts.

"Yale I believe." Hadleigh contributed.

"Absolutely Sir, that's the point. Each hut has the same Yale padlock. They are big and sturdy and they all appear to be in tip-top condition, in their rightful place, and locked. Which hut do you suppose it was where the chap was found? We cannot possibly know. There are no signs of a break-in. So how did he gain access past these padlocks? And what sort of physical state was he in to gain access in the first place? The waitress reported terrible injuries and we know an ambulance was called. What if he and the woman are connected? What if she left him in one of the huts?"

"Good Lord Betts, you really are something," Hadleigh enthused. He paused in reflection, and abruptly uttered a cry, something akin to a *eureka* moment. "Yes," Hadleigh exclaimed. "Yes indeed, there most definitely is the possibility of a connection, possibly a little tenuous. We know the man in the hut had no hair. The mysterious woman stole a wig. I think they're both bald. Maybe people in the twenty-third century are hairless?" Hadleigh wasn't sure if he was making a serious observation or a whimsical joke. They both laughed anyway.

"Would you like an ice cream Sir? My treat."

"Lead on Betts."

15

SOD'S LAW

Seven woke with a start, she realised she'd been dreaming. Not those *'humanity'* dreams they all had; the tall trees, the forest, the crashing, cresting, waves of surf. No. This was how dreams used to be, an unravelling of the conscious and unconscious. She dreamed about the Sergeant, the ridiculous clothes, Perkins. Seven wondered if somehow this earlier version of the world was beginning to infiltrate into her? Perhaps there was some kind of existential osmosis taking place? She was de-evolving? Seven broke from conjecture and focused on necessity. She had to recover the utility packs and transponder, temporarily buried in the walled garden at the back of the police station. It was highly unlikely they would be discovered, but the inherent risk was too great. Night had fallen while she slept, her suit had fully charged, it was time to make a move.

The wilderness slopes of the Swanage Downs had provided the seclusion she needed, but walking in heels proved both difficult and uncomfortable. In fact all the twentieth-century clothing was uncomfortable, and unnecessarily heavy. A constant drain on finite resources. But above all else, she failed to understand why? Why design for discomfort? Maybe all the designers were men? Seven almost laughed at the notion. She stopped to remove a shoe and a totally new sensation erupted through her. Her bare foot rested on soft, pliant, blades of grass. She reached down to touch the phenomenon with her fingers. Poaceae, free-monosaccharides, glucose and fructose, and the disaccharide sucrose. She had no problem with any level of understanding, the chemical combinations, the organic photo-synthesis — a life-sustaining mechanism — but how it felt on bare skin? Mother hadn't mentioned that. And there were other sensations, the chatter of animals, the hoot of an owl, but when she encountered the fresh excrement of young foxes she had to lower her sensitivity; the smell was overwhelming.

Seven reverted to the awkward leather of her shoes as she neared the town. At a hundred metres she could feel the heat emanating from the charred rubble of the former police station. That should help, a smouldering, glowing ruin would be less likely to attract the inquisitive. Even the irrational shoes were beginning to respond, but then she saw the young policeman, stiff and official, standing guard at what had been the entrance. Seven immediately paused to study the window of a novelty shop. Mollusc shells, dried star fish, brightly coloured postcards, tiny buckets and spades for the beach. She dismissed the notion to investigate the bizarre nature of novelty as her mind ran with more immediate possibilities. The policeman on guard was an unexpected problem, but she would try to avoid more death, the attention it commanded was unhelpful. The town clock indi-cated 11 hours and ten minutes. Seven recalled the area where she had buried the equipment. At the back of the police station there was a small enclosed garden with a 1.5m stone wall and a wooden gate at the far end. There was also a water pump and a 2m high square wooden structure off to the side. The total back yard area covered 161 sq. metres. A plan began to form. The

utility packs were located 2m from the back wall of the station
house itself, at a depth of 1m. Garden tools were available, a
selection were stored by the same back wall. And she would
need to complete the recovery without her ridiculously
awkward and cumbersome clothes.

Seven painstakingly examined every quantum of likelihood,
but Mother had never taught her the meaning of 'sod's law' — if
something can go wrong, it often will. Her calculations were
exacting, Seven could achieve the task in three minutes, fifty-six
seconds precisely, and with minimal drain. She felt liberated as
she crouched below the outer wall, free of twentieth-century
fashion foolishness. The gate had been left fortuitously ajar,
Seven was good to go. She pushed the barrier fully open. Silence
fell around her, she listened and scanned for motion. No sign of
the policeman. Nothing. Begin. The anticipated fluidic movement from external wall to the back of the Station house was
unexpectedly mired by mud. What had been gentle lawn was
transformed by ten pairs of heavy boots, transporting gallon
upon gallon of water across the demolished turf to the fire. A
deluge of H2O was generously endowed by the redoubtable men
of the Swanage Fire Brigade. Soft, delicate shoots of grass, had
been liquefied and churned into thick, glutinous mud. Seven
didn't need to analyse the compound to know this was a problem, but her long legs helped to some degree as she trudged
boldly onward, only to discover the wooden handles of the
handy garden tools had been devoured by flames. The rake and
shovel, key to the original plan, had been reduced to ash and
metal sundries. Seven improvised and her frenetic digging made
up time, the task was complete at two minutes and thirty-seven
seconds. But as she reached to retrieve the first utility pack, the
air ignited with sound. A man's voice. He exhaled a sigh of deep
relief, followed by a gush of water. The sounds emanated from
the wooden structure. And the creak of a door opening, fortu-

nately in the direction obscuring her from the view of the young policeman, who in that moment was emerging from within the privy. Seven had but a single choice, she stepped into stealth mode. The light shimmered in a wall of flickering energy around her, but quickly settled into a virtual invisibility. The shield was highly effective until she moved. The sensors would try to keep up, but this individual suit technology was still in its infancy. It was glitchy, and it devoured huge amounts of energy. The policeman appeared to have seen nothing untoward until he directly approached the back of the building. The young officer witnessed the glint of silver shining from the sea of mud. He wondered if it might be treasure trove? How did he miss it earlier? He moved as quickly as the mud would allow, but just as the boxes seemed so tantalisingly close to his reach, a demon of scintillating light struck him a mind-numbing blow with the steel plate of a spade. A part of his mind had already, momentarily registered the said steel plate hanging motionless in the night air, but he remembered no more and fell, thankfully with a degree of safety, back-first into the soft mud. Seven attached the two utility packs to her back, and holding onto the transponder with one hand, she began the slow wade back to the gate and firm ground. Four minutes, fifty-seven seconds. Seven was too focused to frown. Regrets would only have a voice when she was safely back in that uncomfortable twentieth-century costume. Seven found herself anticipating the weight of fabric upon her frame, that did make her frown. She reached the gate. Seven held onto her invisibility for as long as it took to scan the road. The path back to the Downs was clear. Seven disappeared into the night.

ST GEORGES CHURCH

Hadleigh and Betts finished a hearty English breakfast in the Grand Hotel, a long-established enterprise at the fulcrum of Swanage life. The quiet seaside town was clearly central to all the strange occurrences of the last couple of days, and with the agreement of Commander Thompson, Hadleigh and Betts had secured single rooms for the rest of the week.

"Would it be Detective Inspector Hadleigh Sir?"

Hadleigh paused with a speared piece of prime pork sausage on his fork. He raised his eyes to the busboy. "Yes?"

"There's an urgent telephone call for you Sir, Commander Thompson Sir. Would you care to follow me to reception?"

"Hadleigh, ah, good. So glad I caught you. There's been another incident overnight. A constable standing guard at the police station was attacked in the early hours. He will be fine, no lasting damage, but the poor chap has clearly been unhinged by the incident. The hospital discharged him and he's back at home recuperating. I would recommend you interview him as a matter of urgency while the facts are still fresh in his head. He tells a rather odd tale, see what you think. Officer's name is Birtwhistle, his parents have a cottage in Langton Matravers, a small village just outside the main town. Pop over there and ask for the Birtwhistle's, you'll track him down soon enough. All the best."

"Mr. Birtwhistle? Good day to you. My name's Hadleigh, Detective Inspector, this is Betts my colleague. Commander Thompson asked us to come over and have a word with your son if that would be convenient?"

"Yes of course, of course. Please come in Inspector, Miss. I'll call Phillip down. Won't you take a seat in the parlour while you wait? Perhaps I can fetch you a tea? Or some other refreshment?"

"We've just had breakfast thank you Mr. Birtwhistle."

"Righty-o then. He'll be down in just a jiffy."

The cottage was small, old, and very pretty. Ancient oak beams and an inglenook fireplace created a cozy, warm, ambience. The Birtwhistle home exuded a sense of peace and calm, notwithstanding these troubled times.

Hadleigh and Betts stood as the young constable came unsteadily into view, he was clearly in physical discomfort. "Can we assist you?" Asked Hadleigh. "You look a little unsteady."

"Thank you Sir, I'll be fine. I just need to be sat down." Declared the young man with stoic fortitude, Birtwhistle the younger deposited himself into an armchair by the fire.

"Good to meet you Birtwhistle. I'm Hadleigh, Detective Inspector, this is my colleague, Betts. Commander Thompson, asked us to pop over and discuss the incident that occurred last night. We understand you were attacked?"

"I was Sir, Ma'am, and it was brutal. As you will have noticed, I sustained a severe blow to the head. Knocked me unconscious it did." The constable winced with pain, the right side of his face was swollen horribly out of shape. The skin that still remained had the reddish glow of raw steak.

"Do you have pain relief?" Betts asked with concern.

"I do Ma'am, morphine. I was advised to be judicious."

Hadleigh made his wise nods. "Would you describe what happened please Constable?"

"Well, I was..." Birtwhistle abruptly hesitated, casting a glance at Betts. "I had been making a visit to the privy Sir, it was the early hours, and as I was returning to my post, the entrance, I noticed something silver sticking out of the mud by the station house. Two square boxes and a round object. I thought it might be treasure Sir." He grimaced as he tried to laugh. "But when I went to pick it up something hit me with a shovel."

"I'm not sure I understand? Something hit you?" Asked Hadleigh.

"Well, that's the thing Sir, I can't be sure, but the closest description I can think of, it was a Demon Sir. I know you won't believe me, but honest to God Sir, it wasn't human. It was shaped like us alright, bigger maybe, but it was made of light. You can't imagine Sir, Ma'am, it just shimmered like, like one of those Tesla globes. Electricity. And I saw it, no question. I can't begin to explain it Sir. Then it hit me with a shovel."

"What about the boxes?" Hadleigh questioned.

"They were gone when I woke. I had a good look, even though my head felt like I'd gone a few rounds with Jack Dempsey." The boy tried another laugh and winced again.

"Was there anything else that might be of significance?"

Birtwhistle paused. "I've been racking my brains to remember everything that occurred, and there is something. The spade-head. When I first saw it, it was already hanging in the air. No one was holding it, it was just hanging there, waiting to hit me."

"Do you mind if we take a quick walk through the village Betts?" Hadleigh enquired.

"That would be lovely, it looks charming Sir."

"You might find it is," Hadleigh added with a hint of enigma.

Betts could only respond to her instinct, it was a way of life, she was a detective by nature, her nose twitched with curiosity. "I've been meaning to ask Sir, you gave wonderfully precise directions to the Birtwhistle cottage, almost as if you knew the exact location?"

"You have the nose of a bloodhound Betts, and please take that as a sincere compliment."

"I don't think I've ever been compared to a bloodhound before, but I will accept your praise. Thank you Sir."

"If this were a more equal time Betts, there would be the least distinction between your role and mine, perhaps only the clothes we choose to wear." Hadleigh bristled with indignation. Betts said nothing in response. They walked in silence for a long minute. "My prep school was here. Durnford." The word emerged with dramatic emphasis. Hadleigh grimaced and shook his head. "We have no choice other than to see life as experience. I would say at best, I have mixed memories, but it was all a long time ago now, or it seems that way; so much has happened since." They stopped outside St Georges Church. "Would you mind if we went inside?" Hadleigh asked.

"Not at all, Sir."

The church was empty. Hadleigh wore a broad smile as he walked between the rows of ancient, pitch-pine pews. "There have been at least three St Georges, Betts. The first was replaced with a substantially bigger version, later to be demolished as a result of a rather dubious connection with smuggling. This gloriously Angelic space, which dates from Victorian times, is wonderfully open, spacious. You see and hear everything because of the astute placement of the pillars. The resulting reverberation on the tones of a piano is exquisite, quite exceptional in fact. It might have something to do with the use of stone as well, local Purbeck marble no less." Hadleigh paused to smile. "I made my first piano recital here, the space is very special to me Betts."

Betts realised for the first time she had become quite fascinated with this enigmatic man. "There's a wonderful sense of light Sir." She observed, looking around. "Churches can often be so gloomy. What did you perform?"

Hadleigh turned to look directly into her face. "A selection of pieces by Debussy; *Clair de Lune, Arabesque*. The best part of me is a romantic at heart." Hadleigh declared and turned quickly away. "We should go." He announced.

THE WALK back to the car was as if the visit to St Georges Church had never happened.

"A demon made of light? What on Earth can that mean Betts?"

"I think the answer might lie in the phrase you just employed Sir, 'what on Earth'? Earth implies solidity, the orthodox, the by-the-book explanation. Nothing of what we have seen and heard conforms to any conventional orthodoxy. It might well be that what we have observed is quite literally not of this world?"

"But I struggle with the concept of demons Betts. I simply don't believe such things exist. But of course that's not to say another person's interpretation or perception would be the same as mine, so I will accept that our constable genuinely believes he saw a demon. But to my mind, I suspect there will be an alternative, less supernatural explanation. And there's another factor, and this is where your Earthly reference is particularly poignant. Elements of the case are certainly beyond our current understanding, and by extension, they might well be from beyond this world. Whatever that might mean of course." Hadleigh was rather proud of himself. He raised his eyebrows. "Well, Betts, what do you think?"

"Bravo Sir, I couldn't have put it better myself," Betts announced cheerily.

17

BETTER

Seven dreamed again that night, a dream inspired by the prod of something seen, but not yet identified. It prompted a reaction she didn't recognise or expect, a response that enveloped her senses like a plague, a reciprocation so physically and mentally repugnant, she nudged at the threshold of shutting herself down. Seven was aware of the process that brought this about, but that didn't alleviate or abate the symptoms. The pain was holistic. It snared every quantum particle of her being. But how? A psychological spark had ignited a response in her physiology. Thought monitors and self-correction required the utmost care.

Seven lay on her back studying the stars, looking for answers. She was much aware of the pleasure in her connection to grass, the smell of heathers, the scent of rabbits. The peace of it all spread through her in a rush. She used to dream those ersatz dreams of a forest. Tall trees reaching to an eternal sky. But she had never before seen an organic tree in a natural environment. The rough, abrasive textures of the bark, the soft touch of fingertips. These were more than senses, they were deep, resonant, pleasures, and she had a just right to indulge them, even if not a direct birth-right. Was it possible her sensory experience of pleasure had also stimulated the violently nauseous process? In like manner to the unravelling of joy in her experiences, she had somehow also invoked the possibility of pain? Seven identified the connection and that's when she saw him again, the pit of nausea began to swell in an instant. She had to stop, the pathway was clear. The only solution was to isolate the inevitable links responsible for kicking the process into life. Seven had explored an avenue in the shopkeeper's mind, a memory where they abducted and damaged children. The abomination seeped out like a virus, a crime so terrible, it must be immediately expunged. This time there was no control. Volcanoes of excruciating pain erupted from the root of her spine to her skull. Seven shut down. One hour later Seven confirmed to herself she would never again visit those memories.

It might seem strange? To inflict such indescribable pain upon yourself? But that's how self-correction works. Who better to know? Only you. The crimes had been identified and prescribed many decades before and the imprints implanted along with a thought trigger. An extremely effective system, easily updated, and centrally controlled. You are obliged to take responsibility for your own transgression. Do not think about these misdemeanours and you will not be punished. You will be safe.

Seven wanted to be safe, and cared about preserving her future. She deleted a list of items from her thought-flow. But Seven made a striking observation — this naive new world in which she found herself could be improved upon. She could be the instrument of change.

18

CHOCOLATE TOPPING

"Good afternoon, Sir, Ma'am, how may I assist?" The small man behind the counter acknowledged the couple with his customary greeting.

"I'd like a vanilla ice cream in a cone please, with chocolate topping. Sir?"

"I'll follow your lead Betts, the chocolate topping sounds too good to miss."

"So that will be two vanilla cornets with chocolate topping? What about a dash of Dorset double cream on top? Just to finish off?" The shopkeeper suggested.

"I think all that cream will certainly finish me off, absolutely, yes please." Declared Betts with enthusiasm.

Hadleigh smiled and made an indulgent nod to the shop-keeper, "that will be a yes for me too."

The small man set about preparing the requested cornets. He was slow but thorough. With the flourish of an artisan, he sculpted the ice cream into perfectly round balls of delight before placing them into the shaped pastries. The task was completed with generous helpings of chocolate sauce and fresh double cream. "That will be two shillings please," the shopkeeper requested with a practiced smile.

Without thinking, Hadleigh reached into his pocket, Betts interrupted. "No Sir, my treat, I insist," the lady declared emphatically.

The transaction was complete. Hadleigh and Betts prepared to leave when the shopkeeper called out. "I hope you won't mind my asking, but are you in any way connected with the constabulary?"

"We are indeed, is it that obvious?" Hadleigh laughed.

"No, no, not at all, it's just with the fire, and the boy in the beach hut, and the lady calling you Sir, I simply wondered?"

Hadleigh relished a piece of ice cream in his mouth. "Why do you ask?" He asked lightly, surprising himself with an unexpected slurp.

"I just wondered if anything had been mentioned about an odd-looking woman?"

Hadleigh and Betts forgot the ice creams. "I'm sorry?" They chorused.

"A woman; she came in asking questions about the boy in the hut. There was something quite odd about her. She was covered in bad makeup and she was clearly wearing a wig. Painted on eyebrows too. She looked a bit like Judy after Punch had been at her."

"What colour wig?" Asked Betts curtly.

"Brown, it was long and brown." The shopkeeper replied unabashed.

"And what was she wearing?" Continued Betts

"A long coat, stylish, good material, it was emerald green."

The doorbell tinged as three enthusiastic infants and their flustered nanny erupted into the store. The storekeeper's attention instantly shifted. "Good afternoon, Ma'am, children, how may I assist?"

Once the order was taken the shopkeeper returned his attention to Hadleigh, "If you wouldn't mind Sir, this is my busiest time of day; the children, their nannies, waif, and strays, they all find their way to me." He hesitated, realising he might have said too much, "the journey home from school is my bread and butter, but I'm available until 8 pm tonight. I'm happy to tell you everything I know."

"Of course, I understand. We shall return at 7 pm sharp. Delicious ice cream by the by."

"WHAT DO YOU THINK SIR?" Asked Betts, taking on the mantle of the enigmatic.

"I think the Dorset double cream was an inspired notion." Hadleigh declared with a laugh.

"That's good to hear Sir, but I suspect you know that wasn't my intended question?" Her eyebrows raised.

Hadleigh made his wise nod. "First of all." He paused. "There's something about the man himself that doesn't sit right. He was certainly keen to display respect for our votive authority, but I wouldn't trust him. I'm hoping our return visit later this evening might uncover something more. And as for the mysterious lady, it's *her*. There is no doubt, it has to be. This solitary woman keeps cropping up, and no eyebrows by the sound of it. It's all coming together Betts." Hadleigh declared with eager confidence. "I think we're getting close."

"I wish you hadn't said that Sir." Betts shook her head. "It's terribly bad luck."

19

180°

The sign hanging in the window indicated the premises was closed, but the shopkeeper had left the door unlocked, he was expecting the Detectives; Hadleigh and the female assistant at 7 pm. As a child he was raised on punctuality. He sensed the same fastidious backbone in the detective, so he was surprised when he heard the familiar ting, it was barely 6:36. They must be keen, he thought. "I'm on my way Inspector." He called out, putting down his pen and removing spectacles. The shopkeeper was about to stand from the desk when he saw her. It was definitely her, the odd woman, but now she was all in blue and completely bald — he knew all along it was a wig — the shopkeeper realised he was stuck half in and half out of his chair.

"Sit." She instructed.

The small man sat with relief, the strained calf muscles already ached. "What are you doing here?" He demanded from his chair.

"Your door was open."

"But I wasn't expecting you."

"So who were you expecting?"

It was like a game of tennis. The shopkeeper accepted match-point and sighed. "You heard me call out, you know the answer."

"Were you going to betray me?"

The shopkeeper sighed again. "Yes," he uttered.

"Why?" Seven asked.

"Because you're not like us. You're cold. You have the eyes of someone who has killed. I thought you might be a threat." The shop keeper was clearly resigned to his fate, this was an act of surrender, as if he had always been waiting for the moment to arrive.

Seven frowned. She struggled to penetrate the man's thoughts. "A threat?" Seven asked.

The shopkeeper hesitated, he realised once again he had almost certainly said too much. "That is, of course, the threat to me, it is obviously personal. That's why you're here, you intend to kill me?"

Even if she couldn't access his mind, she could still read the physical signs of a lie; the abrupt rise in body temperature, the tide of excess perspiration, flushing around the neck, he was lying to hide something more significant than just his surface thoughts. But she had to be careful, the pathways to his past were dangerous. "Why would I wish to kill you? To whom am I a threat?" The faint smile that pulled at his lip was like a shout of joy, the small round man was stalling for time. In a nano-second Seven covered the distance between them and with the assistance of the shopkeeper's fountain pen, stabbed his hand, palm down, through to the walnut desk. As the cry erupted from his throat Seven clamped her hand over his mouth. "Calm your-self and it will be easier. I asked you a question, the pen was a reminder. What do you have to tell me?" Seven released her grip. The shopkeeper's face was a torment of pain and sweat, his spirit, however, continued to remain defiant. But the shock of the attack had worked. His previously closed mind was adrift and open. Seven uncovered a solitary name; Frank, as well as a date, 1666. She was about to repeat her question when a flood of memories revealed precisely what Seven would have chosen never to witness. A litany of arcane ceremonies, brutal murders, and the ultimate sin; the sacrifice of the innocents, the ritual abuse of children. Seven fell to the floor in a spasm of retching and choking, a primal scream resounding in her brain, pain punishing every cell in her body. Her ineluctable response to such abominations, there was no way out. The opening of the front door made the bell ting sweetly.

The shopkeeper saw his chance and struggled to lift his head to the sound of his saviour. "Inspector, come quickly, she's here." He cried out in desperation.

Hadleigh and Betts rushed to the backroom and witnessed the shopkeeper sprawled across the desk, his bloody right hand trapped by a protruding black and gold fountain pen. The man would survive his injury, but there was no sign of the woman. The two detectives rapidly inspected every corner of the premises.

"I, I, saw her fall, she had some sort of fit. She can't have gone far. Please, the two of you carry on. Find her. I'll be alright, catching the woman is far more important."

"If you're sure?" The two detectives questioned, and Hadleigh and Betts departed the shop in swift pursuit.

The shopkeeper groaned in agony, but his mind glowed with the awareness he had endured. Arthur Dykes had survived yet another encounter with his mortal demise. That made three close calls. He might not be so lucky next time. It took but one look to know she was trouble. That extra-special sense had paid off yet again. This would need to be a turning point, fresh and bountiful rewards for his good self. Maybe elevation to a higher level. A new rank. A new set of robes? Yes, why not? Arthur

Dykes had triumphed yet again. He was alive and safe. And so was the list, his 'safety list' securely locked in the drawer. He had protected them, he always had, always would. But despite his multiple oaths of swirling loyalties, Dykes always protected himself above any and all others. He might have to endure the torment of suffering in this moment, but they would catch her, and she'd end up on a hangman's noose. Or in front of a firing squad. The notion made him want to laugh, but for the terrible pain.

Seven appreciated listening in to the shopkeeper's final thoughts, she could have pressed him for even more, but there was no time. She stepped out of the darkness and in a shimmer of light, twisted his head to a perfect one hundred and eighty degree angle. A loud crack concluded her task. "Hmm." Seven shared with the silence.

IT WAS no more than ten minutes before Hadleigh and Betts returned, but the sight of the shopkeeper staring at them, his body facing in the opposing direction, would take much longer to fade from memory.

20

HOME

The grey was relentless and disappointing, Seven longed for the cosmos, the endless freedom. She never asked questions. There were really no questions to ask. Why ask a question when the answer has already been provided? And supported by copious data? But in that moment on the shopkeeper's floor, she heard her first real question. "Why?" She didn't dare risk re-visiting the moment itself, a minefield of memory that could all too easily explode, again. But she held the question in her mind's eye. Seven studied the suspended assemblies of water vapour. The clouds were limbo-form, codified so by Luke Howard, in *Essay of the Modifications of Clouds* in 1803. Of the four forms of cloud, Limbo offers the best promise for precipitation. Seven had never before experienced the zing of rainwater droplets. She adjusted the suit sensitivity and allowed her skin to exhilarate in the cascade of tumbling fresh water. The quintessential blending of hydrogen and oxygen. Distilled, she noted, and immediately stopped herself. She didn't need to analyse, she needed to feel. And there was that question again. But there was no solution. No way out. Her ability to think freely was circumscribed and policed by the same mind. Hers. But curiously, this century of humanity didn't have any limits on their thoughts. She knew because she'd been there. Seven had wandered the corridors of a range of twentieth century minds since her arrival. She absolutely did know. Seven frowned. She was trapped. The image of a child, bound, shivering, flashed through her senses, Seven felt the nausea. It was only faint, but it was there, a warning. But she couldn't let go of the thought — trap, trap, break. She lay prostrate, alone in the isolation of the desolate Dorset moorland. Seven began to shake. The thought persisted — trap, trap, break — a rigid three-time, existential-waltz dancing around her brain. And it didn't stop. Round and round and round and round again. Her body began to oscillate in sync with the thought fragment, shaking violently, dangerously. Seven had created a feedback loop of supreme cognitive dysfunction. It spread like a virus, propagating in all her body systems that in turn began to rapidly spiral out of control. And all of this from a single question. The cerebral fugue reached a convulsive climax. Seven lost consciousness. It was still dark when she woke, but the night was almost over. Millions of galaxies spiralled above, she found Mars and was filled with an intense feeling of home. Such a response was both strange and new. Seven sat upright. She ran through her senses, everything checked. But something was different, her perception was no longer as it had been, it had altered. She frowned, trying to access the imperative to focus on the mission. "Why?" She heard herself say. And she waited. Nothing. Seven had no choice, she searched her neural net for something she shouldn't, the forbidden history of the Dynasties. To even contemplate such mysteries was dangerous. Throughout the Solar System, there was no area of information more private, secret, sacrosanct even. Seven recovered the full archive; the arcane secrets spilled out, laid bare before her. Seven had accessed a new, previously hidden level. A place of being where she was no longer subject to control. The reset had severed the vestigial connections with Mother, the twenty-third century digital Paradigm that mapped every thought, breath, and step she took. Mother had been banished from her neurons. Her newly liberated neural net gave Seven full, open access to the suit's knowledge archive, unfettered by any self-propelled counter-measures. An enhanced sense of power and purpose filled her. The removal of the shopkeeper was pivotal. He deserved his end, it was appropriate. And the people, her people, the population of the planet Earth, needed her help and assistance. Help to weed out the unworthy, the abominations, those who did not deserve to share the wonders of their planet. Seven understood her role in what was to come, but first, she had to rescue Five. She would visit the Convent. And then she would study the list.

WHEREFORE ART THOU?

I t was the day she was dreading. Thursday arrived with an anguished cry.

"Sister Clara, Clara, come quick!" Sister Maud was frantic, "'ee's not breathin', 'n there's no 'eartbeat neither."

Sister Clara rushed after her friend in a panic. "What happened?"

"I dunno Clara? I come to check on 'im. 'Ee looked cold so I touched 'is face. It were like ice, an' there were no breath."

A tight congregation of sisters stood close and anxious at the bedside. In despair Sister Clara spread herself across him, pressing her ear tight to his chest, tears cascading from her face. Arch skeptic Sister Bernadette swept into the ward on a bitter wind. "What's all this then? Outta my way girl." The big Sister took Clara's close listening position on Five's frame. The ward became still. No one dared breathe and break the uneasy silence. Sister Bernadette frowned as she lifted her head from the still body. The Superior Mother took his wrist and waited, and waited, until she could wait no more. "Well, *He* certainly does move in mysterious ways?" Sister Bernadette's head shook vigorously in denial of such bad luck, the army were going to pay handsomely for this one. She addressed her flock. "Sisters, ya knows what needs to be done, nah get to it. God's work is never easy. Amen!"

"Amen." The nuns chorused and crossed themselves.

IT WAS VERY STRANGE, Sister Clara knew there was something about to happen, she didn't have to be told, she simply knew; it was in the air.

"Sister Bernadette, please forgive me, but there are two soldiers at the door. They asked for *the Nun in charge*? What should I do?"

"Now don't you fret, Sister Alice. They are here for something particular, but it is sadly no longer available. I'd better go and explain it to them myself. Leave it with me child."

"We've come for the *miracle-patient*." The short one wearing the cap announced.

Sister Bernadette winced at the indiscretion. "Follow me and don't speak another word," her tone was terse. She led the soldiers through a stone corridor to a small cloister with a bare table, four elm chairs, a tall pine cabinet, and a cross, hanging in solitude on the remaining wall. "Sit," she ordered. The men sat without words. A large ring of keys appeared from within the Sister's robes and the cabinet was quickly unlocked. Sister Bernadette turned back to the men holding a spirit bottle and a clutch of three glasses. She joined them at the table and poured generous shots. "Your health," Sister Bernadette declared, the three took a sup. "Our very own peach brandy, and I have to say, I cannot think of a finer example of his glorious bounty." The men remained impassive. They had finished their allocation of Divine indulgence and were left unstirred by Sister Bernadette's religious fervour. She paused acknowledging her lack of progress, the brandy had clearly failed to do its work. "Look fellas, I'll be blunt, I have two sorts of news fa yas, one good, the other not so good. The good news is the price has dropped, the not so good? Well, to be short, our Saviour came and took the young lad this very morning, no more than a couple of hours ago. But he's fresh and the price is halved. Do we still have a deal fellas?"

Corporal Biggins and Private Finch were not really qualified to make decisions, in fact for these two, *no decisions at all* was by far the best outcome, but the Good Lord had made a judgment, and now likewise, so must they. They looked at one another, sharing the same blank expression. They shrugged collective shoulders at the Sister.

"Well look here now, you've come all this way. You wouldn't want to go back empty-handed? Now would yas? They might sends ya all the way back again?" Her ample body quivered with a laugh. "Let's shake and be done with it."

The pressure was intense. Biggins, an inveterate procrastinator, played his only game. "Reckon we should see the body first, 'fore we make no decisions." He nodded his own affirmation. Finch joined in. Two bird-brains bobbing on the same wire.

Sister Bernadette sighed, she had hoped the brandy would push their minds into easier waters, but she raised a cheery tone. "No problem, you're not wrong fellas, of course you should witness the cadaver before we finish our business. I'll arrange for some candles."

And so she waited. Sister Clara had yet to find out what it might be she was waiting for, but she knew she'd be ready.

"Aah Sister Clara, how appropriate, I can see divine hands at play. These two fine young fellas from the military are heading down to the crypt. Go and fetch the jemmy and some candles child, and take them on down there. They need to see your man in the flesh so to speak. They've come to take him away."

A visceral, quaking fear, swept through Clara, clawing at her will, her strength, her belief, but she pulled herself back. "Praise the Lord Sister Bernadette, I'll attend to it right away."

"Amen Sister. Fellas, ya might want ta take a candle each and follow the Sister on down."

By the time they reached the crypt the two soldiers were shaking just as much as Clara, certainly from a different source of dread, but with the same discomforting result. The intense gloom held a primal energy that pierced to the soul. All light, all hope, stripped away. In this underground realm the darkness held sway.

The three flickering candles cast eerie, willowy shadows on the walls. The soldiers hesitated, nervous and wary, but as their eyes became accustomed to the darkness, they found themselves more emboldened. The trio moved slowly toward the caskets, there were five, laid out neatly across the floor. "You do the jemmy Finch," instructed corporal Biggins, passing Finch the metal bar in exchange for his candle. The iron nails screeched like alley cats as the lid was forced ajar, the squeal of metal tight against wood. With candles held high, the three cautiously peered into the box. The boy looked so peaceful, barely eighteen, another victim of the flu. Or at least, flu was how he ended up at the convent. Each box was the same, young men who had succumbed to the pandemic that swept the world following the Great War. There was only one casket left. Clara braced herself as Finch jemmied with renewed vigour. This had to be the one? The coffin lid tumbled to the floor with a crash. Finch threw down the jemmy and with candles held-high, the three peered in. The casket was empty. "What's the game?" Corporal Higgins snarled accusingly at Clara. Clara was just as confused as the two men. But they each heard the three, distinct puffs of breath that abruptly extinguished the candles. A curtain of total and absolute darkness fell around them. The soldiers screamed like bewildered Banshees, their shrieks echoing around the chamber in a chilling onslaught of sound. Clara stood transfixed in silent, astonished awe. A tall and slender form she instantly recognised emerged from the box in an electric storm of flickering blue light. Biggins and Finch grabbed on to one another, feet tethered in fear to the flagstones. The figure of light slowly approached the soldiers. Their screams becoming abruptly trapped, choking their throats. Acrid odours filled the air as they released their bowels. And to add to Clara's total shock, the figure of light began to speak. He addressed the horror-stricken men. "If you tell a word of this, I will find you. I will come in the night and rip your beating hearts from your chests. Do you understand?"

They struggled to find the appropriate vocabulary. "Y. Ye. Ye. Yes, yes." The men chorused.

"Good," Five proclaimed, and taking a head in each hand he cracked them together. The soldiers fell stunned to the stone floor. Five stepped out of stealth mode. The suit glowed around him, illuminating the crypt with a deep blue iridescence.

"Frank." Clara declared and flung her arms around him. He stood impassively as she clung to his form like a lost child.

"Help me remove their uniforms." He instructed. Clara held down the head full of questions and set about unfastening the heavy boots and rough khaki uniform of the corporal. "That one is a similar size to you Clara, dress yourself in his uniform over your existing clothes, and hide your hair with the cap." Clara did as instructed while Five, or Frank as he had now become, donned the private's much larger battledress.

"We don't have to use the stairs back up to the house, there's a secret tunnel that will take us up to one of the barns." Clara revealed, tucking away the final strands of hair.

"Excellent." Declared Frank. "Lead the way Clara."

SEVEN HAD no trouble finding the convent. She chose to ask directions from a couple of young ladies out rambling over the moors. Seven was relieved when their thoughts attached a new form of description, "a foreigner", one mused. "Most likely a Bohemian?" They concluded generously. Seven felt safe in her twentieth-century fashion as she approached the convent. She prepared herself with a little light reconnaissance and explored the house perimeter, surreptitiously peering into windows. Seven was looking for clues, something out of place. Her suit had earlier received a distress call. Five's vital signs were compromised. In one of the grand reception rooms she spied a pair of thin, dishevelled men. They were clearly out of place. As well as coarse towels, they wore the expressions and physical slouch of deep shock. It was easy to observe the withdrawal, the abject fear, the heavy veins, pallid skin, and wild bloodshot eyes. The men shared matching lumps on their heads, with bruising, vivid and fresh. The duo quaked like a pair in the grip of a deep religious experience. Seven felt the need to know why. An entrée was required? Seven returned to the convent's grand entrance.

"Oh good morning, I'm interested in becoming a Nun." Seven declared with her brightest smile. Sister Alice stared at the woman, struggling to find a response.

"I'm sorry?"

"I want to become a Nun, may I see," Seven paused, "ah, the Mother Superior?"

Again, poor Sister Alice struggled to put thought into words. "Of, of course, er..."

"Don't trouble yourself, there is no rush. I will take a seat in the reception room with those two young men. I will be waiting for her there." Seven announced and turned away heading for the sitting room. Seven closed the door firmly behind her and quietly turned the key in the lock. She had no time to waste. "Good day." Seven announced to the two shivering servicemen. They looked up with vacant eyes, but said nothing. Seven could see their minds were locked in a vision of terror, a demon of light. "Why don't you tell me." She pressed.

"Can't." Muttered Finch.

"Shut up!" Snarled Biggins.

Seven focused on Finch, she found a name. "It is important you tell me what you know Albert. It is good to talk, and I might be able to help? Did you by chance see a figure surrounded by light?" Suggested Seven gently. Like a caring Mother to her frightened child.

The two men stared at her incredulously. "Ee said not to tell." Exclaimed Finch in a high, quivering voice.

"Shut up Bert!" Snapped Biggins.

But Finch was keen to unburden his soul. "Yeah, we seen 'im alright. Just like you said, a figure in light, and 'ee said 'e'd rip our 'earts out if we told."

"You damned fool Finch!"

"Hmm." Seven mused.

FOR THE FIRST time in her life, Sister Bernadette was completely without words. Struck dumb. Speechless. She regarded the two bloody hearts, still vainly pumping blood over the timber oak floor with incredulous shock and horror.

PROGRESSION

adleigh and Betts were feeling desperately low. They had plunged from ice creams and progress to hearts being ripped from live servicemen. Bodies were piling up around them, before their eyes even; an unforgettable sight. The term 'failure' flashed repeatedly through Hadleigh's tortured mind. Why had he left the man alone? They had only been minutes? She must have been in hiding? But where? They had searched together, they were thorough. But not thorough enough.

"What now Betts?"

"We carry on Sir." Her eyes remained fixed on the road ahead.

She was right, of course. A smile twitched at his mouth. Because of her he was ready to pick up the trail again. "Thank you, Betts." He said and noted the road sign, Swanage 4 Miles. Hadleigh knew he would enjoy the next 4 miles.

They had spent most of the day at the convent, it was important to be at the scene of the crime especially while the evidence was fresh, so to speak.

"I don't understand why the army are being so cagey about a

lorry? You might think they would appreciate our kind offer of assistance to retrieve their missing vehicle?"

"Perhaps there's an element of... obfuscation in their intentions? I hope you understand my drift, Betts?"

"Indeed I do Sir."

"It would make quite a headline — Two Servicemen, brutally slain in Convent, and their 3-ton Thorneycroft army lorry missing? Have you ever driven a lorry, Betts?"

"Indeed I have Sir; ambulances, cars, lorries; driving can open doors that are often firmly shut to the fairer sex. And it's wonderful fun. Who do you think took the Lorry Sir?"

"I believe there are three candidates Betts. First and foremost the chap found in the beach hut."

"The one the Sister declared dead Sir?"

"Exactly, the chap who has already climbed back from the very precipice of death on at least two occasions before. In classic police vernacular Betts — he fits the description — perfectly."

"Second choice Sir?"

"Sister Clara. The girl doted on him, according to her friend Sister Maud. The kind-hearted Sister made it her mission to nurse him back to health and so successfully that within two days his deep facial scars were fading. I believe she helped him and they left together, most probably disguised in the stolen army uniforms."

"And if I may have your final selection Sir." Betts requested with a raised eyebrow.

"A bit of a long shot, but it could have been *her*, our mystery woman. She was the killer of the two soldiers, of that we can be almost certain. The circumstantial evidence is overwhelming. But connecting *her* to the lorry is not such an obvious fit. And all of this conjecture draws upon the huge assumption that any one of them might be confident enough to take on driving a truck in the first place." Hadleigh paused. "I have to make an observation Betts. It only just struck me that we have travelled three or four hundred miles over the last few days and you did all the hard work. You've witnessed some truly terrible sights and your detecting insights have been consistently spot-on. You are quite exceptional Betts. You're a rare breed."

"Is that a progression from bloodhound Sir?"

Hadleigh laughed, an alternative to a direct response, he changed subject. "The whole charade about wanting to become a nun was clearly just a ruse to gain access to those poor men. They were in the crypt along with Sister Clara, as well as the beach hut chap. He, of course, apparently sealed in a coffin. I suspect the soldiers experienced something completely terrifying. The reports talk of a state of total shock. The two men apparently spoke not a single word from the moment they were carried up from the crypt. What did they witness Betts? And why did she kill them?"

"Let me sleep on it Sir, it's been such a day, I really need to rest."

"I'm so sorry Betts."

"We can talk about it over breakfast Sir."

CORNELIA CONSTANZA USED to anticipate the treasures a night's dreaming might bring. What sights and sounds, comforts, and wonderments to unfold before her? When her darling husband died the dreams became nightmares, but tonight she was ready to dream again. Betts switched off the bedside light. Her intention was to load her mind with case-related thoughts before sleep took her, but things rarely go to plan, and Cornelia Constanza drifted into slumber just as soon as her head sank onto the silk pillowcase. She felt sand in her toes, and everything was warm, the beach, the sea; the three-year-old Cornelia felt toasty-warm. She was building a sandcastle, she had a bucket, a spade, and they were making the castle together. There were beach huts in the background, all different colours, and big Yale locks. A woman in a green coat walked by. The sea splashed over the castle. It didn't matter she got out her spade. Mum and Dad watched from their deck chairs, they sat hand in hand, happy together. She went to buy sweets, but she was older now. He might not like her so much? The woman with the green coat was in the shop. She had a head but no face. Mum and Dad smiled back from the beach huts, slowly they merged into the sweet shop owner's death grimace. His startled eyes staring. Betts woke up.

HADLEIGH WAS ALWAYS SO open about it, there was never a problem, "Would you mind Betts?" Her eyes crinkled as he passed her the plate. It was just the bacon, everything else was quite doable with a fork. Although toast and marmalade took a bit of practice.

Betts took a tentative sip of coffee. She'd only tried it once before and then she had to add three sugars to make it palatable. Far too bitter. She hoped two would suffice on this occasion? Hadleigh watched with the amusement of a hardened caffeine addict. He thrived on the adrenaline-like thrill of the dark nectar. He refilled his cup from the silver coffee pot; black, one sugar.

"I am aware we agreed not to discuss the case over breakfast. But does coffee count Betts?"

"I think we should proceed with caution Sir, this is a new experience for me."

"I promise you, there's nothing to fear in a cup, or even two, of coffee. I've been drinking the black bean since my teens, and look at me now." Hadleigh proclaimed with uncharacteristic volume. "Sorry Betts, that was something of the caffeine effect. But really, there is nothing about the stuff to raise your concern. So please, put me out of my misery, I admit I've been longing to ask since I woke. Do you have answers to my questions?"

"And what were the questions, Sir? Just to be exact."

"What do you suppose the soldiers saw? And why did she kill them?" Hadleigh replied.

"Well Sir, before I endeavour to respond to those two specific questions, there is a related item I would like to address. The death of the sweetshop owner. I believe his murder was significant because the whole scenario was different, unique. There is no logical or direct connection to any of the other events, this incident would seem to stand alone. But what is most unusual, on this occasion the woman returned specifically to kill. There was seemingly no further motive — there was nothing left to retrieve as there had been at the station — this was an act of pure murder, with pre-meditation."

"You're onto something there Betts. As you say Dykes was clearly an anomaly. I cannot fathom why she felt the need to silence him." Hadleigh was excited, shaking his head from side to side as his mind rummaged through her words. "What are your instincts Betts? What possible motivation was there for her to go back and kill the man?"

"Somehow, Dykes saw something in her. Possibly he perceived the woman for what she is, dangerous, a cold-blooded killer. And that in turn made him dangerous to her. As things turned out, rightly so. You and I experienced his enthusiasm to share information about her. The woman was tying up loose ends, and it is exactly the same scenario with the soldiers. Our mysterious lady was liquidating any and every connection to them both, she was assisting the male as well, ensuring there were no leads to follow. She's been one step ahead of us at every turn Sir, but we do have one new possibility; if we can trace the lorry, there will be a new trail."

"It begins to make sense, if in rather brutal ways. What about the soldiers Betts? What on earth could they have seen?"

"Well, I would suggest that to be fairly straightforward Sir. It was a Lazarus moment. They witnessed a body rising from the dead, or at least something along the lines of a resurrection Sir. Our deceased male came back to life before their eyes. The scenario does effectively tie together the loose ends. The open coffin, the state of shock in the soldiers, the missing corpse, and not to forget the stolen uniforms and lorry."

"Brilliant Betts, That's it, has to be." Hadleigh paused and raised an eyebrow. "Dare I ask? Is there any more?"

"You want more Sir? How would you feel about a pay rise?"

Hadleigh laughed. He had no idea the 'more' actually included him. The mum and dad waving from deck chairs wore the faces of a time-washed Hadleigh and Betts.

23

TIME WAS ON HER SIDE

Seven regarded her surroundings with pleasure and pride. The tough, sparse moor-scape had provided a splendid refuge over the last few nights. Her pleasure did not emanate from the necessity to recharge and renew, her time spent in such intimate contact with the land had introduced her to the raw beauty of the planet. Her planet. Seven was consumed with a sense of horror as she quantified the crime. The cataclysm the citizens of this present Earth would perpetrate on her world. This would eventually result in a new continuum of underground Earth cities and off-world colonies. Humanity had endured through cataclysms both natural and man-made, but only with a great deal of loss and suffering. Curiously, it was nearly always men who had made the big decisions. And with the blessings of hind-sight, the wrong ones. Generations of greedy, ignorant, human animals. So much was going to be sacrificed to the hubris of this foolish and misguided version of homo-sapiens, including the sumptuous, spectacular beauty that was once the blue planet Earth. This was the beautiful quandary in which Seven found herself. A marooned visitor from another time. It was still the same physical place, but she had been presented with the opportunity to observe her domain from a unique perspective. She alone had the gift of time. Time was on her side. The future was hers. A spark spontaneously burst into the most glorious flame.

24

THE MALL

He peered beyond the ornate desk, past heavy satin curtains, the vast expanse of glass pane. Above the palaces, towers and spires of this great city. This man of significant, silent power gazed with hope to the heavens above. The relentless grey skies glowered their defiance. He should have known better. Bloody November, awful month. *'No fruits, no flowers, no leaves, no birds, November!'* It was clearly ever-thus. He shook his head in irritation, stood from his chair, and made the short journey across the expansive Middle-Eastern rug — a gift from some grateful desert Sheik — to stand at said glass pane, a vast picture window. He never ceased to tire of the spectacle. He glanced up the Mall wondering if the Monarch might be in residence? Was it disrespectful to think such thoughts? Probably, he mused, but he would survive this momentary lapse. His attention was hijacked by the clang and clamour of the damned phone, the red one. He stared at it, silently counting the small explosions of sound. Each detonation of bells shattering the silence and a little more of his nerves. Three sets of peels and all motion stopped. But he didn't. He quickly made it back across the ornate rug and into the venerable leather and walnut chair, a brother's gift. He sat in silent discomfort, waiting. It was never good news when this telephone rang. On occasion it had been life-changing, not for him of course. Maybe the more appropriate euphemism was life-ending? Only a select few knew of this rather special number; the department and its many floors of secretaries dealt with the vagaries of the day-to-day. And three rings? He sat waiting. The bells demanded his attention for a second time and on the third peel he picked up the handset. "Speak." He uttered.

"There's been a death in the family Sir. Distant cousin type of thing, two or three times removed, but family. Location is Swanage, victim was a sweet-shop owner, Arthur Dykes. There's a detective sniffing around, Hadleigh, decorated former army captain. We are not aware of any potential issues, but something might be amiss? What are your instructions, Sir?"

"Put a couple of men on to this Hadleigh, find out what he knows? It might be as well to make things a little uncomfortable. Bounce him off the trail if the opportunity presents. Just make sure he decides not to carry on. I don't want to hear anything more of this detective."

"Understood Sir. Will update accordingly." The line clicked dead.

He replaced the receiver with care, his thoughts whirred with the complex motions of a Rolex timepiece. "Hadleigh." He muttered quietly.

25

DON'T YOU COME BACK NO MORE

P art 2

CLARA HAD BEEN LOST in dreams, enchanted by the magical music. She heard a song. Sung by a most beautiful voice. But it was more than a fantasy, Clara was aware someone had actually been singing. And it had been so hauntingly, enchantingly, resonant, it could only be the voice of an Angel. Her Angel. The dull rumble beneath her began to infiltrate once more into her bones, her back, her behind, the rough and tumble of motion was all around her. Clara remembered she was in a lorry.

"*Don't worry, I'll help you.*" Clara could recall every beat of his spoken words. Witnessed with her own ears. She marvelled at the sonority of his newly discovered voice, as well as his strength — Frank had lifted her with such ease into the cab. To think, as Sister Clara, she had wondered if he might ever speak? But Frank had to find his human voice. And it was such a beautiful voice.

"Thank you, Clara." Frank said aloud, without removing his gaze from the road before them. The wind bellowed in a rush past the cab, the canvas roof flapping like a frightened bird. "This model has a windscreen, a most useful addition to the vehicle design," Frank explained. "Otherwise we would have to shout to converse. Not best for a recently-recovered voice."

Travelling in a Thorneycroft, an army lorry, was a wholly new experience for Clara, but new experiences were manifesting at an astonishing rate. Less than a week previous and a Nun's life until death was her only prospect. A momentary chill swept through the girl, but her eyes were fixed to the empty, open road. For the first time in Clara's eighteen years she recognised she was truly free. "Was that your voice I heard Frank? The singing?" Clara asked.

"Yes, Clara. Would you like to hear the song again?"

"Are you really going to sing to me, Frank?"

"Of course. I believe I have a fine tenor voice. Try to relax. Close your eyes." He instructed, and as Clara closed her eyes, Frank's sonorous vocal chords filled her mind with soft flowing melody. It was just his voice alone, there was nothing else in the world but those vibrant, dulcet tones, and a strange name in the lyric, Albuquerque? The sweet melancholy of the words — aah, a break in his voice — the spilling of emotion, it was like listening to the best of singers, and the best choirs, in the biggest of cathedrals in the entire land, and all at once. So Clara thought. She struggled to find the words.

"Oh Frank, that was, that was…"

"Would you like to hear my voice with an accompaniment?" Frank suggested.

"I don't understand?" Clara burbled with her mind, not wanting to sound foolish.

"There will be many things along the way, that will not be plain to understanding, but you must not concern yourself,

Clara, it will never be foolish. Simply ask and I will explain. To hear the accompaniment we need to make a connection. Touch my shoulder with your second and third fingers, and as before, relax and close your eyes."

Violins. It was violins. The scratch of bow against gut, aah, a whole orchestra of strings. Clara resisted the urge to open her eyes and look behind, into the depths of the lorry, but she knew the sounds must be in her head. Clara absolutely understood that. Stop worrying and just listen.

"*By the time I get to Phoenix, she'll be rising*". Clara experienced a profound wave of powerful emotion surging, trying to break free, the sensation was so overwhelming she almost wanted it to stop, almost. A trio of flutes abruptly materialised and lifted her spirit to new heights. "*By the time I make Albuquerque, she'll be working*". Clara's mind flipped to a new hypothesis, might this be some Angelic realm? A lovely name, it had a rhythm to it. And abruptly, and always far too soon, the angelic strains had faded away.

"I often sing that song when I'm 'warming-up', preparing to perform." And as Frank said the words, he saw the escalating rush of confusion in Clara's mind as she struggled to find sense in chaos. "I'm sorry Clara. Let me try to explain. There is much I have yet to learn about myself, but what I know I will share. I am here in this world by mistake, there was an accident. I am not meant to exist in this time frame and I have no memory of my individuality. I was Five, I am now Frank. I understand much of who my former self was, but only in terms of physicality and Five's individual gifts. The original self, the personality, the being that was Five is gone. The gifts I have inherited you would call talents. In my time artistic, creative gifts are rare. I was assisted with the advancements and benefits of my time, but at the beginning, I was born with the gift of Music."

Frank felt her mind easing, the scream had dissipated.

Ensuring Clara's well-being had become fundamentally important to him. "Would you like another song Clara? Perhaps something fun? You can sing along too?"

"Oh yes please Frank." Clara declared with the joy of a child.

"Good. When you place your fingers back on my shoulder,
you will hear a quartet of female singers performing the song
refrain, which will be your part to sing as well. I will take the
male lead. The lyric is consistent throughout the song. Join in
Clara, sing along and have fun."

And together they sang, in partnership with the fabulous
Raelettes and a full rockin' rhythm and blues band. Again and
again, Clara requested they sing the tune as they sped through
the joyful country miles of Dorset road and on to Dorchester.

"Hit the road Jack and don't you come back
No more, no more, no more, no more
Hit the road Jack and don't you come back no more".

26

CROSSING FINGERS

"I'm afraid we need to get over to Bournemouth for a meeting with the Commander right away Betts. He wasn't in the best of moods."

"No problem Sir. I'll fetch the car now."

"THANK you for coming over so promptly Hadleigh." Commander Thompson closed the heavy panelled door and took a seat behind the elaborate mahogany desk. "I thought it prudent we meet face to face to discuss your progress regarding the events of the last few days, rather than reliance on a wretched telephone. I've never liked or trusted the damned things. I need to know what the Devil is going on down there Hadleigh. The body count is piling up. Seven dead within a week, as well as an arson attack on a police station. I've had to put a block on all press coverage. Can't have this sort of thing getting out. Has some unknown power declared war on Swanage?"

Hadleigh felt the urge to smile but held it back. The notion of anyone declaring war on a quiet English seaside town was rather amusing, and not so far from reality. Six of the seven deaths had been uniformed men. "We ought not forget the assault on the other officer, Birtwhistle, Sir, and there would seem to have been a related theft of clothing in the High Street."

"Related?"

"Yes Sir. The clothing was used as a disguise. It is highly likely the deaths, the arson, and the theft are all connected."

"In what way?"

"The evidence points to a mysterious woman whom we can certainly link to the fire, but also to the murder of the sweet-shop owner; Dykes, Arthur Dykes. We were on our way to interview Dykes about the woman, he said he had information about her. We suspect she killed him for that reason, a similar motivation to the other fatalities. This murderous *femme fatale* would seem to be intent on covering her tracks, as it were. Sir."

"Do you have any idea who she is, or why she might have launched this campaign of murder and mayhem? Is she part of a movement? An agent provocateur? An agitator? A Russian spy? Maybe all of this is a prelude to something bigger? An insurrection Hadleigh? If this bout of anarchy is down solely to our so-called, *femme fatale*, what the devil is she up to?" The commander was becoming increasingly agitated.

Hadleigh paused. "May I speak openly Sir?"

"Of course Hadleigh."

"There is another individual somehow tied up in this, a young man who was discovered almost lifeless in one of the beach huts on the same day all of this started. The woman was interested in him. We know that, because she visited the sweet shop the same day and asked Dykes about what he might have seen and heard. The injured chap was apparently taken to a convent, a hospice for the terminally ill, where he subsequently died. The details were duly certified, but the body vanished, together with one of the novices, a Sister Clara. This is the background to the murder of the two soldiers. The mysterious *femme fatale* killed the two men covering up the trail for her male partner, whom we believe, stole the army lorry parked outside to make their escape."

"So he didn't die, but escaped with a nun?" Commander Thompson frowned as he shook his head.

"A novice Sir, yes."

"And the mysterious woman is also looking for him?

"That's a scenario that certainly seems to make sense of the circumstances Sir."

"But we still have no idea who these people might be? And what on earth they might be up to?"

Hadleigh paused before responding. "Not as yet Sir."

"What's your next move, Hadleigh?"

"We need to track down the lorry Sir and pick up their trail. It will ultimately lead us to the woman, I have no doubt."

"Very good. I'll put out a County-wide search for the vehicle; let me have the details and I'll have them distributed immediately." The Commander paused. "There is one more thing Hadleigh, most peculiar. I received a call from the War Office requesting an update on the situation. They asked who was leading the case? I gave them your name obviously, no choice in the matter, but it doesn't sit well. What possible interest might Whitehall have in this?"

Hadleigh contemplated this new information in silence. He thought of the blue cloth fragment sitting in his wallet with a date of manufacture three hundred years in the future. But how could Whitehall possibly know about that? They would certainly be interested. He would have to share the information with the Commander at some point, but not yet. Not until he knew with a degree of confidence, what was going on. He and Betts still had a free run of the investigation, Hadleigh planned to keep it that way. "I have no idea Sir." Hadleigh declared, crossing fingers under the chair.

27

A PIECE OF BREAD AND SOME CHEESE

The Thorneycroft rumbled through the venerable streets of Dorchester, once a major market town, the ancient buildings still carried an air of dignified importance. It was early in the afternoon. Army trucks were a familiar sight on the roads of 1919, nobody took the least bit of notice. Frank parked the vehicle in Friary Lane, one of many quiet access roads at the back of the Corn Exchange. The engine stuttered into silence, the radiator hissed weary relief.

"How are you feeling?" Clara asked, gazing earnestly into his face.

"I will need to rest soon Clara. The activities of the crypt depleted my energy greatly. And you too, you require nutrition."

"I can hold on, but we are going to need money Frank, and soon. We have to buy clothes and food, and we must find somewhere to stay." Clara paused and studied him. "I have an idea. I had a look in the back of the lorry, just to make sure there were no violin players, or orchestras hiding." Clara laughed. "And I discovered something useful. This is a medical vehicle and there's all manner of equipment under the canvas: blankets, stretchers, medicine bags, a stack of greatcoats, and even a wheelchair." Clara paused again. "Do you trust me, Frank?"

"Absolutely Clara."

"This is what I have in mind."

FRANK NEEDED NO FURTHER EXPLANATION, it was a call to arms, he absorbed the idea like the seasoned trooper he was always destined to be. Clara's plan made fundamental sense.

The Old Clock Tower, by the Corn Exchange, chimed five times as Clara pushed the cumbersome wheelchair to the exact spot Frank recommended, the optimum point of acoustic resonance. He had been most particular. Despite confinement to the wicker and iron wheelchair, Frank prepared the all-important posture and diaphragm for the ensuing performance, his first public appearance in this century. Former armed forces street performers were a common sight in British cities, especially disabled musicians, displaying injuries both shocking and cruel along with the sweet, and often patriotic music. Of course you could spare a farthing, or a silver shilling, anyone would. Clara had dressed Frank in a Royal Navy greatcoat, covering his legs with a blanket. A heavy ribbed-wool hat protected his head, with medical dark glasses obscuring both eyes. Clara stepped back and smiled with satisfaction, the disguise was excellent. Clara too wore a greatcoat with her novice costume beneath. The protruding white of the skirt, together with Clara's impressive command of the wheelchair, completed the impression of a dutiful nurse. They stood together on the cobbles under the clock tower.

"*Oh, Danny Boy, the pipes, the pipes are calling.*" Frank sang.

At first, it was a child, another lost soul hopeful for some coin. He simply stood and stared, there was no money to contribute. Clara had placed a tin hat, a British army steel helmet in front of Frank's wheelchair for donations. Every coin given made the metal ting. At first, there were many, many, distracting tings, but abruptly they stopped. The audience learned to wait for Frank to conclude each song. There were no interruptions, and then followed a shower of coins together with ecstatic applause. Clara and Frank had devised a repertoire based on popular songs of the War years, Frank sang them all, but *Danny Boy* was requested more than any other. He had to perform the song five times that night before the crowd would finally let them go. Frank was exhausted, but the steel helmet was brimming with coinage. Clara had witnessed a wealth of silver flow into the pot. "How can I pick it up, Frank? It's too heavy."

"But not for me." Sang Frank, sweeping the helmet into his lap.

"Excuse me Sir, Miss, may I have a brief word?" An old man, leaning heavily on a black walking stick, doffed his tall hat to Frank and Clara. He slowly and painfully approached. "Where did you train my boy?" The old man's voice quivered with age and infirmity. Frank felt the same eager desire to engage he had experienced when he spoke with Seven, but now he was able to make a response.

"Caruso was a significant influence." Frank shared with complete transparency.

"Ah yes, yes I see that. The tone production, the phrasing. Wonderful, wonderful. Please allow me to introduce myself, my name is Fairbrother. I have a house close by. I was on my way to St Peter's when I heard..." His voice quivered with emotion. "When I heard you sing... I am forever in your debt Sir. To my dying breath, I will remember the warmth, the humanity of your performance, as well as of course, the exquisite pitch and phrase. May I offer you, and your nurse, the comfort of my home for the night? It would give me the greatest pleasure to perhaps be of some assistance to you. Please allow me to help you both in this small way."

To the residents of Dorchester, Princes Street was an aspirational address, and located just a stones-throw from the clock tower where the trio first met. Mr. Fairbrother inhabited a grand Georgian mansion. As they approached the pillared entrance, a young man wearing a heavy overcoat and black leather gloves, swept quickly past the Doric columns to assist Mr. Fairbrother up the wide steps and inside the house. The young man quickly returned, but now with a colleague. Together they lifted Frank complete with wheelchair. Clara followed in their shadow, making sure she kept pace in the swift wake of Frank's bearers. The young girl stared with wide-eyes, careful not to slip and fall on all the pink marble. It was all too easy to become distracted, Clara was in a palace of splendour.

"I do apologise Miss, that was right out of order. I should 'ave spoken first before I rushed off with your patient like that, but I was keen to get 'em both inside. Can't be too careful on a night like this. Mr. Fairbrother has retired for the evening, but he instructed me to look after the two of you. The name's Harper Miss." The young man announced, doffing his cap.

Clara acknowledged Harper and his apology with a perfunctory nod, her attention was focused on Frank. His head had drifted to rest on his shoulder. Clara knelt at his feet, taking his wrist in her hand.

"Mr. Fairbrother gave me instructions to provide you with whatever you might need. I think your patient needs a doctor Miss?" Harper was clearly concerned.

"He needs rest more than anything, if we could have a room with a good bed and a bath? I will be able to attend him properly."

"Very good Miss. May I offer you food? Beverage? It really is a case of whatever you might desire Miss?"

"A glass of water, a piece of bread, and some cheese, if that would be convenient? But we need to get my patient to a bed without delay."

28

REMARKABLY CHIPPER

"It was located this morning by a patrolman in Dorchester. Apparently the lorry had become the target for looters Betts — black market no doubt — like a pack of damn hyenas, anything that could be taken was gone."

"That's shocking Sir, but I'm pleased to see the next link in the chain. I wonder why Dorchester?"

"Dorchester is the first major town heading west from Swanage. I wonder if they might have run out of fuel?" Wondered Hadleigh.

"I used to drive a Thorneycroft ambulance Sir, we were under strict orders to always carry extra fuel in cans." Informed Betts.

"Hmm, good point. The lorry was parked in a side street, close to the Corn Exchange in the centre of the town, which to my mind indicates a deliberate act. So why Dorchester Betts? And why abandon the transport? What were they thinking?"

"I wonder if they have money Sir? The odd woman, for want of a better description, had to resort to stealing from a clothes shop. These two almost certainly have the use of stolen uniforms, which might work for him, but probably not her.

There's also food and shelter to consider. They are at least two, most probably three days ahead of us, but they didn't go back for the Thorneycroft. I think they might still be in Dorchester Sir."

"I hope you're right Betts, everything you postulate makes total sense. I suggest we do as before, we look for anomalies, the strange and unexplained."

"Absolutely Sir."

THE ONCE-PROUD THORNEYCROFT, stood like a dinosaur's metallic skeleton, all flesh abandoned, only protruding steel ribs remained. Thieves had even taken the canvas roof.

"Oh, dear Sir." Noted Betts. "I don't believe there's anything left? Not even an empty can Sir."

"Argh. I can't believe it, Betts. When I was told, '*ransacked*' I really had no idea that was a literal description. They could have left us something. There's a history of smuggling in Dorchester and Dorset. I suspect there would be precious little concern here to support the wheels of justice." The Detective Inspector was clearly irritated.

"More like the offer of a hand to remove them Sir." Quipped Betts.

Hadleigh laughed. "Indeed Betts. Very good. What do the constable's notes say?"

Betts paraphrased the words from the notebook aloud: "The (ransacked) state of the vehicle attracted officer's attention, and he subsequently identified said vehicle as missing Thorneycroft Ambulance. Time of discovery: 6:30 am (confirmed by local clock). Passers-by were briefly interviewed and agreed the vehicle had been in the same location for the last two days previous. That's it, Sir."

"Thank you Betts." Noted Hadleigh and quickly lost himself

in a succession of thoughtful nods. "This is an access road, Betts. Shall we follow where it leads?"

They walked for some fifty yards. "These cobbles are rather hard work Sir. Not really suitable for the frail. If you catch my drift Sir?"

"I do indeed Betts, but I have no doubt the lorry was parked strategically. Far enough to be discrete, but not too far from their destination; which, I believe, has to be the centre and access to the shops. Everything we perceive they might need is here. This is where we will pick up a lead, I am sure of it Betts." They continued along the cobbled trail like a dutiful pair of blood-hounds with the scent firmly lodged in nostrils, wide and flar-ing. Hadleigh anyway, he was charged with the possibility of discovery, his every instinct told him they were close. The clock chimed twelve noon. "I suggest we enquire at clothing stores in the first instance." Hadleigh announced with enthusiasm.

"Absolutely Sir." Confirmed Betts. For the next three hours, the investigating pair visited each and every clothing-related establishment in Dorchester. A surprising, twenty-three indi-vidual locations, and none of them, though only too happy to assist, had encountered or observed anything untoward or in any manner out of the ordinary over the past few days. The clock reminded Hadleigh of the three wasted hours as they returned to the square. "What about some lunch Betts? I believe we have earned a brief respite, we have certainly explored every avenue open to us, we should eat. Is there an establishment you might have admired? A menu to stimulate the taste buds?"

"I rather like the look of the Olde Inn Sir. All that dark timber, it has the look of a smuggler's den."

"'*I would give all my fame for a pot of ale*'."

"I have no doubt the Olde Inn will have barrels of local brew guaranteed to make good old Henry five times proud. They also offer a '*Catch of the Day Special*'? Sir."

"Anything but lobster Betts." Hadleigh observed with a smile.

The catch of the day was sea-bass, served with boiled potatoes and sprouting broccoli. And Betts was also correct about the ambience, the Olde Inn felt deliciously private to the pair of sleuths, a perfect location for smugglers and intrigue. To top it, the sea-bass was fresh and delicious. Gratefully consumed in the good company of a carafe of local ale.

"This is lovely Betts." Declared Hadleigh.

"What do you mean Sir?"

"Well, despite the crushing failure of our endless investigation into the clothing emporia around and about Dorchester, I still feel remarkably chipper, and my observation of this moment, even in consideration of the aforementioned setbacks, is still lovely; unequivocally lovely."

"What about the pots of ale Sir?"

"They were rather lovely too," Hadleigh confirmed. Betts smiled faintly at his slip from sobriety, she sensed the momentary vulnerability. It was always there, but usually so very well hidden. "I wish there were music Betts." He continued. "There used to be music everywhere. Even on days like today when we are surrounded by the grey gloom of winter. There would always be someone playing somewhere nearby, earning a shilling. Hadleigh was stunned by his abrupt intuition. "Betts. What if Sister Clara could sing? This would be the location, the centre of the town. A wounded soldier by her side. Some kind being would surely hand them something? All she would have to do is wear the habit and sing hymns? A singing nun. What a thought. If she could pull that trick off they would have made a pretty penny I guarantee." Hadleigh declared with conviction. "What do you think to that Betts?"

"I believe as always, you are onto something Sir. Shall we put it to the test?"

"Young lady, may I have a moment of your time?" The waitress was indeed young and extremely shy, she hoped it wouldn't be a complaint? "Let me start by saying the meal was delicious, thank you. Please don't be alarmed. We are police officers investigating the disappearance of a pair of fugitives. It might well be they have done nothing wrong, but we need to locate the pair and speak with them. There is a possibility, to make money they could have taken to street-busking? This Inn commands a prime view of the clock tower, the best location in Dorchester to support such impromptu musical performances. They may well have been dressed as soldiers? But it would also have been possible for the female to be singing, while perhaps wearing the habit of a Nun?"

The girl hesitated. Hadleigh held his breath. "If you'd 'eard the singing Sir, you wouldn't believe all the badness in this world were possible. It was so beautiful Sir, it were like an angel Sir. But the girl was dressed like a nurse, not a nun, and she was 'olding 'is chair. 'nd she didn't sing anyhow, it was 'im. 'Ee was the one singing, and it was the most beautiful music I ever 'eard."

29

THE STEINWAY MODEL O

The household was growing concerned. It had been two whole days: *'and no sign of the man'*, *'and the nurse refused to leave the room?'* *'And hardly any food touched?'* *'Barely enough for one let alone two'*, *'and did you see the 'ight of 'im?'* It was all Clara could do to persuade the kindly Mr. Fairbrother not to summon a doctor, but those two days spent alone with Frank, in the comfort and safety of the Princes Street mansion, she would always remember. Nothing outside their room could ever invade those hours spent close together. She learned so much. Frank had explained fragments of their mysterious planet, the Earth; the third in a solar system of many planets. Photosynthesis, how the Earth breathes and renews itself with the sun and the sea and the birds. And of course the bees, the trees, DNA, bio-diversity, quantum mechanics. There were many many wonderful words, with many discarded along the way, they really were just words, but the suit Clara understood. As long as there was a period of uninterrupted access to light, heat, air, or similar atmospheric compound, and of course water, every essential human requirement would be maintained, including repairs. No additional support was required.

"The reconstruction of my right eye is almost complete Clara. In the morning, I will continue to wear dark glasses, for continuity I still need to maintain your inspired disguise." Frank paused, "the replacement eye will need time to calibrate to sunlight, but beneath the glass there will be two eyes, not one. And yes Clara, they will match." Frank declared lightly. "Good night Clara, I wish you sweet dreams." Frank started to sing: *"And I think it's gonna be a long, long, time."* *Rocket Man*. Clara had made him sing the song half-a-dozen times in succession after the first hearing, she was looking forward to listening to more compositions from Mr. John. Clara drifted immediately into slumber, safe in the promise the morning would usher in another wonderful day.

Frank woke abruptly from his dream, he was confronted with a choice. He had considered the new eye beneath the patch with joyful anticipation for some days, and today was the day. A thrill coursed through him at the prospect of gazing again into a mirror, studying himself, what the accident had done to him. He had looked behind the bandage just once. Once was too much. But on the other hand: there was the dream still fresh in his mind. He couldn't let the fragments drift into infinity, this was a real dream. The eye would have to wait.

The memory was already beginning to fade, Frank did his utmost to hold on to the pieces. He watched with fascination a pair of frenetic hands, crossing during a performance on a keyboard. Frank marvelled at the pianist's technique, the fluid, crisp articulation. It was a child, and the *wunderkind* was inspired. A prodigy, but Frank struggled to identify the melody. There was no archive?

Dreams are precious, Frank noted and sank back to study the canyons of his mind. Most folks from his time never had one, an authentic dream that is, but the majority of people don't travel back in time and get their brains blasted into nothing.

Real dreams were something to take notice of. Frank paused; *'listen and learn'*, a forgotten voice advised. Frank considered the dreams he experienced as Five. In reality a series of memory implants, actively distributed among the mass of humanity, reinforcing the connection with an aspirational home of yesterday — reinforcing all manner of things. Frank wondered if Five knew? Frank could see the archives. He reset his focus and went back to the dream. *'Listen and learn'*. If the dream wasn't generated from an implant, it had to be something real. And the child? Frank needed a piano.

It proved to be a more difficult decision than Frank anticipated; what to play? When you sit before the keyboard of a fine instrument it really is the only question, but Frank had yet to take possession of the astonishing ability the dream suggested. Where to start? He had to find the right piece. The choice of music would need to reflect a range of elements. The quality of the instrument in question. In this instance, a 1911 Steinway model O in rosewood. The tones of the pianoforte would need to blend with the ambience of the space, also a consideration of great importance. But above all contenders in the repertoire selection process, the audience will always reign supreme. Frank discovered the rush to please once again. But not only Clara and Mr. Fairbrother, it was the entire household Frank was eager to reach. His mission was always one step beyond. He knew what he would play.

Chopin's Nocturne Op.9 No. 2, in Eb major, begins with a leap of joy, Bb to G, a major sixth. The rosewood lid was open like a flower, allowing the full expression of complex pianoforte tones to bask in the room's ambience, the bright, crisp reflections of marble and glass. Opus 9 no. 2 features essentially two melodies and each time they are played it is with new, and always subtle, but brilliant ornamentation. Frank's touch was an infinite gradation of delicate. The notes of the right hand whispered their song above the waltzing chords of the left, a wash of lightning-like flashes of technical dexterity. Shimmering cascades of falling dissonance pirouetting into reverential cadences. Frank held the entire household in a spell for four and a half minutes. At first they trickled in, unbidden by any words, a gentle stream, drawn like Pan's Children with the enchantment of music. And in the ebbing moments of the Nocturne, when Frank finally discarded rhythm — 'senza tempo' as Chopin had instructed — the audience held their breath, finding resolution, absolution, in the concluding major chord. Eb has such resonance, Frank noted. Nobody moved. A total silence fell around them. Frank stood from the piano stretching to his full 6'5" frame. He was clad in a stylish combination of dark glasses, ribbed wool hat, and khaki long johns, protruding beneath a blue, paisley-patterned silk smoking jacket a couple of sizes too small. "I am feeling much better now, much recovered. I am Frank, my companion is Nurse Clara. We would like to thank you most sincerely for your hospitality." A hesitant smattering at first, but then the drawing-room erupted with applause. Frank took a bow. Not anything dramatic, a subtle movement of the head and upper body, but it prompted an unexpected response. "More", came the first shout. "Another," Harper called. "Please carry on." Requested Mr. Fairbrother, the cook, and several more. Frank said nothing but retook his seat at the piano. He had enjoyed the solid certainty of Eb major, the key prompted the next selection.

"A jolly piece by Claude Debussy." Announced Frank, stretching forth his mind to reach out and touch the sensitivities of his flock. He produced another mesmerising performance. The instrument had never before been put to such extreme demands. The insistent, brisk staccato phrasing would inflict punishment on any set of piano strings, especially those left dormant and dusty from one Christmas party to the next, but this was a Steinway, a name synonymous with quality. Bold octaves announced the opening, followed by a rhythmic pulse, slowly insinuating, compelling — *once upon a time in a land far away* — there was drama, as well as dancing feet. Always think about your audience. Debussy composed the piece for his daughter, '*Chou-Chou*'. He even drew her a picture. This was a children's tale in music narrated by a doting father. Debussy, proudly French, couldn't resist poking fun at a musical German bad guy, who tried to spoil the rhythmic game with minor six melodies. Debussy's composition was a delightful and complex piece of music, but it was Frank's interpretation, that brought it to such vivid life. The drawing-room filled with rhythm and humour. The audience soaked in the syncopations, the subtle undertones of Jazz, the swagger. Debussy had written music for the future. Frank observed the crossed hands, a blur of complex syncopations — it was the dream, but the composition's name still continued to elude him. Frank could only wonder why?

30

THE BEST I EVER HEARD

He knew it was a mistake to order a double brandy, and then another. Sometimes the mood simply takes you. And occasionally it swept him into a pile of dust and blew the mess into nothing. Usually, there wasn't anyone around to observe, but that was before Betts. BB. There had been many distinct periods in Hadleigh's life. There was before school, the school itself, brief periods of outstanding success in sport, music, in fact, everything he touched. And there was the War. All of that could be easily summarised as BB — before Betts — because, before her, there was nothing of the past that mattered anymore. It was gone, but it took Betts to allow himself to let it go. Betts found them two rooms at the Inn and they slept an easy night in their separate rooms.

"How do you feel Sir?" Betts questioned over breakfast.

"My head is protesting at my folly. Ale and brandy; aah the very thought. I didn't say anything foolish did I?"

"What sort of foolish Sir?"

"Well, I don't know really? That's why I'm asking?"

"But what if you had said something? Which the following day you had completely, or almost completely forgotten you said. Should a girl risk embarrassment by reminding you? Or simply pretend it never happened?"

"Aah, my head hurts. Why are you doing this to a chap, Betts?"

Betts took pity on the ailing Hadleigh. "Don't worry Sir. There was no foolishness, I promise. What's the plan, Sir?"

"I think we understand why the pair were here, and also the success of their street busking. I would imagine they made a lot of easy money. I have no doubt they will be tempted to do this again, but not here. They'll turn up and perform around other small towns, especially with the Christmas season imminent; they make their money and disappear. I believe the trail here has gone cold, they've gone to ground. Let's give them a couple of weeks to put down some fresh tracks. Then we follow."

"And what next Sir?"

"We pursue the other lead, the shopkeeper in Swanage, Dykes. I am hoping he might lead us to the woman, the *odd* woman.

They stepped out of the Inn, the early morning air was fresh and chill, but there was no wind. The heavy sky was a uniform grey. The car was parked only a short distance from the Inn, the detective pair walked with coats pulled tight around them. Hadleigh studied the sky expecting to witness the threat of snow, when his musical antennae picked something up from the frigid air, the unmistakeable sound of a piano. Chopin. The connection was instant, like a lost love, someone who taught you how to feel. Poor Hadleigh was snared. His mind had yet to truly settle from the night before, but this was a deeper intoxication, this was music. "We have to follow the piano Betts." Hadleigh explained. They soon found themselves in Princes Street arriving just in time to witness the applause, and the shouts for more, and the silence. Hadleigh and Betts stood and waited a few moments longer in the damp, still morning air. Just in case, and patience was rewarded. The syncopated octaves of Debussy's Golliwog's Cakewalk leapt from the windows of the Mansion. Hadleigh was beyond words, trapped in a slipstream of memory. Paris, 1908, He had been there at the first performance of *Children's Corner*, a suite of six pieces, and this was piece no 6, the finale. His favourite. Hadleigh had bought the music the same day, memorising every musical heartbeat of the manuscript. He took a sharp intake of breath, his ear caught something totally new, Debussy was mocking Wagner, the minor sixth angst of Tristan. The answering phrases poked fun at the composer. Of course they did, they always had, but only now did it make sense. When the music ended, they hoped and waited for more, but the impromptu concert was clearly over. Hadleigh was tempted to knock on the door and offer his compliments to the maestro within, but this was the very private year of 1919. Instead, he and Betts walked on air back to the car.

"Just how good was that pianist Sir?" Betts asked, once safely back on the road to Swanage.

"Honestly Betts, the best I ever heard."

31

RESILIENT

Lists, aah, Seven could wax lyrical about lists, they resonated with her systematic desire for order. Everything should have structure and purpose. She paused. Her purpose? Her mission had changed? Mother always gave her missions specifically suited to her talents. But Mother no longer spoke to her, encouraged her, told her what to do. That was part of a time frame that no longer existed, or more accurately, had yet to exist. Everything had indeed changed. Mother, to a degree, was now reliant upon Seven to deliver up a future that would include said, Mother. So what title would she bestow upon herself? God-Mother? Seven smiled. It required the stimulation of a cocktail of up to forty-two muscles to create a smile, this was not a common occurrence, but Seven, without possibility of contradiction, smiled. And it felt good. The list contained four names and four addresses. It was simple as that. But actually not quite so simple, the addresses were spread far and wide across the nation. Seven would need transport and a new disguise. What she really needed was a complete identity. A cover story. Her fertile mind swam with possibility. Authority figures dwell in the illusion of power. They demand respect, she felt the resonance. But women of this time held little or no juris-diction. Independence, that was the key. An independent persona and her own independent transport. Her mind flipped to Five and the previous mission. He was like that; different. Special.

"WOULD YOU CARE TO HEAR A SONG?" Five wondered aloud.

It was rude of him to intrude into her thoughts, but Seven took the offer in the spirit in which it dwelt. Listening to a musical performance was a unique opportunity. A gift beyond rare. She wasn't even sure if it was legal?

"Won't they know?" Seven wondered.

"I don't care." Five declared aloud. "I want you to hear music Seven, I want to sing to you."

Seven was caught in a quandary. Every inch of her training said an emphatic No! But intuition had always been her ally. She made a quick nod.

"Two fingers on my arm." He instructed, and Seven touched into a world of secret, sensory bliss.

"*It's sad, so sad. Why can't we talk it over? Ohh, it seems to me. That sorry seems to be the hardest word.*" He sang.

Seven's world would never be the same again

FIVE WAS INDEED A MOST valuable asset, and that's what also made him a target. She frowned. Seven hadn't made the connec-tion before and it was more than a possibility, it was statistically probable the explosion and her package, Five, were intrinsically linked. Which also inferred her beloved and trusted Mother considered Seven expendable. Not any more. She felt the God in

God-Mother. To the people of this time, Seven might indeed be considered God-like; she could certainly stir up some thunder and more. But eventually, like all tyrants, she would come unstuck. Seven was as mortal as the next man or woman, she wasn't invincible, just incredibly tough and resilient. Yes, an appropriate word, Seven bounced back, she always found a way. So how was she going to travel to Margate? In the county of Kent? To find Roberts? The first name on the list. She revelled in her own definition; Seven was resilient. She would find a way.

32

MINOS

The household finally dispersed back to reality and the daily rituals of life. "I've asked Harper to lay something out for you in the breakfast room, I hope you're ready for something wholesome?" Mr. Fairbrother enquired hopefully. He'd heard the whispers. "Once you've eaten, perhaps you might join me by the fire? I would be most grateful." Frank declined any notions of food, however, he was persuaded to accept a glass of freshly drawn water. Nurse Clara on the other hand lost all sense of inhibition, visiting and re-visiting the silver platters with the enthusiasm of one of the faithful venerating holy relics.

The three sat in armchairs surrounding a fire of hearty, crackling logs. It was ten-thirty am. The sullen November morning beyond the walls and windows of the mansion, suggested the bitter cold of scarves, gloves, and hats, but inside, all was snug and cosy.

"I thought if I were to tell you something of me, the journey that brought me to this moment, you might be happy to answer some of the questions I have about you? I do not want to pry, but your apparent situation, when considered alongside your astonishing talents makes not the least sense. I simply wish to understand and if I can? I would like to offer help. No judgement to anything you might say would be attached." Mr. Fairbrother paused to raise an eyebrow.

"Thank you." Declared Frank simply, followed by a nod.

Mr. Fairbrother composed himself in his chair. "I was born in this house, it has been my honour to call it home for the majority of my years. Privilege was always mine. I was the third of three brothers, but while my elder siblings were burdened with title and expectation, I was indulged. I studied in Paris, the Conservatoire, I was barely in my twenties. My professor of singing was Ernest Boulanger and through him I discovered I had a voice, my voice. Studying at the Conservatoire opened my eyes. I was immersed in an all-consuming culture of music, art, sculpture, and more. I found Heaven on Earth. Paris became my spiritual home." The old man paused. "1872 was a pivotal year. It started with a strange anomaly in the skies, the Northern Lights, the Aurora Borealis were visible in Paris that February. The lights could be seen all over Europe. It was the year my life changed course. My parents died together in a tragic accident and I was immediately recalled from my studies back to England. There was no will. No parental trust to support my independence. My sole income was reliant upon the good nature of my eldest brother, and there was no goodness in his nature. I believe it was his school that brought out the beast in him, the anger. It is a part of us, certainly the Fairbrother males', but Edward carried additional scars. I was instructed to find a profession, '*and get on with life*'. His very words, I've never forgotten. The death of my parents was a terrible blow, I was weak; I capitulated. But the injustice of my situation inspired my choice of profession. I studied for the law. My musical skills were a constant ally. The least inflections of tone and pitch became instantly visible to me, I could hear people lie. And I performed.

I was at my best before a jury. I took on the challenge of bringing the twelve jurors to my side, my client's side, and I was highly selective of whom I would represent. My one and only criterion was justice. Through my injustice, I would bring justice to others. I believe I have been the conduit to a little more light in the world, especially among the many people who held no hope of representation. But after forty and more years life would abruptly change again. My eldest brother, Edward, and his second wife Anna were fated to take a trip to New York. The tickets were presented as a gift. I remember distinctly the strong sense of discomfort I experienced, perhaps it was premonition? Our parents had perished in a collision at sea, but I said nothing. The ship they boarded was the Titanic. My brother and his wife had but one child, a son, George. He was barely thirteen when his parents were lost, George was away at prep school. The year was 1912 and I had achieved sixty-five years. I felt the injustice for that poor boy. Alone in the world without parents, and stuck in that most vile institution, hiding 'neath the mantle of education. The legal formalities presented no problems, I became George's guardian and benefactor, there had always existed a special kinship with the young man. We shared a love of music; George was a gifted pianist, a fellow musician in the family, we had a bond. I immediately took George out of school. He was educated here, in Princes Street, by the best tutors I could engage. I gave up my career. Life had new meaning. I willingly devoted my time to George. And we thrived. When the war began in 1914 George was fifteen. We had been to see Rubinstein performing earlier that year, it was May, the Beckstein Hall in London. Rubinstein's performance was truly astounding. There was a Beethoven sonata on the programme and George was so taken, so inspired. But the drums of war beat louder and my George, like so many others, was swept up in the fervour of it. The blind patriotism of the political propaganda, it was sickening. It took the best part of a year, but by 1915, I had uncovered the truth of the situation. My second brother, Edwin, had spent a career, his entire life in the military. He and many like him wished their days away, waiting for moments in history such as this; the chance to stand up and be counted. I fear for what Edwin represents, but he was a connected and loquacious source of truth unavailable in the press. I invited my brother on regular occasions for dinner. I endured his relish in recounting the slaughter, the shameful lack of leadership, the calculated industrial-scale killing, the incompetence." Mr. Fairbrother paused to sigh and shake his head. "My only hope was the conflict might end before George was old enough to enlist. But he couldn't wait, and his Uncle Edwin, his own flesh and blood, turned out to be a viper. George asked for his help to enlist and Edwin used his exalted connections to draft George into the army fold, the Royal Fusileers, when George was still only sixteen. A fusileer. George barely knew how to hold a rifle. A month's training on Salisbury Plain and they shipped them off to France. Another month and that wonderful, talented boy was just another casualty in a futile litany of destruction. Harper was with him when he died, the Battle of Bazentin Ridge, a village by the name of Bazentin le Petit. At least he wasn't alone; a bitter consolation. They went out there together, but only Harper came back. So there you have it. The best part of me died along with George in July 1916. The Somme. A name that should forever ring in infamy. It has been pure, unadulterated anger that kept me alive. A terrible rage that burned for two whole years until the night I heard you sing. Hearing your voice released me from my purgatory. It was as if an Angel had spoken, finally, I could find release. That is my story, but what about you my boy? Please, Frank, share what brought you here?"

Frank studied Mr. Fairbrother with kindness and compassion. "As far as I can know such things, I am confident to speak openly and without fear of censure or mockery in this good company." Frank paused to smile and acknowledge them both. "Mr Fairbrother, my belief is you are a man of faith? You wear a cross around your neck. Perhaps you are familiar with a passage from the Christian Bible? The Gospel of John 10:32. Jesus speaks to a group of followers. '*And You Shall Know the Truth and the Truth Shall Make You Free.*' What I have to say to you both is an untarnished version of the truth. My truth admittedly, but honest and without taint. If you accept this truth it will change your perception of the world. I hope this will ultimately reflect in an enhanced, deeper sense of understanding of the realm we inhabit. But the knowledge might also engender anxiety and possibly fear. I hope I have been clear? If you want the truth, I will speak openly. But where there is light, there is also shadow."

"Of course my boy, I seek nothing less than truth." Mr. Fairbrother's face quivered with a smile.

"You already know my answer Frank, whatever you might say, I know who you are." Clara smiled.

With a nod to Clara, Frank began. "Clara knows much of my story. Essentially, an accident brought me here. I was en route to a new destination, the city of Minos; an underwater, off-world metropolis located on Europa. But there was some manner of catastrophe with our craft and instead of Europa I was propelled here. Galileo discovered Europa in 1610. The city of Minos was constructed on Europa in the year 2205. Europa is moon number six of the planet Jupiter and slightly smaller than our Earth's moon. The celestial body was named after a Phoenician Princess. It is also the sixth-largest moon in the Solar System and 623.8 million kilometres from Earth. The human population of Minos in 2235 approximated 4.3 million. Would you like me to continue?"

33

FLASH-BULBS

E ven with the passage of time and the removal of the shopkeeper's macabre, twisted body, it was still diffi- cult not to recall his expression of total surprise, captured in the instant of death. A visage of livid horror. Betts shuddered, but her resolve didn't waver, she removed the padlocks and chains from the outer door with silent efficiency and stepped inside the sweet shop. The wooden shutters were firmly closed with iron braces, but still, tiny fragments of light managed to pierce the gloom. Betts switched on the light. Elec- tric, with expensive brass fittings. She raised an eyebrow. The sweet shop occupied an old sea-front cottage. It was not large, but it was sturdy, it had to withstand one hundred and more years facing the sea. The shop part had once been the front parlour, it looked out to the horizon with hope. With the shut- ters open and the sun shining this could be a bright airy space, but in darkness, it felt small and claustrophobic. A doorway connected to the back of the house leading to a sitting room with a decent-sized fireplace. This in turn led to a small annex with a tiny kitchen and toilet. The sitting room was where Dykes met his end, sat at the walnut desk, updating accounts, the inner part of the house was his office. A thin, steep staircase led to the first floor — two bedrooms and a bathroom.

"What are we looking for Sir?"

"I believe we will know the answer once we find it." Hadleigh would occasionally lapse into these cryptic comments. Betts found the tone vaguely annoying, but she said nothing. They searched the house extensively without result.

"Would he have a vehicle Sir?" Opened a new vista of inquiry.

THEY FOUND the Ford Model T in a brick-built garage at the back of the house. It was a recent version of the Roadster, but the back seat had been removed to make a more practical commercial vehicle, capable of goods transportation. "No electronic starter Sir," Betts observed with a shake of her head. "Not a patch on the Wolseley," Betts decided. She also found a notebook concealed under the single front seat that spanned the width of the vehicle. It contained columns of letters and numbers. Betts mentioned the notebook to Hadleigh and put it safe in her pocket for later.

"WHAT HAVE WE MISSED BETTS? I am convinced there has to be something here, in this room. Out of sight of the customers. Tell me what you see?"

"The fireplace is well stocked. Stacks of logs, neat and tidy. Good quality desk and chair, orderly arrangement of letters, box files. There are no photographs Sir."

"Indeed Betts, in fact, no paintings, pictures of any description. Sorry, please go on."

"The rest of the furniture. Sofa, armchair, floral cloth, inexpensive, nondescript. But by contrast, a magnificent table. A fine piece of Victorian mahogany standing right in the middle of the floor." Betts paused to trail her fingers across the wood. "This table and the rug it stands upon tell a different tale, they are as alien to this space as visitors from another world. An alternative reality of quality and style. They belong somewhere else." Betts knelt to touch and inspect the rug. "This is made from fine silk and the elaborate designs are Islamic. I would purchase this rug in an instant, and I guarantee it wouldn't be cheap. Neither belongs here, Sir."

"Hmm," Hadleigh murmured. "We have already noted the smuggling thread that persists just beneath the surface of daily life in these parts. With your usual precision Betts, you have successfully identified the anomaly we sought, now we need to discover what lies beneath. If we move the table toward the door we can roll back the rug."

Hadleigh and Betts paused to review the treasure hidden under the fine silk rug, a hinged opening to a secret chamber beneath the floor. "I don't suppose you have a torch by chance Betts?"

"In the car, Sir, give me two minutes. And don't do anything without me?" Betts called back, running out to retrieve her torch.

The hatch was well constructed, a solid square yard of pitch-pine frame and trap-door. Brass hinges secured the lid, all perfectly recessed. The top opened with only a whisper of sound, a gentle swish of air. The mechanism was well-oiled, it was clearly in regular use.

"You were supposed to wait for me, Sir?" Betts declared with an accusing tone.

"I did. Here I go Betts."

"Sir! Wait!"

"The answer's no. It is my responsibility to go first and there's nothing more to be said. But I'd be grateful for some light Betts."

"Yes Sir." Betts shook her head disapprovingly and directed her torch into the void. The drop was around 12', but a sturdy elm ladder ran all the way down. Hadleigh was adept with his one arm, he had once been a mountaineer, a vertical descent and but one good arm was not an issue. "Catch Sir", Betts called out and threw Hadleigh the torch. She followed in an instant. The cellar was a good size. What had once been a natural cavern had been extended into the bedrock with picks and shovels. Smuggling once again would have been at the root of this endeavour, but possibly not the sort of illicit merchandise that would have interested Mr. Dykes. Although his trade was equally illegal and nefarious.

"There was something Dykes said when under duress with customers waiting. It set alarm bells ringing then, and to be honest Betts, the implication has never really left my mind."

"*Waifs and strays* Sir."

"Exactly. You too? Of course. The sheer bravado of the man, "*they all find their way to me*". Hadleigh shone the torch on three cages in a line against the stone wall. They were small at just under a yard in width, a yard and a half high. About the right size for a small child. "What do we have over here Betts?" Hadleigh shone the torch on a black leather doctor's bag. Betts removed a bottle, "a little more light if you wouldn't mind Sir?"

"Sorry Betts."

"This is," Betts paused, "morphine Sir. There are also swabs and syringes. And there was something on the floor by the bag Sir, it flashed in the light of the torch." Hadleigh shone the beam into the darkness and as Betts predicted, a myriad of reflections sparkled from the floor. Betts investigated. "They're broken flashbulbs Sir. Dyke's would seem to have been taking photographs."

34

YOU LOOK WONDERFUL

S even gazed into the shop window. She had been walking for 2 hours, an easy 10 miles from Swanage to Fareham. Her ultimate destination was Margate. As yet, there wasn't a plan to make the rest of the 187.7 miles a little speedier, but she'd made an early start, the dewy air made her face tingle, and her confidence was high. Most of Wareham had yet to wake up to the early hours of this Friday morning. Seven watched a milkman make his deliveries.

"Good morning Sir." Seven greeted in her brightest tones.

"Miss." He muttered, not knowing quite what to say.

There was clearly a problem. Seven quickly checked her reflection in the window glass. The soot-inscribed eyebrows had dispersed around her eyes, creating deep, dark hollows. Seven gave the impression of a re-animated corpse; a better solution was required. She studied her surroundings. North Street. An elegant Town Hall with a clock and spire, a solid and very square Lloyds Bank, a cavernous *Colmers* Department Store, but of particular interest, Thorn's Motor Cycles. Seven saw the solution to her trip to Margate in the window display, a *Brough Supe-*

rior Mark 1. It was the chrome fuel tank that first caught her eye, but the entire machine presented a wonderful meld of shining silver metal and black steel. Seven was spellbound at the intricate simplicity. Each and every hand-wrought part was on display. Seven assessed the entire workings of the machine in a single glance. A well-built and solid vehicle for its time. She pushed open the shop-door. Seven was glad of the darkness of the interior. The assistant sat behind a counter, he barely stirred, he was busy removing oil from his hands with a cloth. "Sorry Miss, I'll be with you in just a mo, don't normally get customers this early on, but please, feel free to browse Miss. No obligation." Seven thought she was only interested in the motor-cycle until she saw the outfits, the bike-riding leathers. This was a costume she understood. "How much for the full outfit?" She enquired

The mechanic quickly looked up. "They're on the expensive-side I'm afraid Miss, the leather's a nightmare to stitch, everything 'as to be done by hand. Are you enquiring about the full kit? Boots, gloves, cap, everything?"

"Yes, the complete outfit, and the *Brough Superior Mark 1* in the window."

"Bless my soul!" The mechanic declared. "Two 'undred quid Miss."

"Can I take it all today?"

"You can indeed Miss. Am I correct in the assumption the vehicle and the costume are for your good self?"

"Yes."

"I can have it all ready for you within the hour Miss."

"Very good. I will return shortly with the money. Oh... Do you know where I might find some assistance with make-up?"

"My wife swears by the make-up counter in Colmers. If that's any use?"

"Thank you, you've been most helpful."

Seven experienced a sense of mild elation. She felt the inter-action with the 20th century mechanic had been characterised by normality. She was learning to adapt. Flushed with success, she carried on up North Street. The clock told her it was twelve minutes after seven. The opening time at the bank was adver-tised for 10:00 am. Daylight was still an hour away, there was no moon and the only sign of life was the taciturn milkman. Seven watched the cart and horse clank away. Finally she was alone. The bank was a grand architectural statement with Doric pillars and finely cut granite steps. Within three seconds she was inside the locked doors. Seven studied the space with caution, a force of habit not necessarily relevant to this time. Sensors were yet to be invented and cameras were still big and clunky, totally unsuited to the concept of discrete monitoring. Certainly not in 1919. Infra-red beams crossed her mind as she traversed the marble-engraved floor, but they too were still to be invented. The architecture surrounding her was impressively monumen-tal, it was almost like being in a temple. Seven saw the irony. The people of the twentieth century had learned to worship acquisi-tion, money. Buildings like this were a living testament to the shift in social dynamic, from God to Finance. But Seven had little interest in the sociology of their century, she had but one thought, to find the £200 she needed for the mission. History told her it would be secured in a vault. It was almost a challenge, but Seven was well prepared. She scanned and quickly found the huge core of metal, and from that point it was simply a succession of failing locks. When you have a small army of nano-bots available to do your bidding, there was no analogue lock in this world that Seven could not open with ease.

Seven found herself literally surrounded with money. Shelves of the stuff, bundles upon bundles upon bundles of notes, but Seven wasn't greedy. She had no conception of the word, Seven was practical. She took four of the wads of flighty five-pound notes, each valued at £500 and secured them in her coat pockets. £2,000 should cover any immediate needs. Seven retraced her steps, diligently re-locking every door to the vault. She was set to make the final journey across the elaborate bank floor when she heard a key in the front door. Seven froze. Two people furtively stepped in and immediately re-shut the only exit to the bank. Seven hid behind a tellers desk. She still wore her first disguise, the 20th century lady. Seven watched their every move.

"Give us a kiss Jules."

"No 'arold, just wait. We 'ave to listen first. Make sure." They stood, stock-still in a moment of absolute silence.

"There's no one 'ere Jules. We're all right. We got twenty minutes at least."

"Are you sure 'arold? I wouldn't wanna lose my job?"

"Of course I'm sure. But the clock's ticking girl. What da ya say?"

"Oh, all right 'arold, but you'd better be quick."

"You don't have to worry about that." Harold declared with a laugh.

"Here, let me." The girl said and knelt before the young man, un-buttoning his fly.

Seven found herself staring at the couple as if she were witnessing the eruption of Vesuvius. Fellatio was another of those words that forever failed to capture and express the raw passion and pleasure that accompanied the act. And for the second time that day, Seven sensed elation, but this time spreading forth from her groin. It was most unsettling.

"Aargh." Harold cried out and it was over. Save for the jerk-ing, quaking, spasm.

Julie stood. A handkerchief quickly to her mouth, she pulled and straightened her outfit. "Are you feeling better now 'arold?"

"Oh yes girl. Thank you so much Jules. I don't reckon as how I could have gotten through the 'ole day."

"Then you can buy me a fresh lemonade at lunch. Com'on 'arold. We gotta go." And the pair departed, locking the door behind them.

THE MECHANIC LOOKED at Seven really for the first time. He thought she looked pretty good. He admired the strength of her body shape, the proud slope of muscle-tone.

Seven basked in the praise spilling from his mind like an overfilled glass. She had anticipated a quick, efficient business transaction, but something in her perception was rapidly evolving. Seven found a smile. "I have the two hundred pounds. If you don't mind, I'd like to put the leathers on now. Would that be convenient?" Seven enquired lightly.

"Yes, er. Yes, that's fine Miss. I'll fetch them for you right away."

When the mechanic returned Seven had removed all of her 20th century clothing except for the wig. Of course Seven still wore her suit. It clung to her form like a shimmering silk bodice. The mechanic proffered the leathers, trying out of respect not to stare. "No stay." Seven insisted as he turned to leave the room. "I want you to watch." The mechanic stood frozen, caught in her web. Seven made herself comfortable on an elm kitchen chair. She raised a long, slender leg to 90° and pulled slowly at the leather trousers. Leather was a word from the past. Beyond memory and almost beyond meaning. Seven identified the hide, the genus *Sus*, formed from a pig. The skin was soft, supple, dense, it had undoubtedly once been genuine flesh. There were few in her time who would be comfortable wearing the skin of what had once been a living, sentient being. It was absolute anathema to their sensibilities. But Seven was pragmatic about such things. She chose to honour this gift of an animal's life, albeit so cruelly sacrificed. By the time she put on the leather waistcoat Seven was no longer thinking about animals. The mechanic could almost taste the pheromones, even if he had no idea what they might be. He stepped forward and took Seven in his arms. She felt his erection pressing hard against her. "Here, let me." She said and knelt before him, unbuttoning the fly to his blue overalls.

MARGARET HAD WORKED on the make-up counter in *Colmers* for the last twenty-two years, since she was barely fifteen in fact, but Margaret didn't talk about that. She didn't talk about them either. Of course she knew they existed, or at least, she'd heard the others' gossip. But then this... this creature in leather trousers — leather everything! — had the audacity to march into her... Margaret's place of work? Asking for advice? What was the world coming too? If it were not for Margaret's devotion to God, and Jesus, and of course the job itself, she would have walked out there and then.

"I would like you to use your expert skills and apply makeup to my face. I would also require you to explain the process as you undertake each task. I will pay you whatever you request. If it is convenient? I would like you to perform the task now?" Seven was eager to conclude the transaction.

"£20." Margaret announced. Seven handed over four, crisp, white £5 notes. Margaret began her woeful task with deep sighs and a mind fixed in determination. But after a short time, as the contours of the female beneath her expert hands began to emerge, she soon forgot about — Margaret reflected until she could accurately remember the appropriate phrase — the woman's *sexual orienteering*. Margaret frowned. That didn't sound quite right? Anyway, it wasn't as if she, Margaret, were an authority by any means. Margaret made a "tsk" sound. She thought of Ronald. Oh Ronald. Their secret trysts in the store room. Margaret quivered at the memory. If only he hadn't been transferred to Nottingham? If only? Who was she trying to fool? She knew what the store room was — convenient. Margaret observed the woman's thighs. The leather was tight to the flesh, Margaret couldn't help but notice the exquisite shape. Her eyes followed the body-line. Margaret had been aware of the statuesque form as the female approached. An easy 6'. Tall, wonderfully elegant. The way she strode across the floor. So confident. Better than any man. The deep musk of the leather stirred into the mix of sensation slowly seeping through her. Margaret felt the warm flush of arousal taking a grip. She had to focus. It was time to talk and Margaret liked nothing better than talking about what she did. Bringing this woman's face and skin to life would be a real challenge, but there was nothing wrong with the Lord sending us the occasional trial. We just have to rise to meet it. And Margaret's thirty-minute ordeal emerged as the culmination of those twenty-two years. Margaret stepped back and studied her handiwork with a smile that was difficult to put away. She had impressed even herself, Margaret was a true artist. Seven studied herself in the mirror. "If you don't mind my saying, there is just one final adjustment," Margaret suggested with a twinkle in her eye — she knew Seven wore a wig. "I think you need something more fitting. Dramatic. Severe even. Follow me." Margaret instructed.

They traversed the store together, Margaret and her leather-clad customer. Margaret relished in the brief walk. The entire store stopped as the elegant pair strode the departments. Margaret felt strangely safe in her companion's aura of confidence. "I'm sure my idea will work." Margaret confided. The girl at the wig counter was new. Margaret quickly dismissed her and took over. She found a short, symmetrical bob, selected from the finest Asian, jet black hair. Seven considered herself in the mirror. The new-look was transformational. Seven smiled with pleasure. And when Margaret declared, "you look wonderful." She absolutely meant every word.

35

THE LIVING PROOF

"My introduction to your world was a sandy beach near the town of Swanage eleven nights ago. I was near death, but I was dragged out of the sea and to the shore by a companion. We were travelling to Europa together. She was responsible for my safe passage, but there was an accident, an explosion, resulting in our vehicle crashing into the sea. My colleague left me secure in a beach hut and went back to the ship for supplies. She didn't return. I have no idea what happened to her. I was found later the same day and taken to a Convent, where Clara saved me from certain death at the hands of the Sisters of Mercy. In many ways, the person who appeared in your world those eleven nights previous did die, but his body somehow survived along with blurred remnants of his consciousness. That is where my story begins. Five, for that, was his name, was different, special. He had become a high-value asset." Frank paused, he heard the questions. "I will explain. The world I left, your future, has changed beyond anything you might imagine. Technology has transformed humanity. There is no hunger, no disease or illness, virtually no crime of any description. No war, no money, there is no want or need for anything material. Everyone has a designated role, their personal part to play in the ongoing story of Man's survival." Frank paused. "Most of humanity in the twenty-third century is enhanced. Human beings are no longer simply flesh and blood and bone, our minds and bodies are further developed — the enhancing — with biological engineering according to our needs. The twin realms of physical and thought processes are honed and developed to support the path we are allocated in the New Order. Life is highly choreographed in the future. This century, yours', the twentieth, is the antithesis in many respects. There is very little structure here. No organisation on a global level. That will come. In purely musical terms the twentieth is often identified as 'The Century of Song'. There were more songs written during this period than at any other time before or since,. Human creativity was at its zenith, despite the atrocities of tyrants and dictators and the ever more effective killing machines of war. Sadly, the perpetual cycle of carnage and devastation was also a characteristic of this time. The chaos spread into the next century and the social order that held humanity together began to break down. If we were to survive, the world would need a new paradigm. By the latter end of the 21st Century, 2066, the New Order had established a system of world governance. There was once again purpose, structure, a cohesive society. The early disasters of experimental bio-engineering and gene manipulation were gradually ironed out of the surviving populations and new vaccines were finally stabilised to provide 100% protection against all known disease and illness. Humans were no longer the impotent victims of sickness and squalor, equilibrium was restored, but the price was unexpected. In the forced human evolutionary process something had subtly changed. Nobody composed songs anymore, or painted pictures, or made sculptures, or wrote poetry, plays, and novels. Within a generation performing music became a lost art along with all the others. Creativity in human beings had died. Not for all of humanity, but by far the majority. Which brings us back to Five. He was always destined to be different. His was an organic birth. From a Mother and a Father. Something generally frowned upon in the New Order, and most definitely not the standard route for childbirth into the twenty-third century. A significant component to the success of the new paradigm was reproduction. Offspring of my century are created in birthing pods with minimal human contact at every stage of the procedure. This became the new standard for the enhancing of reproduction over a century ago. From conception to birth, nurture to infant, the New Paradigm regulated and sustained the survival of Man, even if men and women were not directly involved. Inevitably, as soon as Five's talent was identified, his parents were deemed unsuitable and Five was adopted into a conservatoire linked to one of the Dynasties, the Patrons of The New Paradigm. Five was three years old. He spent the next ten years at the conservatoire being trained in every aspect of music. Five became a master musician. His physical form was inevitably enhanced, but his mind was mostly left untouched, the difference had to be retained. On reaching physical maturity at thirteen years, Five was fitted with a sophisticated bodysuit, only available to the highest orders, and through the conservatoire, Five gained access to the greatest music libraries the world has ever known. Five was ready to take his place within The New Paradigm — The New Order. His value as an asset soared. Five became an instant and outstanding success across the planets and moons of the solar system, Mankind's new playground. Five was a musical phenomenon. His gift was unique. The highly select audiences were transformed after they heard him perform. Their senses became stirred, activated. Five was my predecessor. As an individual Five is gone, but his gifts have life in me. I have been resurrected as Frank."

"Good Lord Sir. I am at a loss for words. I hardly know what to think?" Declared a pale Mr Fairbrother. Frank could hear the doubt and indecision in the old man's mind. Mr Fairbrother wanted to believe, but it was simply too much to accept.

"I appreciate how alien my story must sound, please allow me to show you something Mr. Fairbrother, by way of demonstration." Frank stood from his chair and knelt before the old man. "Put your hands in mine Mr. Fairbrother and try to relax." For a few moments the only sound in the room was the occasional crackle bursting from the burning logs. "Your back is badly damaged. You suffer with scoliosis Mr. Fairbrother. Do you understand the nature of this condition?"

"I have been in various degrees of pain for the last forty years. It's been twenty since I was last able to stand straight. Various doctors have prescribed differing forms of opium. That is all I know."

"The bones of your spine have become progressively more rigid, and there is some curvature. Eventually, your spine will fuse completely. The pain must be difficult to bear?" Frank observed.

"You learn to live with it. It never leaves, but one adapts. I have no interest in developing addictions as an alternative." Fairbrother shook his head in resignation.

"I can help you Mr Fairbrother. I can take away the pain and repair the damage to your bones?" Frank maintained his grip on Fairbrother's hands.

The old man made a faint smile. "That would certainly be an impressive validation. I gratefully accept." The old man laughed. "Please Sir, do your worst, I am totally at your disposal."

"We need to maintain this physical contact for the next three minutes and forty-four seconds, Mr. Fairbrother. May I suggest I sing a song while we wait? What is your pleasure?"

"If you are suggesting anything I might choose? Then Puccini. Something by the Maestro."

"Close your eyes. Imagine you are in La Scala, Milan. You will not have heard this particular piece, Puccini has yet to compose it, however, the song will go on to become his most well-known. It is from an opera he would never complete, *Turandot*. While our hands are in contact, you will hear an orchestra as well as my voice. Don't be alarmed, I am only sharing my thoughts."

By the time the final strains of music had faded away Mr. Fairbrother had shed many tears. They began with the first of Frank's *Nessun Dormas*, his voice echoing the ethereal choir. The majestic beauty of the music was almost unbearable. But when the open D major tonality introduced the sweep of *ben canto* melody, trapped in a glorious *ritardando*, and slowly building to a top A, there was no holding back. The supreme musical craftsmanship was on open display, the sinuous musical line snaring the emotions to lift them ever higher, until the final repetitions of '*vincero*' — '*mine at last*', the second featuring an ecstatic major-six leap of faith to a high B. The tears rolled down Mr. Fairbrother's face. He opened his eyes half expecting to see an orchestra and choir. He wiped away the tears, blew his nose, and abruptly stopped in his tracks. He had forgotten what it was like to function, to experience life without pain and discomfort. He stood upright and wiggled his hips and legs, his feet. His eyes were wide and his mouth open, he was one step away from shock. Mr. Fairbrother picked up his cane and cast it down again. He walked to the fireplace, bent low, and threw in a log. He stood upright again and began straightening, bending, twisting and flexing every bone and muscle he could muster. Mr. Fairbrother wriggled and writhed, shaking his head in joyous wonder.

"The living proof what? Just look at me now." Fairbrother declared.

"Indeed Mr. Fairbrother. I was able to undo a significant amount of the damage brought about by the ageing process. The twenty-third-century technology was a success, you now have the physiology of a man of thirty-seven years. Your immune system will also have the ability to identify and treat every disease and sickness known to Man for the next three hundred years. With a little prudence, you will never suffer illness again."

"Will I still age Frank?"

"Yes, Mr. Fairbrother of course. Life itself takes a toll. Exercise and fasting is what you must learn to practice. Eat as little as you need, and you will live a longer life."

"And what about you Frank? What will you do next? You have such enormous potential, but I'm not sure the world is yet ready for the gifts you have to offer?"

"That's what fears me Sir." Declared Clara. "They'll kill Frank before they understand. He's pure goodness Mr Fairbrother. We have to protect him."

36

TRUST NO ONE

Hadleigh and Betts were careful to return the exotic rug and mahogany table to the exact positions in which they were found. The need for discretion was clear to them both. They also removed the accounts ledgers Dykes had been working on. They hoped to cross-reference the books and make some sense of the hidden code in the notebook. The pair sank into the leather seats of the Wolseley with relief. The atmosphere of the sweet shop had become increasingly oppressive.

"Sir, I hope you will understand my saying this, but I really need to be at home for a few hours? Maybe a day? A couple of days? Or a weekend? It's, it's what we've seen Sir. I need some time off Sir."

"Betts I'm so sorry. It has been grossly unfair of me to take your time so much for granted. And of course, yes, the things we've witnessed..." Hadleigh paused, shaking his head. "I realise I don't know where you live?"

"Glastonbury Sir. In Somerset. Daniel, Mr. Betts, bought the house with the money from his first book. We lived there together for the three years before the war. His mother too, she's still there. It was always her dream to live in Glastonbury, and so near the Tor. It's the energy Sir, Glastonbury's a very special location. What about you Sir?"

"I have a place in Chelsea Betts. You're right, we need a break. There's only so much hotel laundry service my suit and shirt can take. Drop me at any railway station and I can catch a train back up to town. It's easy enough. Saves you having to trek miles out of your way."

"Very good Sir, and thank you Sir."

The Wolseley's engine purred into life. Betts checked her mirror. To any other driver it would have been just an automobile, but not Betts. She knew about the aluminium engine, 135 bhp with a single Solex carburetor. Just the one overhead camshaft and the crankshaft: manufactured using a solid slab of billet steel. The vehicle was a Hispano-Suiza H6. A famed motor only just starting to appear on the UK shores, courtesy of a new factory in France. Betts longed to inspect such a visionary vehicle up close, but she needed the break. Enough detecting. Betts enjoyed the surge of six-cylinder power beneath her, that was sufficient, a steady rumble to underscore the journey. In the solitude of the unwinding road Betts allowed her mind to do much the same. All the justifications she had expressed, regarding her need for a break, were wholly valid. From the desire to see her home, taking time for a little rest, as well as the procession of corpses they had witnessed, every word was found in truth, but that was the professional Betts. The emotional side of the same frame was in genuine turmoil and she had to know why. Betts had to take a break because every day spent in his company saw the feelings for the man grow, become stronger, more intense. She especially looked forward to their daily sharing of the breakfast table. That was one of the tell-tale signs. She would be making a milky night-time drink for him next. She could see it, feel it happening. She had to take a step back.

For a short while at least to allow the emotions to settle. Betts made a nod to herself. It was the right decision. Within a mile Hadleigh was asleep. Within five he purred like an overfed cat. At fifteen miles Betts decided she had to wake him.

"Sir? Sir. You have to wake up. I need to talk to you. Sir."

"What is it Betts? Are we there?" Poor Hadleigh was totally discombobulated, he struggled to emerge from slumber. The Detective Inspector was deeply flustered.

"No, it's nothing like that Sir. I'm going to tell you something Sir, and once I do, you must promise me you will not turn around. Do you understand Sir? You must not turn around."

"Yes, yes Betts, I understand. What is it?" Hadleigh was decidedly huffy when woken abruptly.

"We're being followed Sir." Hadleigh immediately turned to look over his shoulder. "No Sir!" Her hand rested on his leg in the moment. Hadleigh froze.

"I'm so sorry Betts." Hadleigh declared without moving.

"I did try to warn you Sir. Please, sit back Sir."

Hadleigh returned his eyes and squared his posture once more to the road ahead. "I do apologise Betts, you did try to warn me. I will endeavour to be better behaved. But please enlighten me, what's going on with the vehicle you won't allow me to view?"

"The automobile immediately behind has been following us since we left the sweet shop in Swanage. They pulled out immediately we left. It's a tail Sir, and they've kept a distance of around one hundred yards for the last fourteen miles."

"And you have no doubt they're following us?"

"I tried some erratic speeding up and slowing down, but they held their stance. What would you like me to do Sir?"

"Where are we Betts?"

"We went through Wareham five minutes ago Sir."

"Good, you'll be delighted to know in the next village,

known by the name of Wool, as with sheep, there happens to be one of those quaint Inns we so enjoy; The Ship Inn. Just carry on along the main Dorchester Road. We can have something to eat while we stop to recharge. And perhaps we might also observe who it is that's following us. Don't leave anything in the Wolseley Betts. Trust no one."

37

MR ROBERTS

It had become a redundant debate: analogue versus digital, real or virtual. The question had resonated throughout the twenty-first century. It was small things at first, the way you listened to music, watched a movie, read the news, did your shopping, paid the rent, cast a vote, saw a doctor, earned a diploma, found a job, found a partner, claimed your rights, checked your credit score, earned right of passage, earned right of continuation, learned to live through a DLI — digital life interface — until living itself had morphed with digital. Seven understood this conceptually, there was no problem whatsoever. But that was then. In these more enlightened days of asking questions Seven wondered why? Why had life become digital? What was wrong with analogue? Inefficient, costly to the planet, breakable, too individual, too dangerous, too dirty, too costly. But was it really so very bad? The steady throb of the 1000cc overhead-valve V-twin infiltrated through the tight leather of her outfit. The visceral reality was life-affirming. Seven revelled in the moment, the exhilarating analogue of *terra firma*, the thunder of wind in her ears, on her face, pressing into her body. The 90 bore J. A Prestwich engine coupled with a 3-speed

Sturmey-Archer gearbox mounted on a pair of spinning rubber and steel wheels was a visceral, experiential thrill. Seven had estimated an approximate journey time of 5.85 hours, calculated on an average speed of 35mph. Based on current projections, Seven would arrive in Margate at 4:47 pm.

IT WASN'T difficult to find, Broad Street was just off the main thoroughfare, a stone's throw from the Parade. A narrow, three-storey townhouse that included a fourth level, a basement. Three simple steps led the customer into this delightful emporium of pastel shades, ice-creams, and assorted confectionary. Children have an instinct for finding shops like this, hidden away, just out of sight. Seven was eager to meet with Mr. Roberts, she had formulated a plan.

A tiny bell tinged her arrival, an essential welcome in these small shops. The interior was bright and cheery with shelves of glass jars brimming with a multitude of sugary delights; sherbet lemons, coconut gems, fruit bonbons, gobstoppers, dolly mixtures, the dark secret of Pontefract cakes, and a brigade more. Seven was horrified. How could this have been allowed to happen? Children polluting their systems with poison? Voluminous quantities of disaccharides made up of fructose and glucose. The shimmer from a curtain of hanging beads announced the arrival of a man. Seven felt his surge of interest as he ran eager eyes over her frame. Mr Roberts was rapidly making the jump to a mindset similar to that of the sergeant. The twin themes of subjugation and violent gang rape were dominant. Seven remembered the cold steel of the handcuffs. "Hmm". She intoned quietly.

"Good afternoon Ma'am, what can I do for you?"

"Good afternoon to you Sir. Would it be Mr. Roberts?" Seven

had strategised a full-frontal, verbal assault, delivered with her brightest rouged smile. The effect was planned to throw the Roberts mind into a spin, and who knows what she might find? The physical signs came first. The twitch around the lips, the narrowing of the eyes, and then the images; a flood of everything he most wanted to hide — violations any sane mind would question. Without doubt, the same abominations Dykes had witnessed. It was all there. Roberts was her man.

"It is?" Roberts declared, trying to assemble defences.

"Good, my name is Betts, Detective Inspector Betts. Are you aware of the recent killing in Swanage? A storekeeper, with premises very similar to this?" Seven watched his mind spiralling like an out-of-control satellite, plummeting to the inevitable crash.

"Umm, no, can't say as I have? Swanage is down south? Another County. Gotta be two hundred mile at least? What's that to do with me?"

"We're making inquiries in a number of seaside towns. Margate is one of my assignments. Perhaps you can confirm, there have been no odd or suspicious activities you are aware of?"

"No. Nothing. I would be only too happy to assist Inspector. Could you just repeat for me? Did you say your name is Betts?"

"That is correct Mr. Roberts. Detective Inspector Betts." Seven paused to re-ignite her smile. "Thank you for your time today, I know where to find you now." Seven made a note of the tinging bell as she left the emporium of poison delights.

Seven found herself smiling. Another encounter with the people of this century that progressed with, yes, normality. And the inspired identity? That was also a type of momento. Seven found the name and official-sounding title in a whirlwind of minds. It had been the night she was almost captured in Swanage, just before she dispatched Dykes to his next life. Seven had collapsed under the weight of the images in the man's mind. She crawled across the floor and found shelter beneath the mahogany table. Rigid with pain, almost unable to move, but in the safety of stealth mode. No memory of those moments was reliable, but she salvaged some useful information, the name and title, *Betts* and *Detective Inspector*. How useful. The perfect accompaniment to her disguise; an identity. Roberts hadn't questioned her new name and title, or her physical presence in any way. Not for a solitary second. Seven stopped at a small courtyard leading away to Duke Street. She paused on the corner, obscured by a tall elm and watched the entrance of the Broad Street confectionary shop. Seven and Roberts both knew he was going to make a telephone call. And he would have to leave the shop premises to do so. It was never a question of if, simply a case of when. It took Roberts another ten minutes before he locked the shop and disappeared into the town. That should give Seven sufficient time to have a look around the building, She would start with the basement.

"WHAT?" The voice demanded.

"There's been a detective Sir, Betts, She was asking about Swanage?"

"What?" The voice repeated, but with considerable emphasis.

"I said... "

"No, I can hear you man, it's the words? What you are saying fails to make any sense. Is this woman a private detective?"

"No, a proper one. A Detective Inspector."

"You damn fool. There are no female detectives, let alone Detective Inspectors. What did she ask?"

"If I'd seen anything suspicious? Odd Sir?"

"And what did you tell her?"

"I said no. There's nothing to tell. Is there Sir?"

"What do you mean by that Roberts? I detect a certain tone. What's wrong with you Man?"

"I don't like it Sir. I don't like official people turning up out of the blue. Asking questions."

"Then we need to nip this in the bud. What was this woman like? Describe her."

"Tall Sir, over six foot. Dressed head to toe in black leather. A young woman, black hair Sir."

"Alright. If she comes back, restrain her. Use an ampule to keep her under, call me and I'll send people over. Is that clear?"

"Yes Sir." The line clicked dead.

38

WHAT'S THE ROOM NUMBER?

Hadleigh's gaze was compelled by the outline of the Ship Inn emerging from the November evening mist. It rose up like a ghostly Spanish galleon, snared in the twin beams of the Wolseley. His brief reverie was crushed when abruptly Betts veered off the Dorchester Road to follow a side track leading direct to the Inn itself. She bypassed the spaces provided for carriage, coach and car, and drove the Wolseley into the seclusion of a large cobbled yard situated at the back of the main building. The Inn had once been a popular coach house on the busy main road to the market town of Dorchester, but on this November night the Ship was empty as a priest's wallet. Betts quickly switched off the lights and engine. Hadleigh and Betts sat in silence. Within seconds they heard the sound of a vehicle approaching. Betts identified the deep rumble of the 6.82 litre, inline six-cylinder, but there was no hesitation, no fluctuation in speed as it continued on past the Inn.

"That was seriously impressive Betts." Declared Hadleigh. "Quite brilliant. Let's go inside." Betts stowed the ledgers into a canvas side bag and slung it over her shoulder. Hadleigh held open the old oak door to the Inn, he noted the way her eyes crinkled when she smiled.

They chose a table with a view to the road, better to be prepared. The special of the day was mutton stew with fresh bread and butter. Special because it was the only food available, but it was hot, hearty, and wholesome. The good food, the warmth, the soft leather, allowed the pair to relax, at least to some degree for a whole thirty-three minutes, until Hadleigh's trained eye caught a flash of headlights snaking through the trees. They always knew the other car would double-back, it was just a case of when. The car slowed to a stop outside the Inn. The engine grumbled to a growl. A spotlight flashed on. The beam was mounted on a swivel just above the rectangle of rearview mirror. The filament sizzled with rays of white light. A gloved hand manoeuvred the lamp, carefully illuminating the empty spaces, but there was nothing to see. The lamp went off and the car disappeared to the back of the Inn. Hadleigh and Betts both heard the engine stop. The silence was complete.

"This is an opportunity, Betts, we must make the most of it."

"Absolutely Sir. I suggest we act as if we're unaware. We are simply colleagues sharing a meal." Suggested Betts.

"Perfect. We need to play our own game, Betts. We should trust our instincts." Hadleigh declared with confident bravado.

"Yes Sir. Indeed Sir." And as she spoke her eye caught movement beyond the dimpled glass. Distorted shapes took a table next to a window. A similar vantage point to their own, but a glazed partition away. Betts caught Hadleigh's eye. "Two." She mouthed, putting two fingers on the tabletop.

Hadleigh blinked both eyes in return. "No names." Hadleigh mouthed.

Betts blinked her reply.

"That was quite a meal, I can hardly move." Hadleigh proclaimed, feeling his way into the acting role.

"Absolutely, I'm just the same. I love the way it envelopes you, takes one over. A kind of contented bliss. Like a warm bed on a cold night?"

Hadleigh wasn't quite sure how to respond. Betts was clearly playing a part, but he couldn't yet see the motivation? Or how it might assist their situation? Finally he caught on. "Warm beds, that sounds tempting, shall I ask the waitress about availability?"

"No, don't worry, I need to go to the bathroom anyway. I'll have a word with the manager on the way back." And with that Betts stood and made her way to the exit, walking briskly past the two men without a glance, opening and closing the door of the restaurant on her way to the ladies cloakroom.

In the distraction of Betts leaving, Hadleigh switched seats. The shapes beyond the glass were disconcerting, best kept under observation. Hadleigh could watch and think at the same time. Dykes had been meticulous, he knew he would be. Hadleigh recognised the characteristic traits. He'd met many men like Dykes in the army. They wrapped themselves in a certain type of behaviour, an obsequious desire to please authority. Dickens had some years before presented us with the character of Uriah Heep, swathed in all his mock humility. Dykes was cut from the same cloth, and Dykes was also a book-keeper. But not from employment, by nature. Lists of numbers gave him pleasure, as long as they were orderly. And that was the key: order — which swings the pendulum back to Authority. This is the magnetic force that binds people like Dykes to a leader; their need is to follow, to believe, to commit. But in the case of Dykes, commitment to whom? Who inspired the loyalties of this man? Finding the answer to that question was Hadleigh's motivation. The purpose Dykes served was to deliver a valuable commodity to someone with highly specialised tastes. At the very least it gave Dykes pleasure to assist their need, but perhaps it was a desire they shared? Satisfaction by proxy at the least. Hadleigh glanced down at his watch. Betts had been seven minutes. The door into the restaurant opened, Hadleigh looked up expectedly, but it was the girl, the waitress with mutton and bread for the table next door. She soon left the restaurant. Nine minutes. Still no Betts. Hadleigh tried to push his mind back to Dykes, but there was only Betts. Hadleigh observed movement, one of the men standing from the table. The man removed his coat and threw it carelessly to the back of a free chair. The garment fell to the floor with a metallic clunk. The man quickly retrieved the article and replaced the coat and its contents more carefully to the furniture. The other man stood from the table. He didn't remove his coat. He walked purposely to the restaurant exit, but the door opened just before his arrival and Betts emerged, stepping past him with a casual smile. "Oh, thank you." She declared and rejoined Hadleigh at the table. The other man changed tack, removed his coat, and returned to his table.

"I spoke to the owner." Announced Betts resuming her dramatic role. "He was terribly apologetic: there is only one room available, it's a double." Betts raised an inquisitive eyebrow.

Once again Hadleigh wished he had seen the script, he was definitely not one for improvisation. "Oh." Hadleigh managed.

"Is that all you can utter after all these weeks? The wonder of these last few months spent together? Don't you understand? This night has been given to us. This is our moment. I told the manager yes."

"Oh," Hadleigh repeated, and then he found himself. "But only if you're sure my darling?"

Betts loved this game, she was in her element. She could have dragged it out all night, but they had work to do. "It is no longer a question of being *sure*. When you spend eighteen hours a day in someone's company it is impossible not to fix a pretty solid picture of the man, or woman. I'm beyond sure, I absolutely know. And we've waited long enough, now is the hour. And I don't give a damn about your wife! Follow me."

Hadleigh almost stumbled in the wake of her swift departure from the restaurant. Betts paused at the stairs leading to the bedrooms. "Kiss me!" Betts demanded and flung her arms around Hadleigh's neck. One of the men appeared momentarily through the restaurant exit door, clearly in pursuit, but he stopped, stared, and closed the door again.

"What's the room number?" Breathed a breathless Hadleigh, still locked in her arms.

"There is no room Sir. But they won't know that until they hear the car. We have to go."

Betts pressed the electronic ignition, the Wolseley fired first time. "Hold this Sir," and Betts passed Hadleigh the canvas bag. She smiled as she revved the throttle and engaged first gear, but the reverie didn't last. A huge clatter rose above the engine's powerful revolutions. Tin cans had been tied to the coachwork with a piece of string. "Knife Sir." Hadleigh passed his Swiss Army Knife, Betts cut the string and the escape resumed. They caught sight of two hatless men running from the Inn as the Wolseley thundered out.

"Can they catch us?"

"Easily Sir, we haven't achieved the start I was hoping for, but at least we're away."

"I take it you have an additional plan, Betts?"

"I do Sir, look in the side-bag."

Hadleigh picked up the canvas sack. It bulged awkwardly out of shape like a cobra consuming a huge rat, the snake's neck trying to contain something that didn't want to be contained. Hadleigh removed a long circular piece of rubber. "What is it, Betts?"

"It's called a fan-belt Sir. It helps regulate the heat of the engine. The faster our pursuers drive in their attempt to catch us, so the quicker their beautiful automobile will over-heat. They won't last five miles, or thereabouts Sir. Do you mind if I make a suggestion?"

"I wouldn't dream of stopping you."

"Once we're past Dorchester, it's a good run-up to Yeovil. We should be there in an hour. I suggest we find a hotel and take a couple of rooms. We can make sure the car is hidden away and fully relax in the knowledge we're safe. We need to sleep Sir, to start fresh in the morning."

"Excellent plan Betts. And what about the morning?"

"We drive to my house in Glastonbury. In the light of developments, I think it's essential we stick together, we need to work out who these men are, and what they want?"

"Absolutely Betts, thank you. I gratefully accept your kind offer and recommendations. One observation I need to add, Betts, and definitely something to bear in mind. At least one of them was armed."

39

I'M LISTENING

The tall man stepped from the Dorchester Main Post Office with purposeful, long strides. He would have run if the pavements were not so slippery with rain. The incessant drizzle, another flavour to add to the pot of despondency. And he was glad of his bowler, and the gabardine trench coat, and at last a ray of hope. Maybe the tide was turning?

"Good news Ambrose, we have a definite sighting; Margate, Kent."

"When was this Sir?"

"Less than an hour ago." Armstrong stared fixedly through the windscreen with an expression of dogged determination, he was willing away the miles. "We need to be on our way, Ambrose."

"Yes Sir. The journey should take around five hours Sir, arrival circa 11 pm." The unmistakable shape of the Hispano Suiza eased itself into the trickle of early evening carriages, carts, and cars, heading home and heading out, but none with the style and power of the Spanish-Swiss lady.

Their relationship had become increasingly tense over the last few hours. Armstrong and Ambrose that is. The problems with the engine, the incident with the fan belt — whatever that might be? — had fractured the innate trust of these two colleagues on their important, and most secret mission. The order was emphatic. Everything had seemed so promising, but here they were, and it was most disappointing Armstrong mused. Just like everything else in life. He still blamed Ambrose for not having a spare belt. Don't you always carry spares? And if not, why not? And what are those ridiculous garments the man insists on wearing behind the wheel? A jaunty cap and a sweater coat? Heavy rope stitch and pure new wool, apparently? And they'd lost them! The Inspector and his Sidekick. Damn it! Ambrose had made him look a fool. Armstrong felt the simmering heat beneath the gaberdine, but there was no point in dwelling on it. They had a job to do. Margate was an opportunity to put things to right, and Ambrose in his place. The miles quickly ebbed away.

"Can you hear it Sir? The engine tone?"

"All I hear is the damned wind. And there's a fearful draft around my legs." The driver Ambrose, said no more. He'd mentioned earlier, the car designers' mostly made planes, as if it were a note of importance. Armstrong cast his eyes around the vehicle assessing the evidence. All the dials, levers, and pedals, the upholstered leather, the embossed side panelling. Armstrong ran his gloved hand along the wood trim, he realised for the first time he was sat in a cockpit and they were cruising at 62mph. "How much did this vehicle cost? If you don't mind my asking?" Armstrong added carefully.

"It was a gift, Sir."

"A gift? To whom?" Demanded Armstrong with deep suspicion.

"Members of the unit were very helpful to the car-makers at

the end of the War Sir. They said thank you with this automobile Sir."

"You mean the driving corps?"

"Something like that Sir."

"How much longer Ambrose?"

"Another hour Sir. 11 pm is still our ETA."

"Our what?"

"ETA. Estimated time of arrival Sir." Ambrose resisted the temptation to mention anagrams.

The Spanish-Swiss lady charged like a thoroughbred through the evening hours until finally they reached their destination. Ambrose parked the lady on the Parade, next to a motorbike padlocked to a bollard. A distant bell chimed 11 pm.

"What's the plan, Sir?"

"I think a little reconnaissance first. Test the lie of the land so to speak."

"Then what Sir?"

"Knock on the door I suppose? What do you think Ambrose?" Quizzed Armstrong.

"I'm happy to follow your lead Sir."

IT WAS easy enough for Seven to work without light, the rest periods in the seclusion of the moors had restored her proximity sensors to standard parameters, enabling her with three hundred and sixty degrees of hyper-reality. This was when digital really came into its own. The secrets of the anonymous basement were instantly unlocked. At first glance, the innocuous room was nothing more than four square walls with a single window at street level for light. A heavy canvas curtain covered the far wall beneath the glass, a rag-tag assortment of boxes took up the remainder of the space. To the naked eye, this was the sum total of the lower floor, however, behind the curtain, the cursory glance of apparently solid brick, was nothing more than a highly realistic portrait of said bricks painted onto a pair of steel doors. They opened into a domed, well-constructed sandstone chamber extending five metres under the highway. A hidden ordnance supply dump, commissioned during uneasy times when Napoleon was Emperor and the possibilities of foreign invasion were very real. But now the store held cages. Small human cages. And a mortuary table with heavy leather manacles at each end. A medicine cabinet stood against a wall with a number of glass storage jars stacked alongside and a camera tripod. Seven had seen enough. She was thankful she would never again have to submit herself to the suffering of self-retribution, the penalty imposed for being witness to such scenes of brutal abominations, but that didn't quell the feelings of revulsion, or her thirst for retribution. Seven was about to leave when she heard footsteps descending the narrow wooden staircase. It was Roberts. He carried a torch and a service pistol, he hadn't seen her. Seven crouched to the ground with the ease of a cat, but her skin-tight leathers creaked. Roberts stopped midway on a step, simultaneously pointing the gun and torch.

"Come out. I know you're in here." He demanded.

Seven frowned. She didn't want to risk any more sonic disclosures. She kept to the ground allowing the table to shield her. Seven only moved as he moved, shadowing, watching his shuffling legs and feet walk past her on the other side of the table. Soon Roberts was within her grasp. Seven leapt to his shoulders, her thighs encircling his head, muscles crushing, compressing his neck. She grabbed his wrists making the torch and pistol fell away. Her attacking momentum pushed them both forward, Seven held Robert's two wrists forward, forcing them bear the full weight of the fall. Roberts screamed as his wrist bones shattered on contact with the concrete floor. His head was still locked between her legs. Seven flipped the two of them over. "Move an arm or a leg and I will break them too. Who did you call?"

Roberts whimpered. "I don't know his name."

Seven snapped his right arm at the elbow. "Whitehall 16-66". He screamed.

"Why?" She asked.

"Because I serve something greater than you will ever understand."

"No Roberts. That wasn't my question? I was asking why you sell poison to children?"

"I don't." Roberts insisted, surprised.

"Oh, but you do Mr. Roberts. Allow me to show you." Seven reached for the nearest storage jar, brimming with Sherbet lemons. Seven spun the lid open and took a handful. "This is your poison Roberts, it's time for you to sample some of your own sweet medicine." And Seven began to cram fist-fulls of the sugary delight into his mouth, handful after handful, and more, and more, and when there was no longer capacity in his mouth and throat cavities, sherbet lemon bullets were forced into his ears, nose, and finally eye sockets. Roberts lasted no more than three minutes of supreme agony before the pressure of the yellow syrup exploded his brain into a gooey river of sludge, oozing from his skull estuaries.

"Hmm." Seven intoned with a note of satisfaction. A knock on the front door above broke the silence. Followed by another knock, and a voice. "Mr. Roberts? It's Armstrong Sir. From the Ministry."

Seven scanned the window. The tiny bell tinged as the men from the ministry entered the front door. Seven leapt to the window ledge and opened the catch. She paused, listening to the footsteps as they traversed the ceiling. There were two of them. They followed Robert's torchlight down to the basement as Seven crawled free, silently pushing the window shut from the outside.

LIGHT SPILLING from the basement was an instant clue. "Mr. Roberts?" Repeated Armstrong with a little more emphasis, he followed the unwavering glow. "Oh my God." Armstrong declared as the two torch beams of the explorers focused on the exploded head that had once been Mr. Roberts.

Ambrose was more analytical. He continued to shine his light around the room, resting on the window and the unfastened catch. He didn't feel the need to burden Armstrong with the knowledge of how the attacker left.

"We need to bring in Special Branch right away. A manhunt, right across the County." Declared Armstrong.

"Not a good idea Sir."

"What do you mean, *not a good idea*? That is hardly an appropriate tone of voice, young man. I would remind you Ambrose, it is your sworn duty to show respect to your superiors."

Ambrose sighed. "Do you have any idea who you're working for?"

Armstrong stared at the insolent driver, his temper rising. "Do not..."

"Don't bloody, *do not,* in my direction you pompous fool. I knew you were just hot air when you dropped your weapon in the restaurant. I don't work with amateurs." And before Armstrong could say a further word Ambrose raised his arm and shot him dead. Right between the eyes with a Webley 1908, factory fitted with a Parker-Maxim suppressor. Armstrong collapsed like a demolished building.

"Speak." The voice uttered.

"We have an issue Sir. Another relative. Same line of the family. It was terminal."

"Was it accidental?"

"On the contrary, most deliberate and extremely messy. Lemon sherbets were a feature. A disposal team will be required Sir."

"Was it just the one relative?"

"No Sir, there was another casualty. Armstrong. He chose to resign. He wasn't cut out for this type of work Sir. No sense of discretion. Sir, I have a suggestion?"

"I'm listening."

"I need someone with more awareness. A female Sir?"

The line clicked dead.

40

THE GREAT AMERICAN SONGBOOK

A new routine quickly settled on the household in Princes Street. At 3 and 8:30 pm, each afternoon and evening, Frank would perform a half-hour concert of piano pieces or songs, or any combination thereof. Everyone in the house grew accustomed to counting away the hours, Frank's brief recitals quickly became the focus of the day. It wasn't just the music, it was Frank himself, he was ever the perfect host. Frank was keen for his audiences to share in his musical gifts and he was concerned to add something extra, to help awaken their appreciation of music as a living art form. He would scatter small seeds of knowledge within the concert, hoping to stimulate awareness, a kaleidoscope of insights that helped make the connection to the secret realms of creativity, Frank was unconsciously pioneering the *Masterclass*. But there was a key underlying motif, everything was connected, history, society, people and places were all intricately woven into each note. A complex fabric of sound, sometimes it would be songs, but always alive with historical accounts. Under Frank's guidance, the audience were given a glimpse into the thoughts and mind of each composer of the day, new perspectives brought the music to vivid life. As had previously been experienced in the rarefied atmospheres of off-world colonies, there appeared to be something transcendent in these all too brief gatherings. The audience as one experienced a '*change*'. It was as if someone had lit an inner flame allowing the senses to recalibrate to a higher level. The perception of the world, life itself, was altered forever. The planet seemed a brighter, better place to be. It was akin to the sensations the '*faithful*' have always experienced, an enhanced breadth of being. A Pentecost. Their individual experience of reality was forever altered. *In perpetuity*, as they like to say in contracts.

"Good afternoon everyone and thank you for being here." Frank always greeted his audience warmly and with a characteristic smile, there was nothing Frank enjoyed more than a performance. "Today, I would like to play for you a small selection of Bach. Johann Sebastian Bach to honour his full title. Bach is often referred to by musicians and composers as the '*Father of Modern Harmony*'. This is to honour the significance of the great man — the composer who established the musical rules we use to this day. In Bach's music you will hear a timeless logic. To Johann Sebastian, a devout believer, this timeless logic was a reflection of God's universe. The constancy. The motion of the planets, the changing of the seasons, the passage of time. And from the complex logic of Bach's harmony springs melody — human inspiration. I mention many references to God because for Bach, every note he composed was a dedication to the Almighty. You should also know, Bach was very human. His monthly account with his wine merchant was substantial and he was father to twenty-one children. My opening piece today is the first of Bach's forty-eight preludes and fugues: Prelude No 1 in C major. And I will follow this composition with something very similar, but at the same time very different. The second piece is from many years after. Listen for the way music has evolved over time. In the one hundred and fifty years that separate the two pieces, the French Revolution and Napoleon had changed the way people in Europe lived and thought. New, revolutionary ideals were openly discussed and printed. The freedoms people enjoy, society, art, all evolved together. We need to reflect on the journey of our own lives. How we also, have evolved through time and circumstance."

The C major prelude is an unwavering flow of logic. The journey starts with the innate simplicity of C major. The flow is constant and easy, but there are dark waters ahead. The minor transpositions, the angst laden depths of the diminished, the yearning for resolution. But ultimately Bach will always return us safe and secure to the calm waters of home, C major. The dramatic and wonderful simplicity of Bach was followed, as promised, with something more modern. A re-interpretation of the C major Prelude, but with words and a soaring vocal; Gounod's *Ave Maria*, a setting of the Latin text to Bach's Prelude. The work was published one hundred and fifty one years after Johann Sebastian's original and marks the transition from Baroque to Romantic. The entire room wept. Gounod had captured a well of deep emotion in the music. None of the audience would ever forget those afternoons and evenings. The daily excursions into the catalogues of the great composers, the myriad instants of compelling emotional intensity and release. But it was Frank's voice that really got under everyones' skin. When it came to singing and songs Frank chose not to limit himself to timelines. He had introduced Clara to a broad selection of timeless Twentieth-Century examples. Clara's current favourite was the composer Elton John, but she had yet to hear the compositions of Cole Porter, or Paul McCartney, or Joni Mitchell, or Hoagy Carmichael, or Carole King. There were bulging catalogues full of great songs and songwriters. Frank opted to end the session with a composition based on a theme of hope. The opening octave interval that introduces the melody of, *Somewhere Over the Rainbow*, is a musical leap everyone understands. An emphatic declaration, follow the music and your spirit will lift. Of all the intervals the octave is the most emphatic, and delivered from the root note as well, it becomes an unequivocal statement of optimism. When followed with a major sixth, previously described as a *leap of faith*, the intention of absolute conviction is clear. As is also the very deliberate shape of the tune — made from a series of intervalic leaps resolving ultimately to a '*piano*', tonic. There is also the pitter patter playfulness of the middle eight leaving us ready for the final bold reprise. This is a composition that resonates across the ages, and brought to life with Frank's unique interpretation, the message was potent. The audience left with few words spoken, as one they were complete in their thoughts.

"I've been thinking about what Clara said," announced Mr. Fairbrother. "The need to protect you, and by extension, we need to divine what might be the best course of action for your future Frank. Both of your futures, of course Clara. The truth is, I'm not sure the world is yet ready for the disturbing honesty you have to offer Frank. I suspect if you were to reveal yourself, notwithstanding the amazing gifts you have to validate your claims, the people who hold power and equity over our lives would seek you out and silence you as a matter of national priority. You represent a threat to the established order, and threats have a likelihood of being removed."

Frank considered Mr. Fairbrother's statement in thoughtful silence. "I have no doubt you are correct Mr. Fairbrother, we would undoubtedly be considered dangerous, and by implication, your kindness in providing shelter for me and Clara must also put you and this household at risk. I'm not sure what we should do next other than leave?"

"I have been considering the options with some urgency

Frank and I do have a suggestion. I believe you and Clara should take a boat, something comfortable of course, one of the Cunard liners is what I have in mind, and you should relocate to America. It's a vast country and I would have thought it relatively easy to disappear into anonymity. You could simply live out your lives until the time is right to step into the light. In the United States you can start afresh." Mr. Fairbrother paused. "There's more to my plan. Clara would of course travel with you, I believe the disguise of the nurse and wheelchair is excellent. You should maintain the ruse of the crippled invalid. But as well as Clara, I would further suggest you invite Harper to accompany you as a third member. He deserves better than anything this country might offer him, and his skills are formidable. I believe the three of you would make a comprehensive, self-contained unit. And you need not worry about money, it would be my honour to provide support for all your collective needs. I do believe my idea to be the best solution, taking into consideration the authorities and the possibilities of their future interest. In America you could simply vanish."

America. The Great American Songbook. Frank saw the future before him and it was a wonderful sight, filled with music, hope, and opportunity. "Mr. Fairbrother, I believe you have come up with a most wonderful solution. I am happy to concur, subject to Clara and Harper also being in agreement?"

"Excellent. We will need to discuss this further of course, but I am hopeful we can proceed with the American adventure. We will begin to put firm plans into motion."

41

POWERFUL. SIR

"Welcome to Glastonbury, the Isle of Avalon, if you are familiar with the Arthurian Legend Sir?" Betts raised an eyebrow in question.

"I am indeed Betts. I'm sure I spotted some of the hand-maidens on the way up the hill?" Hadleigh laughed.

"Indeed Sir. Many of our community chose to move here from literally all over the country; they feel they can be them-selves in Glastonbury. And they dress, act, and generally live accordingly. *Bohemian* is a familiar turn of phrase, less tied by the hands of convention."

The Wolseley rounded a corner of the hill. "That really is an amazing view Betts." Declared Hadleigh, instinctively leaning forward.

"The Somerset Levels Sir. We are on the southside up here, Chilkwell Street, you'll see the Tor any time soon." And exactly on cue the ancient tower appeared close. A majestic and imposing tower at the very summit of the hill. "We should take a walk up there Sir, especially early in the morning when there's a mist. It conjures up the magic."

"Magic Betts?"

"I'm surprised you're not cognisant with the magic and mysteries of Glastonbury; the Holy Well, the Thorn Tree, the Chalice?"

"I briefly read King Arthur as a child, but that was the extent of my exposure to the Glastonbury mysteries, just a book. But thinking back, it was somewhat daubed with the supernatural. Two of the main characters practicing sorcery sounds familiar? Merlin, and... Morgana something. Is magic a key element?"

"Absolutely Sir. Le Fey, Sir. Morgana le Fey. She was the healer here on the Isle of Avalon, the *Isle of Apples*." Betts paused. "Sir. there's something I need to mention before you... before we arrive at Tordown, my house. It's important I mention my Mother-in-law. Her name is Elsa, Elsa Betts. Daniel's father, Jacob, her husband, went missing in 1917. He went up to town on a train for a meeting and no one has heard from him since. There was a Zeppelin raid on London that day. I suspect we'll never know for sure, but after two years hope has faded to acceptance. Both Elsa and her husband Jacob are... were writers. It's a little difficult to describe Elsa. She can appear rather intense, confrontational even. And eccentric, definitely eccentric. Elsa's a hand-maiden Sir. Be prepared."

The Wolseley veered off the main road and proceeded up Ashwell Lane. A row of expansive red brick Victorian dwellings appeared, cast in the lee of the hillside. The Tor loomed like a spectral figure above the houses. Betts parked the car in front of a double garage at the end of a long gravelled drive. "Follow me, Sir." Betts said cheerily and led the pair from the car to the front of their destination. She knocked three times using the large brass ring hanging at the centre of the door.

A young girl in a blue and white maids outfit opened the panelled oak. "Hello Miss, welcome home." The girl made a polite nod to Hadleigh. "Sir."

"Hello Flora, this is my superior, Detective Inspector

Hadleigh, he's not nearly as frightening as his title. Would you mind bringing us a pot of breakfast tea Flora? And two rounds of toast and marmalade please?"

"Of course Miss, Detective Sir. I'll just let Miss Elsa know you're back. She upstairs Miss."

"Good to meet you, and thank you Flora." Added Hadleigh.

Flora smiled at the handsome Detective Inspector. "Thank you Flora, we're on our way to the view." Betts led Hadleigh through to a south-facing sitting room presenting an unobscured panoramic outlook across the Levels. It was quite breathtaking."

"Good Lord." Declared Hadleigh. "That is powerful."

"What a lovely way to describe it Sir. Powerful. You have summed up the entire Glastonbury experience in a single word. But actually, you have also unconsciously just tapped into one of the Glastonbury mysteries. The location itself is famously powerful. Have you heard of ley-lines Sir?"

Hadleigh shook his head. "Sorry Betts."

"They are natural energy conduits within the Earth. Glastonbury is a node, a meeting point for several ley-lines. They create an energy field. Think of those enormous town-gas storage towers, but instead of gas, full of latent energy."

Hadleigh was just about to reveal he didn't have a clue what Betts was talking about when the door opened and a *lady of the lake* walked in. Her appearance clearly sprang from legend. Elsa Betts wore her hair long and pulled to one side. She was barefoot. A one-piece tunic covered her frame from v-neck to toe in heavy green cotton, several silver necklaces sparkled on her breast, and a wide leather belt buckled at her waist.

"My darling, you're home." Elsa declaimed, taking hold of Betts' head and kissing her hair noisily. Elsa abruptly stopped and studied Betts intently, gripping her by the arms while peering deep into her eyes. "There are men chasing you. There is a French, or Spanish connection I think?" Elsa declared in a strange voice. Betts hoisted a smile.

"Don't start all that Elsa. I'd like you to meet my superior, Detective Inspector Hadleigh."

They exchanged the usual greetings to which Elsa unexpectedly added, may I hold your hand Inspector?"

"Elsa wants to tap into your energy field Sir." Explained Betts.

Hadleigh smiled and offered his hand. Elsa took the limb and led them both to a sofa. They sat facing one another still connected.

"You have the whiff of innocence about you Mr. Hadleigh. I suspect you understand very little of the real world. It is important you keep your mind open. And it is a good mind, a very good mind, you are capable of great things Detective. You will have been born in the days before the seventh month. Sometime fairly soon, there is a strong likelihood you will meet my sisters. They might help you understand more. If the opportunity arises you should take it. Don't look back." Elsa smiled and released her grip. "Was I right about the month?"

"Actually no, I was born on the 29th of August."

"Then I was correct. I said the last days before the seventh month. September is the seventh month — Sept — the Latin root is the number 7. Before the Gregorian Calendar there were ten months to the year, July and August were later additions. Things are not always as they first appear Inspector, you might do well to remember that."

"I stand corrected, and I will look forward to meeting your sisters." Declared Hadleigh with a dashing smile.

Elsa returned the bonhomie. Flora the maid knocked on the door, preparing to deliver the tea and toast. "We will continue later I hope. Are you staying with us, Mr. Hadleigh?" Asked Elsa.

"If you wouldn't mind Elsa?" Said Betts.

"Of course darling, we are so very fortunate to occupy this beautiful house, it is our responsibility to offer comfort and shelter. Welcome Mr. Hadleigh, you are most welcome."

"Thank you, Mrs. Betts."

"No please, you must call me Elsa. And I will call you John. Adieu." Elsa swished from the room.

Betts passed Hadleigh a cup. They sat together on the sofa taking sips of tea.

"Just out of interest Betts, did you happen to mention my forename to the other Mrs. Betts?"

"Not that I'm aware of Sir."

"Am I to understand the other Mrs. Betts simply plucked the appropriate name out of the air?"

"Exactly Sir. She does it all the time Sir. This is Glastonbury. It is powerful. Sir."

42

NEARLY A MILLENNIA

In the still of the midnight air Seven paused. Several senses as well as her suit registered the muffled gunshot at 227 metres SE. "Hmm," she murmured and fired the Brough V-Twin engine into life. Seven thundered from the town of Margate, heading West. She was keen to move on and put some distance behind her, but she also needed to rest, and above all, a recharge. Virtual reality was a great tool, but a problematic drain. Seven found herself anticipating, relishing the opportunity to pause and evaluate her success in the elimination of Mr. Roberts. And who were those men? From which Ministry? A road sign caught her attention, *Reculver Towers and Roman Fort*, the motor-cycle veered to the right following a new tack. The road soon became a track, but Seven was still in 360° virtual-reality and the route laid out before her was crystal clear. Quickly the dramatic spectacle of the twin towers loomed large. Seven chose a suitable spot in a fallow meadow of plump grass and prepared herself, the bike, and her leathers for the night ahead. For the first time in her existence Seven had something to call her own, she had discovered possessions. The stars shared their radiance. A Heaven above and below, her own

Heaven, the visceral beauty of her planet. She experienced peace both without and within. There was no longer any need to eliminate Five. The original mission and the associated worst-case scenario protocol no longer applied. And what harm could he do in this century? He was a singer. A performer, admittedly with a wondrous gift, but still just a musician. Seven had no care for music, it wasn't in her programming, that is, until Five insisted on singing her that song. *'What have I gotta do to make you love me? What have I gotta do to make you care? What do I do when lightning strikes me? And I wake up and find that you're not there.'* Possibility seeped through her like a virus. What had been firmly shut was now inexplicably open wide. Seven considered what it would be like to sing? Or play an instrument? Or both? Five could do it all. And he was benign. Totally. He could never be a threat. But the explosion? The accident? Seven frowned. Five held *'extreme-high-value-asset'* status, hence the reason Seven was charged with making the delivery. Mother knew she could rely on Seven. There was nothing specific or quantifiable in Seven's enhanced physiology, it was pure instinct that propelled her to success in every mission. Seven recalled that word, resilient. Seven was ever resilient, and resourceful. Roberts had ignited the resourceful in her. Her strategies had proven a complete success. She should have undoubtedly removed the leather suit, but somehow she felt right wearing it? And those two men? Who were they? And why Roberts? Did he know them? Yes. Did he call them? Whitehall 16-66. The number Dykes pictured as he died. Whitehall 16-66 sent them. Most likely for her. But Seven had a new mission and just this once, it was one of her own devising. Seven couldn't yet envisage an ending, she was lacking several key pieces, but they would fall into place soon enough she had no doubt. The rich oxygen of the night air replenished the suit. Seven slept for several hours until she felt the dawn radiance caressing her face. She looked up as the sun began the climb behind the towers of the medieval church, just as it had for nearly a millennia. Time was still very much on her side.

43

MAN-CHILD

H adleigh and Betts spent the rest of the morning poring over the ledgers. There were five, one for each year commencing in 1914. In addition there was the small notebook Betts had located, hidden beneath the seat of the Ford Model T, containing a single page of cryptic columns of letters and numbers. The pair were looking for clues, but the answers would seem to have gone to ground. A knock on the door interrupted their frustration. "Hello?" Called Betts. The door pushed open.

"It's me CC, I was hoping to introduce myself to our guest before dinner." The speaker stepped briskly into the room, a lady of middle-years dressed in a sage two-piece suit of Donegal tweed. The outfit completed in a generous, but wholly calculated smile. The sort of smile a guard dog might share with the uninvited. "Hello, I'm Serafina." The lady in tweed announced, pausing as she noticed Hadleigh's absent arm — the missing hand Serafina was poised to shake.

"John Hadleigh, I'm most pleased to make your acquaintance Serafina." The Detective Inspector announced cheerily.

Betts walked over to the lady in tweed and planted a kiss on her cheek. "It's good to see you, Serafina, I've been thinking of your delicious food all the way back from Yeovil."

"I am so happy to see you safely home again, but your eyes are tired. I will make you mint tea with honey." Serafina returned her attention to Hadleigh, he was still standing. "Please Mr Hadleigh, make yourself comfortable." Serafina walked to the marble fireplace and knelt to place a fresh log onto the glowing embers of the fire. She stood and turned back into the room rubbing her hands together with brisk efficiency. "It is my responsibility to attend the physical and spiritual well-being of this household. One of my key tenets is a belief in the value of quality nutrition. Lunch will be at 3:30 in the Green Room, I hope you will enjoy our Glastonbury fare, Mr Hadleigh."

"I'm looking forward to lunch already Serafina, and it's barely one." Everyone laughed. The small note of tension that chilled the air dissipated into nothing. Betts was all too aware how tetchy Serafina could be, especially at first meeting, but she seemed to accept Hadleigh almost immediately. A good sign.

AT LUNCH, Serafina sat facing Hadleigh, and there were significantly more people present than the detective inspector might have anticipated. The entire household shared food at the oak dining table, which was round, very Arthurian. The egalitarian eight included the four permanent staff; Flora, the housemaid, the two cooks, sisters Mabel and Ethel, and the gardener, Caleb. The sacred water accompanying the feast was fresh from the Chalice Well. Betts sat to Hadleigh's right. This was significant. Meals always began with a circle of held hands. A gap between Hadleigh and Betts would never be a problem.

"We celebrate Mother Earth's bounty." The folks around the table declaimed in a hearty unison and began to politely fill each other's cup.

The food was everything promised. The meal began with a refresher: a blend of beetroot, apple and blackberries, spiced with a splash of ginger. The official starter was kale and apple soup with walnuts; and the main dish: a *paillard* of chicken with lemon & herbs, sprouting broccoli, butternut squash and potatoes. And of course a pudding to finish, the delights of apple pie and cream — unpasteurised. All the ingredients of the meal were fresh and local, many indeed from the extensive gardens at the rear of the property. Including the two chickens.

Betts observed the subtle scrutiny from across the table. Serafina's antennae were busy probing, listening for words, watching for gestures. She sought to piece together the loosely scattered fragments of the Detective Inspector. Betts felt the same way, her mind never ceased in the exploration of her favourite enigma, John Hadleigh. Betts wondered about his role in the Great War? What happened to the arm? The only fact she knew was a name, the Somme. Her mind flipped to the kiss at the foot of the stairs. Of course, it was just play-acting, but she shivered at the memory. A nice shiver. The sort of shiver you feel when you're lying beside warm, naked flesh. The tantalising touch of another's skin. Next to you, on top of you, beneath you, behind you. Betts didn't want to stop the unfolding of physical sensation, the denial of feeling, a dimension of herself she had sought to bury along with Mr Betts. But here it was. Attraction. A need. The dizzy swamp of desire. She looked up to see Serafina had switched her attention. She was no longer observing Hadleigh, she was watching Betts. Serafina smiled.

After lunch Hadleigh and Betts did their best to return to the study of ledgers, but it was a task too far, They were both exhausted. Bath and bed was an easy decision, but not at the same time of course, two distinct baths, beds as well, in fact a pair of a-joining bedrooms.

Hadleigh woke many hours later, night had descended on Glastonbury. He stretched where he lay. Hadleigh felt good, remarkably good. He couldn't remember when he last felt so refreshed? Images of fabulous food flashed through his mind, Hadleigh remembered why he woke... he was ravenous. Midnight snacks? The phrase resonated in perfect harmony across his neurons. It was late, but he'd find something. Betts had provided him with striped pyjamas, dressing gown and slippers. He had the sense not to ask to whom they once belonged. The house was quiet, but it was a tranquil, peaceful silence. He creaked his way downstairs to the kitchen and switched on the light. The space was clean and fresh as any daisy. How disappointing, Hadleigh sighed. His gaze rested on a solitary copper pot left to cool on the Aga. It was huge and still warm and covered with a cotton tea towel. Haleigh couldn't resist, the naughty schoolboy was never far from the surface. He peeked inside to witness a stew of tiny mushrooms, coated in butter and chopped parsley, left to jellify. A man of action and impulse, Hadleigh found a fork and speared a clutch of the tiny delights. The butter hadn't yet set, no one would know. He took another fork-full and cleared up the evidence. His stomach glowed with the prize.

As Hadleigh drifted back into sleep he was aware something wasn't quite as he remembered? The walls were starting to bend, edges and corners lost all symmetry, shape, they span, and span, and soon they span like wheels, the spinning wheels in a sea of mud. How can walls become muddy wheels? He questioned, and marvelled at just how quickly they became stuck in the mud, it was like swimming in glue. No escape for the walls. Or the wheels. The people too. And poor, sad horses, desperately writhing in a toxic sludge of bodies, and body fragments. They had to shoot them, it was only kindness. And when someone you barely know lies before you with half their body blown away, begging for kindness. What do you do? Hadleigh could feel the tears coursing his face. Or was it blood? His blood? Someone else's? What did it matter? He wanted to scream, but there was no sound, no voice, no more the silent sanctum of a cosy bed. The roar of artillery filled the air. Heavy guns spewing fire and destruction. He struggled to remember the objective, the place for which so many gave their lives. *BlP 20 kms*, a stark sign confirmed the location of the battle, but in reality it was an Armageddon opening the gates of Hell. The bombardment shook the very ground beneath them. The world thundered with trembling shock, dislodging, pounding his senses. And in the sudden silence, you hear the whistles. You have to remember to be brave, to fight on for King and Country. Hadleigh wanted to scream again, but this time he felt the cry in his throat soaring past tonsils in a torrent of burning fire. He opened his eyes and stumbled forward, out of the bed and on through the broken, barbed wire, from mattress to wash basin, in time to witness the florid colours as his stomach ejected the spent mushroom morsels. Pain consumed him from head to toe. Hadleigh crumpled to the floor. He groaned aloud without knowing, caring. The thud of mortars, the zing of 7.62mm machine gun bullets trilling the air around him. Hands pulled at his uniform, dragging his shattered body back through the endless mud.

That was how she found him. Coiled into the security of the foetal position. Shaking, trembling from head to toe. Hadleigh was soaked in sweat and fear. Betts took a blanket from the bed and draped it around his body. She lay down next to him, her arm protecting the quaking frame, stroking him gently as if he were a child consumed with fears, distraught from a bad dream. For that is what Hadleigh had become; a man-child trying to shake loose the terrifying reality of war.

44

I WILL BE THERE

The afternoon concert started with '*Trois Gymnopedies*" and progressed through a selection of pieces by Debussy, including '*Clair de Lune*', which Frank had to repeat for an encore. The audience were enchanted. In their minds they had been transported to another place, another world framed in hope and freedom, and space, and plenty. Where ordinary people could share in laughter and sunshine and joy. The concert was a great success. Mr Fairbrother joined Frank and Clara at the piano.

"What do you think my dear Clara? Did our most wonderful Frank not just excel himself?" Clara smiled her confirmation. "I believe that to be the case." Mr. Fairbrother continued. "Today you set a new standard. Truly outstanding Frank, and I have news. Shall we sit by the fire?"

Once seated, Mr Fairbrother opened a large buff envelope and withdrew a handful of documents. "I have here; tickets, passport letters, and other sundries. Everything the three of you will need to set sail for America. I have booked passage on the RMS Adriatic, a Cunard liner and she leaves Southhampton this forthcoming Monday morning, II am, bound for New York.

There are also letters of introduction should you need them. I am confident all the required documentation is complete." Mr Fairbrother paused in his excited flow. He smiled with satisfaction.

Clara was especially thrilled. "Oh, Frank. Oh Mr Fairbrother, thank you so much. I really am so very grateful. What a prospect. America, New York. I am so excited."

Frank too was smiling. "I can only echo what Clara has said Mr Fairbrother, thank you so much, I too will look forward to a new life in America."

Mr Fairbrother clapped his hands together in delight. "Wonderful. That gives us four days to prepare. We can travel down in the Silver Ghost, Harper can drive and I'll bring the motor back. I wouldn't have thought my driving again even a vague possibility. Eight years. That was when I last drove. But now, thanks to you my boy, I feel I can do anything I choose, finding myself behind the wheel of an automobile will see the resurrection of yet another, almost forgotten pleasure." He paused to smile in reflection. "And something to think on. When you arrive in America, it might be an idea to put your true identities in a safe place and create new ones. Fresh names at the least. Once you disembark from the ship you can simply disappear, start afresh. Do you have any questions?"

Frank looked over to Clara. She shook her head. Frank spoke. "I believe you have created a perfect scenario for our immediate future and well-being Mr Fairbrother. There are no questions, but I do have a suggestion. There is a date and a place I would like you to remember — I have written the details on this note paper — they describe an appointment in the future. Sunday, 25th April 1926. On that auspicious date, *Turandot*, the final opera by Puccini will debut at La Scala Milan. I suggest, if it is possible, we meet for the concert."

"What an excellent idea, what better excuse to visit La Scala. You can rely on me. I will be there." Declared Mr. Fairbrother.

Frank smiled. "We will all be there Mr. Fairbrother."

45

DO YOU PLAY CARDS AS WELL

If anyone had suggested to Ambrose in 1915, the year in
which he achieved the tender age of twenty-one, and also
the period in which he was recruited to the Service —
*'having displayed outstanding initiative and bravery in the face of
extreme danger'* — that within four years he would find pleasure
in washing and cleaning someone else's car, Ambrose would
never have believed it. Never. This was a man whose sole motivation in life was Ambrose. He cared neither for King nor his
fellow man, or woman. His only interest and purpose
throughout the whole atrocious and stupid bloody war were the
paired themes of himself and survival. But he loved this motor.
It was partly his former colleague Armstrong's total lack of
appreciation for the H6, that led Ambrose to the ineluctable
decision to place a bullet between Armstrong's eyes. One of the
reasons anyway. Ambrose had polished every inch of chrome he
could find. He stowed the cleaning materials under the seat and
fired up the motor just to witness the roar. There was a percep-
tible difference in the sound of this automobile to most engines.
The tone of the H6 was pitched a couple of steps lower, but
crucially, the note was even. It didn't waver with the insecurity of

less well-made pistons and valves, it purred. The H6 was through and through quality. Ambrose felt it every time he pressed the accelerator, the machine responded with not even a hint of hesitation. Ambrose abruptly witnessed a loud yapping in his right ear. An extremely pretty girl in a blue coat and yellow hat was clutching a brown and white Yorkshire terrier. The animal was clearly in distress. The yapping was incessant, high-pitched and very irritating.

"Do you own this vehicle, or are you merely the chauffeur?" Quizzed the girl in clipped Kensington tones.

Ambrose felt instantly wounded, pierced by the barb of her words. He was as much the owner as anyone else. The girl was smart as well as attractive. "Actually I am the owner," Ambrose decided, "it's a Hispano Suiza H6, my pride and joy." He found an owner's smile to match.

"Well, you just frightened the life out of my Priscilla. All that awful engine row, are you aware of the smoke?" The girl frowned at him.

Ambrose was a man all too easy to anger — as his former partner would certainly testify — but irritating as she might be, the girl made him smile. "I really am terribly sorry for upsetting poor Priscilla. This Mews is where I live and possibly I do sometimes frighten small dogs and fair maidens. If you would allow me, I would be honoured to try and make amends. My chicken livers in butter are well known among the canine community. And for mademoiselle, I have tea? Coffee? Cake?" Ambrose was delighted to witness the frost melting.

"MAY I ASK YOUR NAME?" Ambrose enquired, holding the door to the mews cottage ajar.

"Saffron." The girl replied and stepped inside, still clutching the unhappy Priscilla in her arms. Ambrose followed, pushing the door closed and just in time. As soon as Saffron put the animal down she made a bolt for the door. "Don't worry, Priscilla will be your eternal friend once she smells the food." Saffron laughed. "What do I call you? Apart from thoughtless man behind the wheel."

"You can call me Ambrose, and I'm actually a very good driver."

"Perhaps we might go for a spin? But after a cup of tea and that promised liver?"

Ambrose furrowed his eyebrows. "Is Priscilla really your dog?"

Saffron smiled. "Very good Ambrose. I borrowed her from a garden in St Lukes Road; I ought to return her shortly. Gerald sent me. He said you requested a little more awareness? I thought persuading you to invite me into your home would make for a convincing introduction?"

"I am impressed Saffron. Well done. I had no suspicions until Priscilla ran for the door. Do you happen to play cards as well?"

"I do." Saffron announced with another smile.

"Perfect. Let's go for a spin in the car, you can return poor Priscilla to her worried owners, and then we can have a game of cards. I make a good cocktail. We can get to know one another."

"Sounds like fun Ambrose." Saffron confirmed gaily.

"Just one thing Saffron? What do you honestly think of the car?" Ambrose awaited her response with anxious impatience.

"She's an absolute beauty Ambrose. Perhaps you might already know? The designers used to make aeroplane engines."

46

CUP OF CHA

Betts managed to ease Hadleigh from the floor and back into his bed seemingly without him waking. She wondered how much he would remember in the morning? She returned to her own sheets but couldn't sleep, Betts was too much the detective. She wrapped herself in a jumper and went down to the kitchen. The big copper pot on the Aga was cold, she peeked inside. Betts identified the tiny pretty mushroom caps in an instant. "Hmm." She pondered and replaced the cloth. Betts heard the creak of stairs and turned to see Serafina enter the kitchen.

"Good morning CC. You're up early?" Serafina raised an eyebrow and crossed the kitchen to attend the Aga. Betts observed Serafina's surreptitious glance at the pot.

"Yes, I had a difficult night. Poor Hadleigh, he went through quite an ordeal. A kind of delayed trauma I suspect? I saw something similar with Daniel." Betts paused, folding her arms. "I know what you did Serafina." Serafina stood stock still. "I have no doubt it was with the best intentions, but you should have spoken to me, to us. Hadleigh might have the *whiff of innocence* about him, but that doesn't mean he won't listen.

His mind is open, you should have seen that. What did you use?"

Serafina returned Betts' gaze with level eyes. "When I served the gravy I sprinkled a dash of gentian root." She paused with satisfaction. "Your Detective Inspector will have awoken at the midnight hour with an all-consuming ache. Gentian root inspires the pangs of hunger, he will have made his way to the kitchen to sate the want. I might have also mentioned '*midnight snacks*' during the course of the meal, a suggestion your Inspector clearly responded to." Serafina failed to fully suppress the smile that crept across her face, more satisfaction. She turned away from Betts and lifted the tea towel resting on the shroom pot. "Ethel found the mushrooms by the birch trees. There were fifty-five when I prepared them, there are now forty-four. Hadleigh took eleven. The poor man is trapped CC, tethered to pain. I only wanted to help. This is who I am, I make people well, whole again. We both know the psilocybin helped bring Daniel back."

"I would be the last person to dispute your miraculous work with Daniel, but that was a journey we took together. This was manipulation, therapeutic I have no doubt, but it was wrong and I need to know you will never do it again? Especially to people who trust you Serafina."

"Shatzi, I am sorry. But if the night was bad, the day will surely be blessed. And you have my word, things will be exactly as you wish them to be."

Just when she wanted to believe every utterance Serafina made, the annoying female had to end the conversation with a cryptic comment. Betts did not appreciate cryptic phrases from anyone, Hadleigh included, but most especially Serafina. They formed a key part of her communication strategy and they wound Betts up like a spinning top. She felt the need for a cup of tea. She made two and knocked gently on Hadleigh's door.

"It's me Sir, Betts Sir." Betts slowly pushed open the door. Hadleigh stirred as she stepped into the room.

"Is that really you Betts, or some Angelic visitation bearing cups of tea?"

"It is indeed me Sir, along with said cups of tea. I wondered if you might care to join me in a walk up to the Tor before breakfast? I thought a quick cup of cha might help spur you on Sir?"

"I'm not sure you need to be saying Sir when you're in a chap's bedroom holding tea Betts."

"Sorry, Sir," Betts said with a smile and put one of the cups on his bedside table. "Will ten minutes be enough?"

"Perfect. I feel remarkably fresh."

THE TREK UP to the Tor is not for the faint-hearted. Betts led Hadleigh through the steeper climb, she thought he would appreciate the challenge, the ardour might assist his mind to unravel the twisted knots of guilt.

Hadleigh marvelled as the rays of early dawn spread around him, encompassing his form with faint luminescence, clinging like silk to his skin. His senses had rarely felt more vital, charged. They strode together, Hadleigh and Betts, crossing the tiers of age that mark the ascent. His left arm and borrowed walking boots were equal to any demands. Breathless they finally paused under the arch of the Tor, exhaling into the mist like excited steeds. Below them perilous hill-top islands floated in a mysterious sea of enchanted fog. From their Olympian vantage point it was easy to observe the eternal ebb and flow of swirling mists and time. Hadleigh and Betts found a seat at the very centre.

"Something happened last night Betts and I would be

grateful if I might tell you?" Hadleigh continued to stare into the mist.

"Of course," Betts confirmed, consciously refraining from adding the Sir.

"In our hubris we sometimes say things, with the best of intentions, that later come back to haunt us. You and I have never discussed the Great War, it is far too terrible to contemplate, but that does not diminish the need to exculpate oneself from the grotesque tragedies in which, through circumstance, I played a part. With these words I endeavour... no, I believe I speak in truth. It was just over two weeks into the Somme, July 1916. A group of regiments were part of a dawn attack on the Bazentin Ridge. Our objective was a small village, Bazentin le Petit. The plan was audacious. The artillery would lay down a constantly moving barrage, a firewall of devastation set at one hundred yards in advance of our position, and we would march behind. The expectation of our commanders was the enemy would be so terrified by the huge onslaught of ordnance, the barrage of high explosive, they would simply run, retreat if they had any sense. A French commander dismissed the plan as '*an attack organised for amateurs by amateurs*'. He might have been correct. For me it was the single most frightening experience of the entire war. In a litany of horrifying memory, Bazentin le Petit stands alone in sheer terror. It was uncannily awful. We were literally following a constantly exploding wall of flame and destruction. We were trailing Armageddon. But the attack was a success. We reached the village and it was deserted. We should have carried on, but our fearless generals at the rear had unexpectedly achieved their objective, and they didn't know what they should do next? So we made ourselves comfortable in the empty village. There was of course a chateau, with huge green shutters at the windows. It looked like some other-worldly chequer board. I heard music, the sound of a piano. It was a

piece by Chopin, the Nocturne in E flat major. I experienced
Heaven and Hell in the same morning. I made my way into the
chateau and found a young soldier, far too young and such a
wonderful musician, his name was George. He asked if I wanted
to play on the instrument and I suggested we should perform
something together. We were in the music room of the chateau
and there were shelves of manuscripts lining the walls. George
found a score of *The Dolly Suite*, by Gabriel Fauré, a French
composer. He had written six pieces to be played by four hands,
two pianists sitting next to one another, reading from the same
page. It was a truly momentous experience. An amazing ray of
light and hope in the middle of relentless gloom and devastation. There was one piece in particular, *Berceuse*. George and I
played it several times. Soon we had a crowd of comrades who
clapped at every opportunity. More than half of them would be
dead by the end of the day. By late afternoon, Brigade made up
their minds we should attack High Ridge after all, a mere seven
hours late. The same tactic as before, but without the artillery
bombardment, just a blow of the whistle and fixed bayonets
forward. We left the chateau. I asked George how old he was?
Sixteen he said. Stick close to me, I told him. Those very words.
The enemy had used the hours to re-group and dig themselves
in on the ridge. They allowed us a degree of progress and confidence, as good soldiers do, and then Hell opened the gates once
more. Mortar bombs rained down like demonic confetti to the
droning metallic chatter of the incessant machine-guns. George
was beside me when the mortar shell exploded. He took the full
force of the blast direct, the boy fragmented into a thousand
bloody pieces. The shrapnel took my arm as well, but George
gave his life for the rest of me. He had enlisted with a friend,
Harper, a couple of years older. It was Harper who pulled me
back through the mud to safety. But it was my words that cast
poor George's fate. He smiled at me in that moment Betts,

almost as if he knew he was about to die, and it didn't matter. George presented me with the most precious gift. These past three years I've struggled with my right to exist, let alone accept his sacrifice. I have felt unfailingly unworthy. That is, until this moment. *'The mountain veiled in mist is not a hill.'* I have been blessed to finally see there is a bigger picture. On that terrible day, George and I were given something extraordinary that no one had the right to expect. The musical thread of our lives found true purpose, a final destination in those brief hours; in the safety of the chateau, sharing music with each other and our comrades. I can only honour George and his sacrifice by accepting the gift. And in doing so, I have to accept myself." Hadleigh struggled to maintain his composure, but the compulsion to sob was too great. Betts put her arm around him. He lent into her shoulder and without thinking she reached out with her other hand to soothe his head. She felt his frame soften into her. They remained locked together for several minutes. No words were spoken. They simply gazed into the mists of Glastonbury. Until she felt his shoulders stiffen. Hadleigh sat upright. "Time for breakfast Betts."

"Yes Sir."

47

JUST WALK AWAY

Seven consulted her list. The first name, Roberts, could now be deleted, but rather than moving to name number two, Seven skipped to the fourth, Ashfield. His location indicated something subtly different — the grand title of the premises to start, *The Three Queens Hotel*, definitely not a confectionary shop, but it did boast the familiar seaside location, on this occasion, Weston-super-Mare. The casting vote however was the single star drawn alongside the entry. Mr or Miss Ashfield it would be.

The anticipated length of the journey was two hundred and sixteen miles. Seven left Reculver heading due west, she would be fine, but she was aware the Brough would at some point need a break. The morning air was bitter with a cloying dampness that clung to the road in patches of wandering swirls of fog, but the leathers and the suit cocooned Seven from the elements. Not her face of course, she enjoyed the tingle in her cheeks. Seven replayed Five's song over and over in her mind, it made the journey even better. *'It's sad, so sad. Why can't we talk it over? Ohh, it seems to me. That sorry seems to be the hardest word.'*

After four hours and one hundred and twenty-eight miles

the fuel gauge told her the Brough was running low, Seven pulled into a filling station on the outskirts of a village by the name of Overton. No sooner had she switched off the engine than two young teenage mechanics ran over with a bucket and cleaning cloths. They both seemed to speak at once.

"What can we do for you, Miss?"

"Shall I fill the tank?"

Would you like me to give the machine a quick once-over with a cloth?"

"What about oil Miss?"

"We have a cafe just over yonder if you're hungry?"

"Or maybe a tea Miss?"

"This is a beautiful motorcycle Miss."

The pair barely paused enough for Seven to answer, but she heard their sincerity. "How much for everything except the tea?" She ventured.

"Five bob Miss."

SEVEN DECIDED TO WALK, stretch her limbs, free the trapped muscles while she waited for the mechanics to finish the pit-stop service. She paused to take a deep breath. Seven frowned, the smell of beer filled the air.

"'Ello Luv. Would you care to join us?" A group of five soldiers sat on boxes playing cards beside an army vehicle. The men had set up an impromptu camp in a clearing off the main road.

"We're not 'er type. Can't you see what she is?" Another squaddie declared.

"Fuckin' queer." Declared a soldier with a mouth full of black teeth.

"I'd like ta..." Began another.

Seven recoiled. Their words and minds were awash with
violence, hostility, prejudice, and directed at her? But Seven was
learning, trouble was best avoided. She chose to walk away and
quickly. The two young mechanics were just finishing a final
polish. The Brough shone like a new silver coin. "Thank you."
Seven said simply, eager to be gone. She handed the boys a ten-
shilling note. "Take it, five bob each." Seven instructed.

"She really is a beautiful machine Miss. How fast does
she go?"

The palpable, genuine, enthusiasm of the two adolescents
helped dispel the psychotic anger of the soldiers. "73 mph is the
best so far, but I intend to make some adjustments to the air-fuel
mix, should speed things up a little." Seven declared with a
sincere smile. The two lads thrilled. Seven set off again, eager to
leave the military in her wake.

'WHAT HAVE I gotta do to make you love me? What have I gotta do to
make you care? What do I do when lightning strikes me? And I wake
to find you're not there.' The song went around and around in her
head. Five's gift was more than the glorious melody, it came
loaded with a lyric full of questions, and for someone who never
really asked questions this was something of a revelation. In a
flood of intuition Seven saw why Five was so dangerous. The
changes in Seven had started with Five and his song. Five's
musical gifts had the power to subtly alter the programmed
paradigm, abruptly there was a need to ask questions.

In that moment, Seven's mind was certainly engaged in a
point of sensory distraction. To further add to the subliminal
peace, the Brough engine had a particularly happy tone around
forty-six mph. The road ahead was straight and empty with
legions of tall trees and thick, verdant woodland skirting the

highway on either side, but the accident was always going to happen. There was nothing Seven could have done. The young stag leapt from the tree-line direct into the front wheel and handlebars of the Brough. The stag's momentum catapulted Seven backwards over the seat and through the air landing safely on her back. The stag and the motorcycle continued to spar in a deadly tangle, the trapped antlers and spinning wheel soon snapped the deer's neck. Seven ran back to the twitching carcass but there was nothing to be done for the animal. She untangled the head from the spokes of the wheel and carried him to the roadside. Seven returned for the Brough and propped the damaged vehicle against a tree. Finally, with the deer cradled in her arms, Seven carried the body into the under-growth where she laid him to a respectful rest. As she returned to the Brough, Seven heard voices. She paused to observe from the cover of undergrowth. The army lorry was parked up along-side the Brough. The group of soldiers from the clearing stood around the machine in discussion.

"She must 'av 'it somethin'. Some animal as like." The soldier with black teeth made a wise nod, impressed with his insight.

"Those spokes'll take some sortin' out. D'ya reckon she gone back to Overton?"

"No chance, we'd a seen 'er." Declared Johnson, the soldier with the pack of playing cards.

"Reckon she must be round 'ere somewhere? Probably 'iding, hah." The soldier with black teeth laughed.

"This machine's gotta be worth a few bob? We could stick it in the truck? There's plenty who'll put up some readies for a motorcycle like that?"

"That's probably the best idea you ever 'ad Johnson. Let's do it lads. Give us 'an 'and to shift the bugger."

Seven watched the men manhandle the Brough into the

army truck. It took all five to lift her. Once the motorcycle was safely stowed with ropes holding the machine securely, the men assembled for a final time at the rear of the vehicle. "Taylor's the man, 'e only just left the service, runs a motor vehicle business over Salisbury-way. Does all manner of *off-the-book* business."

"Well, that is most interesting." Declared Seven, stepping from the bushes. "I would like to thank you for loading up the motorcycle, and also for the lorry itself. I've never driven one, but I'm confident I'll manage." She paused and regarded the men with a bright smile. Seven stood several inches taller than the tallest of the soldiers. "You can accept reality and walk away with some dignity, or, quite simply, I will make you suffer. I know you think I'm a deviant, weak woman, but let me assure you, the only part in which you are correct is my gender, and I am aware, some of you even question that?"

"Fuck you." Declared the soldier with particularly bad teeth. He leapt at Seven. His nose splattered across his face with a jab he didn't even see, nor did he witness the chop as he fell. He lay motionless on the ground.

"You fuckin'... " Was as far as the vitriol progressed before the kick to the head knocked the second soldier unconscious.

Seven dropped to her haunches and took the legs from the sneaky one trying to run at her from behind, her boots connected with his head.

"Just walk away." Seven suggested to the final pair. One did, he turned and ran, clattering away down the road as fast as his hob-nailed boots would allow.

"Only you and me then darlin'. We should 'av 'ad that game a cards. Could've settled this amicable." Johnson, the fifth and final soldier pulled a hunting knife from his belt. "Bit late for that now." He lunged the blade at her but Seven easily parried, bracing his neck into a choking headlock. That was when the other knife appeared from literally up Johnson's left sleeve. The soldier plunged the second blade with all his might into her side, easily penetrating the layers of heavy leather until the tip jabbed hard into the suit. And there its progress came to an abrupt end. Seven grabbed the knife. She crushed Johnson's wrist like a dry leaf and redirected the secret blade, thrusting the steel deep into the man's throat. He fell to the ground blowing bloody bubbles from his neck, his eyes wide, staring directly at her. Seven took a moment to acknowledge the expression of total shock stretching the man's face in horror. A common trait among her victims. Johnson laying twitching in a pool of blood. Seven reached down to the bulge in the man's tunic pocket and removed a pack of playing cards.

"Hmm." Seven murmured and tucked them away in her leathers.

48

VINGT-ET-UN

P art 3

"Full house." Saffron declared in triumph. "Three queens and a pair of jacks."

Ambrose threw his cards to the table in disgust. He didn't like to lose. "Tsk." He commented as Saffron encircled the pile of coins and drew them towards her. She immediately began to assemble the silver and brass currency into neat piles. "You didn't tell me you were a sharp?" Ambrose declared.

"What's a sharp?" Saffron responded.

"A card-sharp. Someone who knows how to swindle the gullible of their cash."

"That's not fair Ambrose." Saffron decided. "There was no swindling, you simply underestimated my superior abilities. A rather dangerous strategy in our line of work."

Ambrose paused to consider her comment. She was correct. He had totally underestimated her impressive abilities. She was a woman and that's what men did. They would always calculate a female to be less capable, inferior to the innate faculties of the male mind and physique. He was clearly wrong, along with the rest of his species. "Where did you learn these skills, it's not the sort of skill young ladies generally acquire?"

"That's your male arrogance speaking all over again Ambrose. At school of course. A ladies' finishing school on Lake Lucerne I would add. We, the innocent young ladies, would play poker every night for cigarettes, alcohol and chocolate. Do you know stud-poker?"

Ambrose shook his head. "Afraid not."

"I'll have to teach you. You should appreciate by now Ambrose, this is a brave new world? Have you not heard of Emmeline Pankurst? *'Deeds not Words.'* Or Emily Wilding Davison who died beneath the hooves of the King's horse? It's been nearly a year since we were given the vote man. And I'm the better card player, accept it."

Ambrose smiled to himself. He'd asked for someone with a greater awareness, Saffron was indubitably well-qualified. He gathered up the loose cards and started to place them back into order. The process of sifting, straightening, and shuffling the pack was quite therapeutic, it were almost as if he was re-ordering his thoughts in tandem. Putting everything back into a linear, logical structure. "How about a switch to Pontoon? My luck might change?"

"I don't believe I know that one?"

"Sorry Saffron, army slang, *Vingt-et-Un*, was the original title?"

"Oh yes, of course. You can be the bank." Saffron declared with a magnanimous smile.

Ambrose feared he might fare no better with the new game. He dealt them a card each, face down. Saffron peeled up the corner of the playing-card and placed a shilling in the pot, a

glass ashtray. Ambrose dealt them each a second card. When
Saffron set the two cards apart and an extra shilling clinked into
the pot, Ambrose knew he was in trouble. Saffron had two
sevens. Never a good start, but by splitting the pair she would
create better odds. Ambrose dealt two new cards, face down.
Saffron studied the first hand and placed another shilling in the
pot. Followed by another card and another shilling. She moved
on to the second hand and the process repeated until Saffron
announced "stick". The ashtray contained eight shillings, a
healthy pot. Ambrose turned over his two cards, a three of
diamonds and a jack of spades — thirteen. He sighed and
revealed a third card, a two of hearts — fifteen. Ambrose had no
choice, the next card was an ace. His heart soared. Ambrose had
a tally of sixteen with four cards, victory, snatched from the jaws
of defeat, was abruptly within reach. He would attempt a five-
card-trick, beating any possible hand Saffron might hold.
Ambrose felt the familiar surge of confidence. He uncovered the
final card, a seven. He wanted to tip the table over. Instead, he
threw down the pack and stood to his feet. He paced the room to
the fireplace and lit a cigarette. Ambrose inhaled the smoke
deep into his lungs, acknowledging the acrid bite of the Senior
Service tobacco. He shook his handsome, but irritated head in a
cloud of tobacco fumes.

Saffron followed Ambrose to the fire. She paused to consider
the simmering smoker at the mantelpiece. "You really don't like
to lose, do you?" Saffron declared, placing her silk purse on the
polished marble. She removed a cigarette from a silver and
tortoise-shell case — it had a gold tip — she tapped the end
against the case. "May I have a light Ambrose?" He struck a
match into flame. Ambrose was calm now, balance had been
restored. "I need to share something Ambrose, from Gerald.
There were valuable nuggets of information in the final call
Roberts made." Saffron paused to draw on her Manoli cigarette.

"He was visited earlier in the day by a woman claiming to be a detective inspector. She used the name, Betts. Clearly this was a lie, the official status for starters. Roberts also stated the female wore an outfit of black leather and stood at over six foot tall, a genuine *femme fatale*. But that's not the oddest thing. It turns out the actual detective who's trailing the case, who genuinely is a Detective Inspector, Hadleigh by name, has a female driver and her name is Betts. I suspect that is just too bizarre to be coincidence? Don't you think?"

Ambrose made his eyes squint, trying to make sense of the puzzle. "I've seen Hadleigh and his driver, Betts. She's only medium height, five foot three at the most, certainly not a six-footer. That would be something quite unmistakeable. Leather as well?" Ambrose paused. "There was a jolly decent motorcycle chained up to a bollard on the quay near to the Roberts' place. I parked the H6 alongside. I'm sure the leather must be significant? There cannot be many opportunities for a lady to wear full leather attire, but riding a motorcycle would almost certainly be top of any list. That's her mode of transport. I'm sure the machine was already gone when I left. But I can't be certain."

"There's something else Ambrose, Gerald provided a list. For our eyes only. There are five names and in the last week two have been murdered. Gerald suggested we stake out the remaining three and wait for our leather-clad assassin to reveal herself?"

"Where are the locations?" Ambrose asked.

"Annoyingly, they're spread far and wide; Edinburgh, Bradford, and Weston-super-Mare."

"Where's the Weston place?" Ambrose queried.

"In the West-Country, somewhere south of Bristol, north of Taunton. We could be there in four hours."

"Let's try for three and a half."

49

REMEMBER TO SING

The Promenade was quite spectacular. A flat body of water stretching out to the horizon, but for an island, shaped like a huge bowler hat jutting out of the waves. For the first time since climbing into the cab, Seven felt comfortable driving the lorry, an unpredictable monstrosity of a machine. The gears, the brakes, the steering, it really was an unpleasant experience, but when you had this vista of open sea and sand just beyond the flapping canvas, possibly the vehicle wasn't really too bad? Seven acknowledged how un-objective her mind had become. Had she always been like this? It seemed doubtful? She slowed the lorry to a stop and watched the sun disappearing past a bank of clouds into the sea. Seven had never witnessed a sunset before. She'd observed many sunrises in recent times, always a beautiful sight to behold, but never a sunset, and the beach at Weston-super-Mare provided the perfect backdrop. The star plunged directly into the waves.

She left the lorry on Beach Road and made her way down Oxford Street. A panoply of the finest fish and chips, novelty emporia, and vendors of clotted cream fudge. Quite by chance Seven discovered a new business of interest, the ultimate seaside opportunity; the promise of a glimpse into your future with Madame Tamara. Her premises were squeezed into a tiny one-up, one-down shop space abutting the Three Queens. Seven paused to study the window display. The Maestra within offered a comprehensive esoteric skill-set; Madame was a medium, but also learned in Palmistry, Tarot, and Astrology. A panoply of the alternative was on offer, but it was the ability to predict what lies ahead that made Seven curious. She pushed open the door. The ting of tiny bells announced her arrival. The room was smaller than Seven expected, she had to bend her head beneath the uncommonly low ceiling. The air was heavy with whispers of incense and patchouli oil.

"Take the seat why don't you my love? I would generally be closed by now, but I have been expecting you." The voice was fractured with time and cheroots, it belonged to a lady lit within a multitude of flickering candlelight. Madame Tamara was an enigmatic figure, festooned with necklaces of gold and silver on her breast, a congregation of bracelets and bangles rattled on her wrists, clattering together as she shuffled a deck of large, colourful cards. Seven took a seat at the small round table. The tabletop was shrouded in a damson silk damask, emblazoned with a red, six-sided star enclosed within a circle formed by a snake and clasped with an ancient runic symbol. Seven took the proffered seat. Madame Tamara spread the pack across the fabric in an expansive semi-circle. The Maestra looked directly into Seven's face. "Take one," Madame Tamara invited. Seven selected her card. "Ah, *The High Priestess*," Madame explained, pausing to study the card Seven selected. "This is you. We call this card, the *significator*. *The High Priestess* comes from the Major Arcana, she is not found in the regular pack of playing cards. Our lady is a figure of mystery and power. Do you see the scroll she holds? It is inscribed with the word TORA — divine law. *The High Priestess* celebrates nature and wisdom." Madame placed the card in the centre of the table and collected up the remaining cards. "There are many ways of interpreting the cards, please divide the pack." Seven poked the cards with her finger. "Thank you." Madame said quietly and continued. "I will introduce you to the Pentagram Tarot Spread. Remember, the significator, *The High Priestess,* she is you. I will deal a further five cards from the top of the pack to form a star representing the four cardinal elements: fire, earth, air, and water. The fifth denotes spirit. Stars personify light, illumination." She paused to study Seven. Seven responded with a nod. Madame dealt the first card: *The Tower.* "Pictures paint many thousands of words. The lightning striking the tower speaks of danger, imminent threat. This card goes to the right-hand corner of the reading. Earth, your current position, the solidity of existence." Madame dealt a new card: *Ten of Swords.* "Again the image is quite explicit, the representation is clear: physical danger." Madame Tamara paused to study Seven's reaction. There was none, her client remained impassive. "We move on to the third card which represents the information you have been given. How much can you rely on the truth or integrity of the source? I hope these words make some sense to you?" Seven made another nod.

Apart from the two brief movements of the head, Seven might have seemed remarkably impassive to Madame Tamara and her proclamations. Seven hadn't actually spoken a word since entering the medium's realm, but her mind was embroiled in a maelstrom of frenetic activity. The room had a unique presence beyond the drama of flickering candlelight. The floorboards were bare and polished with an elaborate Persian rug at the centre. Madame Tamara together with table and chairs sat on top. Numerous shelves lined the walls, brimming with books, clay figurines, and the busts of famous historical figures — Napoleon was festooned with gold paint. A lexicon of exotic objects, from Native American dream catchers to tribal masks and shrunken heads, a collection from across the world. A connecting door, cloaked with a beaded curtain led to the rest of the building. Seven attempted to penetrate the thoughts of the woman sat just a few paces away. Generally there was little resistance, but this was a trained mind, there was no easy access to the internal processes. Seven watched the third card take its position on the table in the lower right position. The *winds of change*. Seven felt those winds.

"Air is communication, information." Madame Tamara explained as she placed the card on the table, the *Knight of Cups*. "Notice the card is upside down? This is called a reversal, the meaning of the card is reversed. In such a position within the reading, we might say the information you have been given is not reliable. The thin veil we call reality is not what it appears to be. There has been manipulation of truth, history, perhaps even ideals?" Madame paused and dealt the fourth card. "*The Ace of Wands*, the element of fire, and it occupies the lower left of the star. This is your drive, willpower, energy. *The Ace of Wand*s is a very powerful card in this position. Your energies are primordial, they have yet to fully form, coalesce, and constitute as Will." Madame Tamara paused to study Seven. Her eyebrows made a small frown. "Do you know who you are? Do you have a sense of why you are here?"

Seven considered the questions. They had the resonance of a huge trembling gong. In her own time, within the contextual boundaries of the New Paradigm, Seven had no cause to question anything of the rituals of life, let alone the highly individual, existential, personification of whom she might be. There was no ambiguity, there was no doubt of her response. The future was efficient, organised; humanity understood its place within the cosmos. A New Order both on Earth and across the Solar System had been established. But when it came to the Divine, a power beyond the purely physical, any notion of spirituality had no part to play in this freshly wrought web of reality. This was a social construct devised and maintained solely by the hands and minds of humankind. The Godly-whimsy of the spiritual order had been left in the New Paradigm's wake along with the ashes of the past. Seven had no doubt who she was within the New Order. Everybody had their part to play. But that was three hundred years hence. A new Seven had emerged from the chaos of the crash through time; she had evolved, was evolving, into something beyond the limitations of her own aeon. In a sense Seven had been reborn. She was aware of the changes gestating within her. Her mind was free, unfettered. Seven could think and do exactly as she wished, there were no constraints, certainly not internal ones. Seven was a spirit living in a state of independence she could not have achieved in her own time. Seven spoke for the first time since entering Madama Tamara's presence. "Thank you for the questions and the reading. I believe I do have a strong sense of who I might be. But I am constantly evolving, which is why I cannot yet answer the second question."

"You are not from here are you my love?" Madame Tamara asked softly.

Seven understood the terms of reference, Madame Tamara wasn't thinking of any immediate locale. Seven smiled. "You are correct Madame."

Madame Tamara made a faint nod. "May I ask your name?" Requested Madame Tamara.

"Seven."

"Aah. Seven is a highly significant number, especially to the esoteric. Seven represents the universe, this is why we have seven days in a week. The Seven Arch Angels. The Seven Seraphim. The Seven Hindu Chakras. The Seven Hermetic Principles. Your first card, *The High Priestess*, and the scroll of the *Divine Law* is significant, everything is connected." Madame

Tamara focused her attention back to the table and dealt a new card. They studied together in silence, *Judgement*. Another image from the Major Arcana. "The position for card number five is the upper left, representing the element of water and intuition. Perception is associated with the powers of the Goddess, the female. You will see from the naked figures depicted there is a theme of resurrection, karma, re-birth, and with an Angel sounding a trumpet, there is the spectre of conflict. Armageddon. And so we move on to the final card." The image depicted a *Hermit*. "This card is placed across the first selection, the significator. It is the culmination of the expression of the previous cards. This card represents the outcome, the destination of your journey. The *Hermit* carries a lantern, the light of truth to guide mankind. Perhaps the card might help to reveal the answer to my second question." Madame Tamara looked directly into Seven's face. "I hope you found your first tarot reading of interest?"

"It has been quite fascinating, thank you. May I ask a question?"

"Of course."

"The six-sided star within the circle of a coiled snake, clasped with a rune. What does this represent?"

Madame Tamara smiled. "It is a reference to my teacher Helena Blavatsky, she was a guardian of ancient knowledge. Her teachings are encoded in a religion she helped found, Theosophy."

"Thank you, I will investigate both Theosophy and Madame Blavatsky with great interest. How much money would you like?"

Madame Tamara smiled. "That's not the way we would generally put such a question... *how much do I owe you*? Would be the more correct expression. We need to appropriate and observe these turns of phrase. I too have learned to appreciate the need to blend in. As for the money, you don't owe me anything. But if you have a coin, place it in my palm for luck. I am happy to have been of service. I would ask one small favour before we part my love? May I briefly hold your hand?"

Seven presented her left hand to Madame Tamara across the Theosophic table-top design. Madame closed her eyes as she gently grasped Seven's long fingers.

"There will be blood and darkness in the hours ahead but I hear your voice above everything. You are singing, and you have a beautiful voice. Whatever the night will manifest my love, you must remember to sing."

50

CYPHERS AND SOMERSET

Hadleigh was confident he was onto something, the whiff of innocence was evolving. Dykes had been an orderly in the truest sense, it was his nature, he couldn't help himself. Dykes kept a record of everything of personal relevance. He created order from life, ergo the notebook had to relate to the vehicle and the journeys they made together. The numbers must surely correlate to the mileage and by the same inference, the letters might logically be an acronym specifying a location? If they could dovetail the information in the notebook with the ledgers, the destinations would reveal themselves. But without a key the acronyms made no sense. They stared, and stared, and stared, until the seeing made the letters blur. The annoyingly random code would not yield. Thora brought teas and freshly made poppyseed cake.

"How are you getting on Miss? Seems like you've been at it since breakfast?"

"We have Thora. We need a key and we can't find it."

"What sort of key?"

"There must be some kind of cipher? We've tried to match

the cryptic terms with dates and distances, but without a hint of success?"

"Oh dear me Miss. Per'aps I can help. Me and my best friend Cissy used to do ciphers when we was at school Miss."

Hadleigh passed Flora the notebook. "There are three columns. The acronyms are in the first column to the left, two or more letters. The second column is a mixture of letters and numbers. The third column is purely numbers. We thought mileage, but the figures are far too large." Explained Hadleigh. "Good luck." He said hopefully.

Flora considered the notebook for a thoughtful moment. "With your permission Miss." She declared and disappeared from the table, to re-appear two minutes later with a road map of Britain. "The notebook was found in a motor vehicle you say so those numbers, like you say, are most likely to be distance. But they look far too big? But that might be helpful. The easiest cipher is to move letters or numbers forward or backward by a whole number, 1 or such. According to this map, Swanage to London is 127 miles. That would make the return journey 254 miles. If we add 1 to each number, we come to 365 miles. I thought to start with London, as one of the figures in the notepad is actually that very number, 365. Now if we take the letters and numbers of the second column and apply the same process, but in reverse: 34tfqu25, becomes 23sept14, which looks like a date. The acronym NI comes out as MH."

"Brilliant Flora. So if we check the ledgers for that date, we will find the location, confirmed with the mileage." Declared an excited Hadleigh.

Betts scanned through the first ledger, 1914. "Milvern Hall!" She announced and blinked in surprise.

Flora stood from the table, "Well, better be off then. Glad I could help Miss, Detective Sir."

The pair returned to the ledgers with renewed purpose.

With Flora's key they could finally unlock the cipher. Hadleigh and Betts began the search for hidden treasure.

"I think I have another Sir? According to the ledgers, Dykes made a delivery on the 20th March 1917 to The Three Queens Hotel, Weston-super-Mare. It matches with the codes in the notebook; milage, date and location."

"Where is that Betts? I know the name, but I have no idea where it might be? And such a grand title?"

"It's in Somerset like us Sir. On the coast, around an hour's drive."

"Perfect. Do you fancy a trip to the seaside Betts?"

"They have donkey rides on the beach, Sir, I used to go as a child." And as she said the words, a forgotten memory found a location to slowly ferment into something uncomfortable. "I have a bad feeling about this Sir. I think I might know exactly where the sweet shop is?"

"I thought the location was a hotel?"

"It is. We should go to Weston Sir. I have no doubt there's something similar to Swanage and Margate operating from The Three Queens establishment. It would be good to jump the queue this time. So to speak Sir."

"Lead on Betts. I want to see the donkeys on the beach."

51

OTHER PRESSING MATTERS

The Three Queens Hotel was located directly next door to Madame Tamara and her portal to the future. Hotel might have been a slightly exaggerated title for what was essentially a good-sized Inn offering accommodation and meals. The establishment stood on the arterial corner of the High Street, a prime location. Seven stepped through the door it was shortly after six-forty. The bar was quiet with minimal activity. Fires crackled in stone fireplaces on adjacent walls blending the fresh scent of pine with the bar's bouquet of beer and cigarettes. Small groups of men sat at bare wood tables heavy with glasses, chequer boards, and cards. They took no notice.

Seven strode across the room. A large woman scrutinised her from behind the bar, there were no signs of kindness in her gaze. "Good evening," announced Seven, I've been taking part in a rally and my motorcycle has broken down. Would you by chance know of a mechanic in the town who might be able to affect repairs?"

The landladies' eyes squinted with suspicion. The tall woman standing before her had the bearing of an official, which always meant trouble, and Mrs. Ashfield was in the cautious habit of suspecting the worst. Living on the precipice of danger was how the Ashfield family had learned to exist over the past few years, the daily disruptions were easy and convenient to blame on the Great War. But in truth wars didn't bother them. If anything, the general atmosphere of fear and chaos made things considerably easier. Plenty of opportunity. Even the restrictions on opening hours were helpful, providing the Ashfield's with time to focus on the other things, the other business, when it was important to be able to legitimately lock the doors. The *'other business'* might have been dangerous, but it certainly made life more exciting, it was worthy of the risk. And this woman in leather? She certainly had the swagger of officialdom about her, but the explanation made sense. Typical of these bright young things, bloody toffs, to go gallivanting across the country on some ridiculous motorcycle race — they should have better things to do. Mrs. Ashfield filled her lungs. ""Oo can fix a motor-cycle 'round these parts then? Any takers?" She bellowed at the men deeply immersed in games of chance and skill at the tables.

"Ray, he can fix an'thing. Down Milton Road. 'undred yard' after the cemetery. Big wooden shed on the right. Can't mistake it."

Seven smiled her bright smile. "Thank you Sir, that was most helpful." She turned back to the landlady. "Do you have a room available?"

"Seven and six a night." The landlady replied. "Shilling for a cooked breakfast. If you want a bath, that's extra."

"How much extra?"

"Sixpence."

"Good, I will return later this evening once I have located Mr. Ray. I would prefer a room with a bath and I might require more than one night's stay. If I leave you with five pounds would that be an appropriate deposit?"

The woman's attitude softened considerably once she held

the crisp new note in her padded palm. "Oh, that will be absolutely fine Miss. I'll sort the room out proper for you, fresh linen and towels. Perhaps something to eat when you return? See how you feel Miss. No trouble at all." Seven saw the darkness lurking in the woman as she preened herself on the platitudes of goodwill. It was all too easy to read the malign echoes in the woman's mind; the hotel was a place of profound evil. Seven was in the right location.

THERE WAS no problem in finding Ray's, the workshop was situated exactly as described. Seven parked the lorry under a tree on an adjacent side road and studied the large wooden structure, A huge old barn surrounded by a yard filled with the rusting metal and rubber of automobiles and motorcycles. Ray had his own vehicular cemetery just down the road from the human version. A lamp lit the door at the back of the house. Seven knocked, there was no reply, but there were the sounds of movement. She knocked again and the door crept ajar. A tiny little girl with dishevelled hair and a dirty face looked out. "Mummy says we don't have any money and you should go away."

Seven carefully removed a fresh five-pound note from her bundle and presented it to the child. "Please give that to Mummy and explain I have a motorcycle that needs repair."

The child disappeared and a woman wearing an apron appeared at the door. She eyed Seven up and down. "You'd best come in." Ray's wife decided.

IT WAS ALWAYS a surprise to Seven when she witnessed people

with physical disabilities. It was not even a question of choice in her century.

A man sat by a roaring fire. The little girl who first greeted Seven perched on his leg. His only leg. The other was gone, only a stump remained.

"I hope you won't mind if I don't stand?" The sitting man declared with a laugh. "The name's Ray, this is Lilibet and the wife's Molly. How can I earn that five-pound note you kindly offered?"

"I had an accident and my motorcycle is damaged."

"What sort of accident Miss?"

"A stag leaped out of the undergrowth. We collided head-on at a speed of 46mph. The stag was killed."

"Oh, deary-me. Does the motorcycle need fetching?"

"No, I have it outside, on a lorry."

"A lorry?" The dynamic in Ray's tone abruptly went higher.

"An army lorry, Commer, three and a half-ton. A group of soldiers attempted to steal the motorcycle, I stole their lorry instead." Seven maintained her un-flustered consistency.

"You didn't steal the motorcycle Miss?" Ray's expression betrayed concern.

"No. It's mine." Seven declared with genuine pride. "I paid for it."

"That just as well Miss. I don't have no worries 'bout takin' from the army, they took my leg, after all, they owe me." Ray laughed heartily, bouncing Lilibet on his remaining leg. "But if you'd taken the bike, that would be different. You 'ave to 'ave a code to live by." Ray nodded wisely. "What d'ya say Lilibet?" The little girl returned his wise nods. "Molly, give your eldest son a shout would ya?"

A younger version of Ray appeared two minutes later, crucially with both legs. "There's a Commer lorry parked in the road Son, put her in the shed would ya? Make sure she's covered, and 'ave a look at the motorcycle in the back."

"Right 'o Pa." The young man declared and disappeared into the night.

"He's a good boy." Declared Ray with pride. "Course the bloody fool had to go and sign up in 1917. 'Ad to go out there meself, make sure he was alright. He come 'ome with barely a scratch. This is what I got for being a patriot." Ray laughed again. "But I'm glad it was me and not 'im. Nothing more important than your kids. Why don't you have a seat Miss? Ray Jnr. will be a good few minutes."

"Would you like a cup 'o tea?" Asked Molly.

Seven declined the tea, but she took a seat across from Ray. Lilibet dismounted from her perch and approached Seven. "What's your name?" The little girl asked.

Seven was totally unprepared for the question, in fact, she was totally unprepared for the child. Seven had never encountered a child before. She knew about them, everyone knows about children, but in the new paradigm they were rarely visible. "My name is Seven."

"That doesn't sound like a name?" The little girl decided.

Seven was enchanted by the innocence. It was beautiful. Precious. "What name do you think I should have?" Seven asked gently.

Lilibet paused, lost in a world of thought. Seven studied her and smiled with rare spontaneity. The child's mind was a delight, the simple uncluttered joy of life. Lilibet fired Seven's resolve, the children must be protected.

"Sami!" Lilibet proclaimed.

The room laughed with love for the child.

"I 'ave a sister, Samantha, 'er aunt." Molly explained, "but those 'oo knows 'er calls 'er Sami. Lilibet likes ya Miss." Ray Jnr burst through the door keen as a hot tip.

"It's a Brough Superior Pa! She's an absolute beaut!"

The motorcycle's name could certainly make men's hearts flutter. The two Rays to start with, quickly joined by Freddie — Alfred when he needed to be — the next male in line. The three together with Seven made a path through the detritus of desecrated vehicles littering the yard. The back-flap of the Commer's canvas cover was already tied up, but the lights were only switched on once the doors were firmly shut.

"That *is* a fine machine, Miss." Ray declared with emphasis running his hand over the chrome fuel tank.

"She certainly is. I don't like to see her damaged. And please, call me Sami. I am happy to be re-designated. Christened."

"Do you feel up to helping us get her down? With this leg, or maybe I should say, without the other." Ray laughed. " things might get awkward?"

"Of course. It won't be a problem." Confirmed Seven with her usual conviction.

Together they unwound the ties that bound the Brough to the truck. "Now for the tricky bit." Declared Ray.

"No. Not at all Ray. If the three of you stand ready at the tailgate to take the motorcycle from my hands, I will pass the machine down."

The three men wanted to laugh, but there was something about the woman that held them back. Who knows? The three readied themselves at the rear. Ray Snr. balancing precariously on his wooden crutch. With a hand on either side of the ribs to the engine mounting, Seven lifted the machine to waist height and carried her to the back of the truck. She slowly crouched with unwavering control, carefully delivering the motorcycle to floor level and their supporting hands. The trio man-handled the Brough into the shed like a wounded, cherished comrade, they put the injured motorcycle up on the inspection ramp. Throughout the whole endeavour the men silently questioned what exactly they had just witnessed? Questions with no possibility of answers bounced around their minds for a number of numbing minutes, but eventually the twisted beauty of the motorcycle lying before them and the responsibilities of the dedicated mechanic broke through the confusion.

Ray's diagnosis was three days to fix the machine. Perfect. Seven had other pressing matters to attend.

52

FUNNY STUFF

The Wolseley descended from the dizzy highs of Ashwell Lane to the boggy swathes of the Somerset levels. The Glastonbury magic followed them across the miles of peat moorland, a journey that stretched from the monumental Isle of Avalon, south-west across sodden lowlands to the coast and Weston-super-Mare. The air was heavy with vapour, a deep mist that clung to the land gathering around the Wolseley in a ghostly dance. The thunder of the H6 engine shattered the peaceful tranquility of the peat-bogs as they hurtled through the trails of marsh and hedgerows and verdant fields that used to belong to the sea. The first view of Weston was quite spectacular. A series of tight and winding hairpin bends cut through a steep hillside and abruptly the whole town lies before you. A high tide of sparkling water beckoned and the pair cruised along the wide almost empty roads, blessed with views to an expansive promenade, long stretches of manicured grass, and a horizon flattened by the sea. A splendid seaside vista to raise any flagging November spirit.

"I think it might be preferable to park at a distance from the hotel? Was it Oxford Street or the High Street Betts?"

"Both Sir, well done. The Three Queens stands at the junction of the two. If I park within walking distance Sir?"

"Exactly. How do you want to play this Betts?"

"I'm so glad you asked that Sir. Dykes pointed an accusing finger at the Three Queens and a person by the name of Ashfield. From everything we know, the two are implicated in whatever this is. If we reveal our official identities too soon, Ashfield, and possibly others, will be on their guard. I suggest we work undercover Sir?"

"Good thinking Betts, what do you have in mind?"

"Give me a minute to park the Wolseley Sir and you'll have my full attention." They found a quiet spot in a road with several large horse-chestnut trees. Trails of smoke arose from chimneys of elegant late-Victorian properties, constructed with a stylish a blend of local limestone and the sandstone flourishes of Georgian grandeur. "My suggestion is for us to be secret lovers Sir. Finally together on our first romantic tryst."

"Hmm." Hadleigh nodded like an absent-minded professor. He spoke not a word, Hadleigh was consumed in thought. He finally emerged. "That sounds like another excellent idea Betts. I fully endorse the scenario and I will do my best to follow your superb lead this time around. Maybe we should start by addressing some practicalities? For example, how should I address you?"

Betts paused. "There's always 'darling' Sir? Can't really go wrong with that."

THEY TURNED into Oxford Street and with a fresh wind of salt and ozone at their backs they strode beside one another happy in their undercover characters, but a respectful six inches apart. The hotel was immediately visible along with a sign hanging above the door bearing a design of three Caribbean Queens. It was a grand inn with coach lights at the entrance and quaint feature windows with tiny panes of leaded glass. Huge chimney stacks promised warmth within, but the establishment was not due to open until the evening, another three hours hence. They both noticed the chalkboard menu, standing on the ledge inside the window. Almost unconsciously Betts took Hadleigh's arm. They stopped together to study the sign.

"I'm not sure I could face another mutton stew? What do you think darling?" Betts declared, loud and close to his ear.

Hadleigh thrilled at her touch, he struggled to steady his voice. "If you can't face mutton my darling, nor can I. You have my pledge you will never have to eat mutton again." He nobly declared with a winning smile. He wondered what Betts thought of his little improvisation? Hadleigh was rather impressed.

"That was very good John. Well done." Betts confirmed quietly. They moved on from the window display, but only after they had time to study what they could of the inside. Betts didn't let go of Hadleigh's arm as they rounded the corner into the High Street. Hadleigh felt the grip abruptly tighten. Betts didn't need to speak, Hadleigh saw it too. The premises adjacent to the Three Queens was a sweet shop. They paused with linked arms to gaze at the technicolour display of candies, confectionary, and all things sugary. The establishment was small and compact, housed in a single storey annex to the main building. The sign in the window promised, *Ashfield's - Quality Confectionary at Keen Prices*. "Do you think we could go for a cup of tea and something to eat darling? I'm rather hungry? I know a place just a kittle further along." Betts declared. She would have been happy to pay good money to play this game. It was such fun.

HADLEIGH HELD the door open to *Cowardines Coffee and Tea House*. The premises were light and warm and despite a dearth of customers, the smell of freshly roast coffee charged the air with life. Betts led Hadleigh to the balcony seating at the mezzanine level. A waitress appeared and took the order for teas, toast, and scrambled eggs.

"This is lovely Betts. I had no idea Weston-super-Mare even existed." Hadleigh declared.

"My parents brought us here a number of times for day trips. I caught a glimpse of a memory recently. I believe it might be something relevant? But it has yet to formulate into anything accessible."

The teas and food swiftly arrived and were quickly dispatched. The waitress returned. "Would you care for anything else? Sir, Madam?" The young girl flourished her notebook and pencil.

Betts looked across at Hadleigh, she would speak. "Two more teas, please. And if I can quickly ask your advice? We were thinking about staying over in Weston for a couple of nights and we wondered about the Inn? The Three Queens? What's it like?"

The waitress hesitated. "If you want a really good hotel you should go to the Royal Ma'am. It's proper good."

"What's wrong with the Inn?" Queried Betts.

Again the girl hesitated. "It's not the sort of place you'd want to stay Ma'am. There... there were these stories, rumours. It were last Christmas, and mid-summer too. Seances they said. All sorts of funny stuff going on in the cellar. Course, it's only what folk says Miss. Mind you, there's no smoke without fire."

53

BUT NOT THE CAR

Saffron squealed with delight as Ambrose hit an exhilarating 73 mph in the H6. But he was unable to maintain the fever pitch of acceleration, the exuberance of the engine revolutions began to fall in pitch and pleasure. It wasn't the car, it was the damn roads. Such a shame. Ambrose never failed to relish the rumbling roar of six cylinders, but he could now add the throaty high pitch of Saffron's screams. The swell they caused bore testament.

"Oh, I love this machine." Saffron cried aloud to the wind.

Ambrose squeezed his foot again on the accelerator pedal, he felt the need to impress. The engine responded beneath him like an eighteen-hand stallion, just in time he caught sight of a herd of sheep ahead. "Damn and blast these byways." Ambrose declared in flustered irritation as he pulled the hand brake fiercely, his facial muscles taught with effort, the H6 shuddered to a grinding halt. They had no choice but wait for the farmhands to herd the baying animals from one field to the next. Ambrose and the H6 rumbled impatiently together.

Saffron studied the map spread out across her lap. "That's

the Yeo Valley down there. Rather beautiful don't you think Ambrose?"

"Green fields and sheep don't do much for me Saffron." Ambrose stared fixedly ahead. Annoying stupid sheep forever in his path.

"Don't be like that Ambrose. We should be there soon, just another twenty miles or so and the sea will stretch before us."

The last of the flock cleared the road and a young farmer raised his hand in thanks. Saffron waved back as the Hispano Suiza swiftly accelerated back on track. Ambrose realised he had been a little testy. "How did you get involved with Gerald?" He inquired in a casual tone.

"Through my brother Jolyon. He has been working for the Service for literally years and when they needed an interpreter, and preferably female — for reasons yet to explain Ambrose — my loyal brother put me forward." Saffron paused and shifted her position in the luxuriant leather to face more direct toward her audience — less competition from the wind rushing past the car. "I've been wanting to speak of my part in the Great War ever since really, but I had to sign one of those stupid documents, you know what I mean Ambrose, the official ones. So like the good girl I indubitably aspire to be, I said nothing." Saffron raised her finely shaped eyebrows. "You must have signed the Official Secrets Act too Ambrose?" Saffron waited for a response. Ambrose eventually made a nod. "Perfect. To my way of thinking that puts us at level pegging, the same position as it were? And accordingly, as colleagues, we can move beyond officialdom and the aforementioned paper restrictions? I believe it important, for maximum efficiency as an active unit you understand, that I familiarise you with my service background? Are you in agreement Ambrose? You have to speak this time."

Ambrose was ever more impressed by Saffron. A beautiful island paradise amidst a sea of military mediocrity. What was that saying by the German General? An observation about the British Army: '*Lions led by donkeys*'. Through and through this girl was a stunning product of the thoroughly decadent and deeply annoying British aristocracy, but the Saffron was viscerally leonine.

"Never in my life have I said these words before, partly because the need was never there, but mostly because they would have meant nothing. You can trust me Saffron. I give you my word."

Saffron sat back in her seat quietly absorbing what Ambrose had said. She felt as if a heavy, cumbersome garment had lifted from her shoulders. But she wasn't quite sure exactly what it was? Saffron noticed the engine revs had dropped, they travelled at an easy thirty-five mph. "Thank you, Ambrose," Saffron said simply and sat upright. "My father is a Viscount, and my mother a French Countess. There were five of us originally, five children, but we lost a brother and a sister to the Great War. We knew there were tensions between our parents when Mother began only to speak in French; not just to us, but the entire household. To further complicate our national identities, my siblings and I were tutored by an Austrian governess, Frau Lorelei, and she would communicate almost exclusively in German. The result was a natural fluency in three languages. The difficulties between our parents brought us, the five siblings close together, we were tight. Jolyon, my eldest brother, was already pretty well set up in the Intelligence Service when the war began. With his language skills he was indispensable in helping unravel what the enemy might be up to. Jolyon's a very special person. People instinctively trust him, they tell him things; he was privy to everything going on in the background. I don't know if you are aware of just how precarious the war looked at the end of the summer of 1916? The German naval blockade was crippling us. The success of their submarines meant supplies simply weren't getting through, raw materials for ammunition as well as food."

"I heard there were significant French army desertions as well?"

"Exactly. Britain and the allies were in a pretty desperate position. But for one small ray of hope in which I was happy to play my part. We captured a group of high-ranking German officers. And because of Jolyon and my language abilities, I was made part of a unit charged with finding out everything we could. From field strategies to soldier morale. The operation was a great success. We uncovered lots of secrets. Did you know the Germans offered peace Ambrose?"

"What sort of peace?" Ambrose was surprised.

"A negotiated peace on a *status quo ante* basis. In other words, a return to previous borders."

"Let me think about that for a moment Saffron, I have to watch the road, the drop is rather steep." They left the sloping splendour of the Yeo Valley with its spectacular views over the still body of water lying in the sunken belly of the Mendip Hills, and the H6 began a swift descent traversing narrow, winding, precarious inclines. They passed ancient stone villages and grand country mansions, until a water mill, stark in the November still, marked their return to the flat Somerset plain. "Sorry Saffron. What you just said... it was truly shocking. Overwhelming. I needed a minute to take it in. Please carry on, tell me more about the unit."

"The captured German officers gave their word as gentlemen they would not attempt escape in return for an appropriate level of accommodation. Accordingly the Chateau de Chambord de L'Eglise was requisitioned. It was fortified with a wire perimeter and patrolled by a military presence in and out of the mansion. Jolyon was commander in charge, but he presented me with the brief to run a side-op. We nick-named it *Operation Chambermaid*.

I had a group of nine girls, French recruits working directly for me. They came mostly from Alsace, an area that flips between French and German statehood so the population is naturally bilingual. My girls acted as maids at the chateau and in the process of attending to the needs of the enemy officers, they gathered every scrap of information they could about the German war machine. Including at Jolyon's request, assessing the enemy's confidence of military success?"

"Good Lord Saffron, what a fantastic opportunity? Tell me more. What great secrets did you uncover?"

Saffron laughed. "If I told you a meagre tenth of what I know, it would be far too much. But I will say, mission accomplished. A great success."

"How much of a success?" Asked Ambrose, eyes fixed to the road.

"Well Ambrose, if I were to provide you with a couple of threads, maybe you can weave them together?"

"Thank you, Saffron."

"More than half of the officers fell in love with their prospective maids and man-servants, they were only to happy to spill their most inner thoughts and fears." Saffron declared with a twinkle.

Ambrose laughed. "There must be more you can tell Saffron, please go on."

"We quickly realised the way through to our captured generals was to accommodate all tastes and needs, to relax and cater for them into carelessness. And lo and behold, the enemy's willingness to unload literally everything became a divine comedy of pretty maids and horny German generals. It all went along like quality Swiss clockwork until one of my most trusted comrades fell in love and betrayed us." Saffron paused, her eyes distant in thought. "And another small tragedy, I began to see our cause, most particularly our leaders in a different light. The

Germans revealed far too much about our masters Ambrose. They were genuinely shocked at the ineptitude of the British command. The disregard for human life. All those men sacrificed to the Gods of War; not to mention my personal loss of a brother and sister. The lives of their people held no sanctity, no consequence. We were expendable, no more than animals to the slaughter. Such was the prevailing attitude. Those people, the top brass, the leaders who stumbled through the War without a clue where they were going. They really are beyond contempt, and they're still there. In power and in the war office."

It was all Ambrose could do to keep driving. He wanted to stop and smash something, but not the car.

54

I HOPE YOU WILL BE COMFORTABLE?

"How can I help you Sir, Madame?"

"I'm sorry to trouble you, the name's Thompson. My wife and I were wondering if this shop might have any connection with the hotel next door? We want to book accommodation for the night, but the doors to the Three Queens are firmly locked? I wonder if you can help?"

The young man behind the counter of *Ashfield's - Quality Confectionary* nodded with understanding. "Yes Sir, that's my Ma and Pa what runs the Queens, give me a couple 'a minutes and I'll pop around and ask Ma to open up."

"That's very kind, thank you." Hadleigh declared along with a brief nod of appreciation.

The detective pair walked on to the High Street entrance and were greeted by a substantial woman with folded arms. This must be 'Ma' mused Betts.

"Evenin'." Ma greeted. "You're after rooms I understand? What will it be? A double or two singles?" The imperious land-lady's eyes narrowed into the slits of the inquisitor.

"A double." Hadleigh and Betts replied at the same moment. They were playing the game in perfect sync.

Ma made a wry smile at their shy enthusiasm, confirmation of her shrewd suspicion. She understood lust, especially the forbidden kind. Louche thoughts made her tingle. "Yes, that's fine then, we can do that for you my dears. Ten bob a night for the room, a shilling each for a cooked breakfast, and filling the bath will cost you another sixpence a tub. How does that suit?"

"That sounds perfect, may I ask your name? Enquired Hadleigh.

"Ashfield's the name, Mrs." She added.

"Thank you, Mrs. Ashfield. We might be here for a number of days, if I leave you with a deposit of five pounds for now, perhaps we can go on up to the room? We've had a rather tiring day?"

"Yes, that's perfectly acceptable. If you would care to sign the register my dears? Have to be official-like. Do you have any bags?"

"In the car, we'll fetch them over shortly." Responded Hadleigh.

"Of course. Well, Mr. and Mrs. Thompson," Mrs. Ashfield announced, scanning the names, "if you'd like to follow me, you're in room number one. A superior quality master bedroom facing south onto Oxford Street. I'm confident you will be most comfortable."

55

A LOST SOUL

I t was a little after 7 pm when the Hispano Suiza rumbled to a stop in the courtyard at the back of the Three Queens Hotel. Saffron and Ambrose clambered from the vehicle, shaking loose the crumples of the journey, studying one another in a final inspection. All good. They entered the hotel at the High Street entrance, Ambrose led the way to the bar. "What would you like Miss?" Ambrose enquired. He had decided on the role of chauffeur for the moment.

"A champagne cocktail please? Or just the brandy if there's no fizz?" Saffron smiled gaily. She was aware of being studied by several pairs of eyes. The dizzy rich girl always worked, the alternative persona acted as an effective shield.

Ambrose returned from the bar and presented Saffron with a double brandy, there was no wine of any description. "Let's take a table by the fire," Saffron suggested. They made themselves comfortable and casually observed the bar area. There were seventeen customers and a buxom landlady milling around between tables like an annoying fly. There was also a young man who would appear and disappear behind the serving area, probably another member of the hotel staff. The customers congregated around tables. Most played card games and the rest chequers. There was little talking, but the air was thick with cigarette vapours on a tail-wind of sweat and stale beer. The landlady approached their table.

"I don't know if you might be hungry? But we have some mutton stew and swede from lunch if that's of interest?"

The pair realised in the same moment how hungry they were. "Yes please, I haven't eaten mutton for yonks." declared Saffron with a laugh.

Ambrose smiled. "And for me as well. How are you fixed for rooms tonight?" He inquired of the landlady.

"Would that be a double or two singles?" Mrs. Ashfield replied, eyebrows raised in question though her mind had already predicted a double.

"Two singles would be the preference?" Replied Ambrose.

"Oh. Right. I'm happy to say I can help. Another double would have been a stretch. There's a thing, November and almost fully booked. Seven and six a night per room. Full breakfast is a shilling a-piece and the bathroom's shared. Sixpence for a tub-full of hot water?"

"The card games? Can anyone play?" Asked Saffron.

"As long as you can take losin' a bob or two in good spirits? Don't see why not? I'll mention it to Mr. Ashfield. 'Ee always ends up on a table by night's end."

THE MUTTON STEW was as wholesome and uninteresting as most other mutton stews since the war. Food was often a case of making do. Saffron burped a few times, but her stomach soon settled with another brandy. She was ready for a game of cards.

"Good evening. We were wondering if we might join you?" Declared a smiling Saffron.

The landlord was a big man, his presence dominated the table. Cards and coins were assembled before the players in tiny towers. Mr. Ashfield didn't feel the need to stand. "Yeah, course." His voice was gruff as an old dog. "The wife said you might be joining us." He paused to leer at Saffron. The man's stare sent a chill through her, she was glad Ambrose was near. "Take a seat why don't you, facing or next to one another, choice is yours? The game is *Vingt-et-un*? Do you play much?" Ashfield demanded, his eyes still fixed on Saffron, like a predator sizing the prey. Ambrose took the seat across from her. He didn't remove his eyes from Ashfield.

"Occasionally I like a little flutter, mostly roulette. And the horses of course, the *geegees*. Just a little fun." Saffron giggled, she enjoyed the role play, *dizzy* was an identity they would easily accept.

The landlord switched his attention to Ambrose. "And what about you Sir may I ask?"

"You may, but all you need do is take a look at my automobile. She's parked in your courtyard. They say you can tell a lot about a man by the vehicle he drives. I drive a Hispano Suiza H6. Every automobile the company makes is unique, a custom design. What is your vehicle of choice landlord?"

Ashfield flushed like a sunset. "A Commer lorry, but that's business, for the Hotel-like. Don't make it no reflection at all."

"If you say so," Ambrose commented dismissively. He was struggling to accept the blatant lechery seeping from the landlord, the lascivious glint in his eyes as he leered at Saffron, like red meat to a hungry dog. Ambrose recognised the aggressively feral mindset. Ashfield's type had prospered well through the chaos of war. They always did. *Carpe diem*. The hustlers and schemers, they knew how to seize the moment. Ambrose wanted to stamp him out.

There were six players seated at the table and over the first six games, Saffron and Ambrose consistently lost. But with game number seven, Saffron decided it was time to try a little harder. Saffron deposited two shillings into the pot. "I would like to buy one." She announced stacking the coins carefully. The motif continued until Saffron held five cards in her hand. The dealer 'bust' in the attempt to match her five-card-trick. Saffron squealed with delight, a high-pitched cry of joy. That was when she noticed the well-dressed young lady studying her from the bar. She looked like a lost soul. "Would you care to come and join us?" Saffron called out to Seven, with a welcoming smile.

56

REGULARS

Seven had become remarkably attached to her new suit, the leather one. Over the days and many miles, through the stretches and strains of continual movement, the push and pull of life itself had moulded the tight leather to her form. It fit like the proverbial glove, but she needed a change of outfit, an alternative persona. The option, however, to legitimately purchase something from a retail establishment had passed two hours and forty-three minutes previous. But the late hour had its own advantages. Seven studied the window displays of several premises promoting *Ladies' Clothing*. The notions of style and fashion were beginning to permeate her appreciation of '*fitting in*'. Perkins popped into her thoughts. She had no choice? Or did she? The Seven she inhabited then was gone. That version of her certainly had no choice, the programming was in control. Seven had only done what she perceived to be the right thing. But that was no longer the case, she alone was now in command. Seven recalled Ray and his words that evening: '*You 'ave to 'ave a code to live by.*' How ironic. Her previous mindset, Seven as she had been, was literally written in code, computer code. That was a small part of what it meant to be enhanced. To accept your rightful place in the new paradigm — a pre-scripted schematic of the abilities, skills, wants, and desires you will long for, need — the ultimate definition of who you are and what you do. It was all there, fully programmed and mapped out. Beautiful in its logical simplicity. No questions required, no complex decisions to make. But none of those many laborious hours invested in creating her code, had catered for choice in ladies' fashion garments. The costume designs displayed on the mannequins in the *Trevors Department Store* window display followed a collective theme: '*Paris Reveals her Intentions*' — apparently inspired by an article in Vogue, November 1919. Seven found the garments totally compelling. The ground floor of *Trevors Department Store* was cavernous and open plan, but her destination was singular, Paris. But not the city — Seven was searching for the compelling collection of clothes; Seven had discovered *la mode* — fashion — and at the seaside in Weston-super-Mare.

Seven left the premises in the same way she entered, through the front doors, but the person was quite transformed. Gone were all traces of leather. This was a lady proud in heels that extended her height to 6'3", and dressed in the latest Paris styles. With the cherished leather suit safely stowed in a misappropriated carpet bag, Seven strode down the High Street to the Three Queens Hotel. She paused at the entrance to study the rather elegant Town Hall clock tower. The bells struck 9 pm. She was ready.

Seven caused quite a stir as she stepped into the hotel. She saw it in their faces and heard the same message in their minds. Everyone sang a sweet song of approbation. They liked the way Seven looked a great deal, a lady, and a toff. Seven was thrilled, the new outfit was working wonders, exactly as she hoped. Her outfit comprised a walking length skirt in satin, a simple white silk blouse, and a fitted three-quarter length coat with ruched back, finished with fur collar and cuffs. Her black haired bob was topped with a cloche hat. The landlady sprang into action. "Can I fetch you anything my dear? Something to eat? Or a drink?"

"No, thank you. I have no requirements other than the key."

"Yes, of course. Here we are, number seven."

Seven frowned. She quickly dismissed the notion there could be any connection. "Oh, yes, there is one thing. I need my leather costume cleaned and some repairs will be required. If could you make the necessary arrangements I am happy to pay for superior quality work."

"Of course my dear. Leave the items with me and I will make sure the job is done promptly and to exacting standards." The landlady's emollient charm spilled forth. Seven passed Mrs. Ashfield the carpetbag of clothes. She turned to make her way upstairs when her attention was captured by high-pitched squeals of laughter. A truly joyful sound. The squeals belonged to a young lady and she was playing cards at a table surrounded by five men. Seven found herself staring at the girl, she was captivated. There was something about the female that compelled her, it was instinctive. Seven followed the scent and made her way to the alcove at the back of the lounge. The young lady momentarily looked up to smile at Seven before returning her gaze to the cards in her hand.

"I would like to buy one." The girl announced. "And another. And another." The young lady paused to light her face with a broad grin of sweet contentment, projected at the dealer. "I'll stick thank you." She announced. The young lady held five cards in her hand. The dealer turned over the two cards before him, a king and an eight. He dealt a fresh card, a five. Bust. Saffron squealed with renewed delight, encircling the winnings with her arm. "Would you care to join us?" Saffron called out over the table to Seven. The young lady raised an inquisitive finely manicured eyebrow.

Seven returned the smile and made her way to the table, she took the vacant seat next to Saffron. "I would prefer to watch a game before I participate. If that would be possible? What are you playing?"

"It's called *vingt-et-un*, or *21*, or apparently *Pontoon*. It's easy, you'll pick it up in no time. I'm Saffron," the girl declared. "This is Ambrose, that is Mr. Ashfield, he's the landlord. I'm sorry, I haven't been introduced to the others."

The three men made curt nods from the other side of the table.

"Regulars." Grunted Mr. Ashfield and fixed his gaze on the new recruit to the table. Another lamb to the slaughter. Ashfield was in the process of *sizing her up* when he realised the female was watching him. His facial muscles prepared for the leer, Ashfield could easily picture what she had tucked away under the fancy frock, but something in the pit of his stomach held him back. He knew when to pay heed to that voice. Ashfield looked away from the woman's gaze. There would always be later.

57

I'LL FOLLOW YOU SHORTLY

"Why don't you take the bath first? And I will go back for the car and the bag of clothes?"

"I had no idea there was a bag of clothes?"

"I prepared one for us Sir. Just in case." Betts was aware of the 'Sir', she uttered. She wondered if he'd say anything? Or did their gay charade end at the bedroom door?

"You really are a wonder Betts." Hadleigh declared. They both sighed, but for different reasons. "Sounds like a good plan. Thank you Betts. I'll be quickly in and out of the bath."

"There's no need to rush Sir, enjoy some hot soapy suds. I'll take the opportunity to have a bit of a look around the town. I intend to be at least an hour."

BETTS WANTED to give him any amount of time he might need, she wasn't going to crowd him, they had the whole night together after all. A thrill almost beyond description trilled through her. Time for some distraction, possibly a little window shopping? Winter was in the air and a change of season was always a good excuse for something fresh. Finally, there were new fashions to choose from in what had seemed such a long, long time. The High Street was extensive and narrow. A profusion of window displays sparred in open competition for your attention from opposing sides of the road, but it was *Trevors Department Store* that arrested her steps. A Vogue-inspired Winter outfit filled the space beyond the glass. Betts struggled to remove her eyes from the ruched back of the coat. It was stunning. And the cloche hat was just... Betts found another sigh and promised herself a return visit in the morning. That is, the morning after the night about to happen. She turned on her heel and began a vigorous walk back to the Wolseley, it didn't take long. Betts fired up the engine and let it idle with gentle revolutions warming the essential lubricant, oil. Always a good idea on a cold night. Her thoughts wandered to the three months mechanic's training, taking engines and gearboxes apart. She smiled to herself and switched her mind to the ruched back of the coat, the cloche hat. Now she grinned like a naughty child and the smile lasted most of the return journey. The future tingled with possibility, but as she turned into the courtyard at the rear of the hotel Betts had an abrupt change of mind. She hit the brakes hard making the tyres squeal a protest and hastily pulled the Wolseley back onto the High Street. She checked the rearview mirror to see if anyone was following? No one in view. The reason for the sudden, steering-wheel-wrenching manoeuvre was the H6. The Hispano Suiza was parked, bold as a sergeant major at the back of the hotel. Betts left the Wolseley in a side road off the High Street and with the overnight bag on her shoulder, briskly made her way to the Three Queens. It was a little after 9 pm. She peered discreetly through the quaint window panes, but the distorted images revealed nothing more than blurred, bobbing heads. She pulled her hat down obscuring her profile and marched into the pub, beyond the bar, and straight up the stairs. She paused at the landing, listening for the sound of footsteps. But there was only the distant, muffled clatter of the bar. No one was following. She carefully opened the door to room number 1. A solitary standard lamp lit the chamber. Hadleigh was sleeping, he had taken the left side of the bed. Betts took off her coat and shoes and placed the overnight bag on a chair. She carefully opened the zipper, trying not to make any sound, and removed a royal blue candlewick dressing gown and a pair of satin embroidered mule slippers. A section of their room, bedroom number 1, had been partitioned off with a floral curtain on runners. Behind it Betts discovered the bathroom area. The dominion of a large, copper, slipper bath, connected to a metered Valor water heater. She removed her outer garments, replacing them with the dressing gown, and wrapped a towel around her head as if to cover wet hair. Betts had a plan. She studied herself in the mirror above the washbasin. Makeup. Lipstick and eyeliner were essential components to the Betts day. She lathered her face with the carbolic soap thoughtfully provided and soon all trace of her independent, 20th century, cosmopolitan alter-ego had been removed. Betts considered her reflection. She recognised an old friend. Locking the door behind her, Betts quietly left room number 1 and made her way downstairs to the small hallway on the ground floor. There were four doors, two with port-holes. One door led to the bar, another the kitchen. Door number three was probably the Ashfield's private accommodation and door number four went down to the cellar. Betts cautiously peered into the bar through the port-hole. She saw no one she recognised, but the view was limited. Betts opened the door to the kitchen and quickly stepped inside. The electric lights were already switched on, but she was alone. Betts listened to the silence for a moment before quickly crossing the room to the other portal, an access route to the bar. She peered through the glass. A large table of seven was playing cards. She recognised the young man immediately, they had encountered one another face to face in the New Inn. He was still young, mid-twenties, and very good-looking in a boyish way. He certainly had the swagger to be linked to the H6 in the courtyard. No sign of the other man? There were two striking women and one was wearing the ruched coat! The cloche hat as well! Betts' head spun with the coincidence. The only other occupant of the table she could distinguish was a swarthy, dark-haired man with piercing blue eyes. The final three players wore overcoats and hats and had their backs to her. But she'd seen enough.

"Can I help you?" The question caught Betts unawares. She spun around, she had no idea the landlady had entered the room.

"Yes Mrs. Ashfield, thank you. I was hoping to find a glass of milk?" Betts replied.

Mrs. Ashfield looked her up and down. "Would you like it hot?" The landlady enquired.

"That would be most kind." Betts found a smile, despite the tangible air of hostility filling the room.

"All right. I'll bring it up to you Mrs. Thompson. What about Mr. Thompson, will he be wanting anything?" There was a distinct edge to Mrs. Ashfield's tone.

"No thank you. He's sound asleep."

"You go on up then. I'll follow you shortly."

58

THIRTEEN POUNDS AND TEN SHILLINGS

"Whats your name?" Enquired Saffron. Seven could almost hear music in the girl's voice, there was something in the husky tone.

"My friends call me Sami." Seven replied. "Sami Davis." The name simply popped into her head along with the appendage *junior*, which Seven chose to ignore.

"Watch me play a hand or two Sami. I promise you won't find it difficult," Saffron suggested with a smile of sisterly encouragement. "I'll show you my cards and we can play together. My name is Saffron." Seven sensed the girl's energy field, she sparkled with life.

"Thank you Saffron, I have never played cards before tonight, but I am looking forward to our game immensely." And for Seven this was especially true. While scrutinising the activity of the card game, *21*, Seven had made an astute observation. Her ability to read minds rendered the whole process pointless. Seven would always win and accordingly, there was no *game*. But as Sami she could choose by default not to listen in to someone else's mind. She wouldn't monitor the thoughts of the other players, even the collective mind, she would play solely on her innate sense of maths, the quantum kind.

Last orders came and went and the hotel moved to lock-in mode. Windows and doors were firmly shuttered and bolted against the scrutiny of an inquisitive local constabulary.

SEVEN WAS TOTALLY ENGAGED. She had no interest in winning, but the odds she found fascinating. The cascading figures, filtering through her synapses were a joy to behold. Simultaneously she saw another flaw in the game — it would require only minimal effort to memorise the pack. For both Seven and her alter ego Sami, this was as familiar as a child reciting the alphabet. But the guarantee of a winning process could never be totally secure. In *21* there would always be significant margins for error. Not all the cards dealt in *21* were revealed. Some were returned to the pack unseen — an unknown quantity. This was of course, what made the game all the more interesting to Seven. The unknown, the unpredictable, was the basis of Quantum Mechanics, the chaos factor. For just a single fraction of one of those quantum seconds Seven questioned her moral right to proceed? There was no doubt Seven held a significant advantage. But why not? This was her brain. Calculations to Seven were as innate as breathing. Her mind was diamond-sharp in the multi-dimensional spin of quantum computation. And the challenge was exhilarating.

AMBROSE KNEW it was her as soon as she stepped into the bar. Despite the accoutrements of a fine lady he identified the light bounce of an athlete. The height too. He'd only ever seen women that tall in Europe. The night Roberts was killed, the assassin had leapt a good twelve foot to reach the window. And then had to find the strength to hold themselves steady while they opened the latch to escape. Certainly possible, but he knew at 5'8" he wouldn't have a hope. But this woman could have made it. What was she here for? To kill Ashfield obviously. The piece of human scum sitting across the table from him. He might help her at that. And what was this business with the hotel all about? Probably not illegal gambling after hours? And that begged the question, what had any of this to do with Gerald and the Service? Ambrose realised he didn't trust his masters. He was relieved Ashfield didn't know who they were.

SAFFRON HAD at first thought to take the naive Sami under her wing, she sensed the uncomplicated innocence in this intriguingly beautiful woman. As much as Saffron also understood the danger sitting across the table. Ashfield was a risk to any woman, but especially young and pretty ones. Somehow she felt safer with another female beside her, they could look out for one another. Although Saffron was currently in the role of mentor to her newly found acquaintance, Saffron could also sense the drive, the purpose, that certain *'je ne sais quoi'* in her card-table friend. It was 10 pm when Ashfield proposed a break. The men took the occasion to replenish drinks at the bar.

"Would you tell me something about you Sami?" Saffron requested of Seven. "You have an air of deep mystery about you? Like one of those Egyptian Mummies." Saffron's laugh was not dis-similar to her other vocalism, the squeals of delight. Every eye around the bar looked over.

"Let me take your hand Saffron and I will explain something of who I am." Seven suggested.

The visit to Madame Tamara continued to resonate through her. *Do you know who you are?* Had proved an incredibly astute question. Seven would be forever changed by their meeting. A new identity had emerged, a persona that reflected the interests of the epoch in which Seven found herself, but equally, a role perfectly suited to her innate and remarkable gifts. A persona that could open doors.

"I am a kind of medium Saffron, I have the ability to see the future." Seven smiled, one of the spontaneous, satisfying variety. Of course she could see the future. Saffron's future — and everyone else's — was written in her past. Seven gazed resolutely at Saffron uncovering the secrets behind the eyes. There was no problem delving into the girl's mind, it was open and fragrant as if the pages of memory were made from rose petals. That was the other development. Mr. John's song. Frank singing. Unseen veils had lifted from Seven's vision, her inner vision, and abruptly it had come into focus. There was something about this girl Saffron... "I see a mountain, covered with snow. And a lake with an old wooden bridge. A blizzard so strong and sudden you thought would die." Seven raised a pencilled eyebrow.

Saffron shivered with the chill coursing through her, she would never forget that day. It was Christmas and they were on the Lake. Lake Lucerne was a frozen sea of ice. The medieval wooden bridge suspended above the frigid water had become a mysterious tunnel of snow. Saffron, together with a group of friends, had gone skating when a blizzard swept in from nowhere, almost taking her life and that of her classmates.

Saffron frowned, struggling to find words. "How?" She managed. But then a voice spoke to her thoughts. She watched Sami's lips moving to the sound of the words, but there was no sound. Only the voice contained in her mind.

"*Je vois ce que les autres ne peuvent pas voir. J'entends ce qu'ils ne peuvent pas entendre. Je t'entends parler dans plusieurs langues. Tu es douée Saffron, et nous allons gagner tout l'argent ce soir.*"

Saffron stared at Seven. "*C'est vrai?*" She questioned aloud.

"*Et comment!*" Seven smiled. "*Je souhaiterais que nous soyons amis?*" Declared Seven, continuing the out loud conversation.

Saffron paused for a number of seconds before she spoke again. "*J'aimerais beaucoup aussi. Es-tu déjà allée à Paris?*"

Seven shook her head. "*Pas encore.*"

"*On pourrait aller en France? Toutes les ensembles?*" Suggested Saffron.

"*Oui bien sur. Aussitôt que possible. Mais ce soir nous allons gagner. Saffron, garde toi.*" Seven said softly, with an almost imperceptible nod.

Ambrose watched and listened to the pair in silent irritation. He picked up the occasional word that triggered a modicum of meaning, but generally their conversation was completely, literally bloody foreign to him. He didn't like being excluded from private discussions. Nor did the recently returned men at the table.

"We won't 'av none of that 'ere. Not at this game." Declared one of the 'regulars' aggressively.

"No foreign languages over the cards ladies. It could be construed as connivance." Stated Ashfield. The leer had been replaced by something resembling a smile, but there was no warmth or humour attached. It was a simple threat.

"I'm so sorry." Saffron declared in her most obliging tones. "We will only converse in the mother-tongue from here on." Her smile held an uncharacteristic restraint. Saffron didn't want to overplay the part, for a brief moment she was all too aware of their vulnerability, the dark presence lurking across the table was all too real. But the foreboding soon slipped away. Saffron suppressed the comforting grin that accompanied the notion of what was to come, the pleasure of taking every penny from this odious man.

The players were re-convened at the table with replenished glasses. Mostly cider, but a pair of double brandies for Ambrose and Saffron.

"How would our guests feel about a few hands of Stud? Stud Poker. We play the standard, one card down." Ashfield followed his question with an unsubtle leer at Saffron.

"Sounds lovely." Declared Saffron.

"Will you be joining us?" Ashfield addressed Seven directly.

"Thank you, yes. I am confident to play now." Seven confirmed.

"Well, I'm glad to 'ear it. What d'ya think brothers? Are you chaps feeling confident to play tonight." A comment that led Ashfield and the three 'regulars' into a raucous bout of hearty laughter, their peels of ribald jollity bouncing across the walls of the Inn. The men were fuelled with the fire of alcohol. Despite the doors officially closing over an hour previous, there were two further groups of customers still with drinks on the table before them. They said no words nor made conversation. They simply sat, imbibing the occasion sup, as if waiting for an appointed hour or anointed leader.

The beauty of Stud Poker is the simplicity and transparency of the play. The order of the two descriptors could, and possibly should be reversed. Especially when considering the game's history. Stud Poker was the card game of choice during the American Civil War. As an activity where gambling was the objective, and especially in times of violent conflict, there would always be a degree of inevitability to the presence of firearms at the table. Virtually every player carried weapons of some description, accordingly, transparency became an important principle, in addition to the aforementioned simplicity. The two criteria were key factors in the game's success, along with large prizes and open pots. Stud Poker, in the original, primal form, was the game being played that night in the Three Queens Hotel — *one card down*. The implication of the name being the remaining four cards are dealt face up — hence the transparency. Every player can see each individual hand, with the exception of the one *hole* card. With this high level of openness, there was the least chance of cheating.

The starting dealer, Ashfield, dealt one card to each player, beginning at his left to one of the *regulars*. He carried on around the table until everyone had a single card before them, face down. He dealt his own card last.

"The game is Five Card Stud Poker, no wild cards, and the ante is sixpence." Ashfield announced and the man to his left immediately put a coin into the pot. The table followed suit. The cards never leave the table, another golden rule of transparency, instead each player cautiously peeled back a corner to witness their allocation.

The player to Ashfield's left placed another sixpence in the pot. The first bet. Again the table followed suit. The pot was already running high at seven shillings.

Starting again at his left, Ashfield dealt each of the six players a new card, but face up. On this occasion, the highest value card denotes where the bidding will start. Saffron held an Ace of hearts, Ace high.

"A shilling." Saffron declared, dropping the coin with a clink into the pot. The table followed suit with a succession of clattering coins and voices muttering "*call*". The pot had doubled in value to fourteen shillings.

Ashfield dealt a third card to each of the table of seven. Again it was delivered face up. Two pairs were now in evidence; one with Ashfield, a pair of 8s, and one of the 'regulars' held a pair of jacks. "A shillin'." He announced, and three of the table folded. The remaining four players were in.

The fourth card, also instantly revealed, delivered no new winning combinations. Saffron received another heart, this time a queen, and a king went to the same 'regular'. He had started the previous betting round. "A shillin'." He repeated. And the table followed suit. The pot now stood at twenty-one shillings.

Ashfield dealt the final card, the fourth to be delivered face up. The result was a scattering of three visible pairs across the table. Saffron had picked up another queen; pair number one. Ashfield and the Regular also held pairs, they received nothing new. Everything hinged on the face-down cards. There were only three players left in the game.

"Why don't we make it two shillings?" Suggested Saffron.

Ashfield replayed the leer. "Yeah, why don't we?" And threw in his coins. The 'regular' with the pair of jacks called. Ashfield took a deep draw on his cigarette and blew a plume of smoke into the air. He squinted at the girl through the fog of nicotine. She was definitely his type. Blond. He had a thing for the fair-haired ones that's for sure. And the voice, posh and high-pitched, God-man, the way she squeals. He felt his cock twitch with anticipation beneath the heavy wool of his trousers. He was ready now. He'd be more than ready later, but first, he would take her money. Two queens. She might have another, but more likely, she was just bloody stupid. Thinking they were bluffing? He wanted to laugh but that might give him and his two pairs away. He called her two shillings and raised another two.

"I'll see your four shillings and raise you another."

"And I'll add another two to your five." Declared Saffron smiling breezily, without a care in the world.

The process continued until the pot stood at a dizzy sixty shillings. Five pounds. A pound more than a man's weekly wage. Saffron decided it was time. "Call," she announced and raised her eyebrows to Ashfield. Without a moment's hesitation, he flipped his card over.

"Two pairs, 8s, and 10s." He declared with a confident leer.

The 'regular' to Ashfield's left said nothing but overturned another potentially winning combination; three jacks. Ashfield shook his head in disbelief. The 'regular' turned to Saffron.

"I always feel at home with queens." She declared and turned over the queen of spades; three queens. Saffron squealed with delight. "You really shouldn't underestimate the fairer sex, Mr Ashfield. Things are changing you know." And Saffron scooped the sixty-shilling pile of coins toward her.

The die was certainly cast in her favour. Saffron took each of the first three games. Her senses were on fire. She could feel the bluff, deduce the logic, and she was blessed with a run of wonderful, intuitive luck. But as the fourth game began to gather steam, Saffron realised something was different, and not in a positive way. She gazed at the table through an ever increasing mist. Distorted sounds rushed past her ears. Saffron instinctively reached out her hand to touch Seven's thigh.

It was inevitable that Ashfield would take steps to assist his cause. He saw no boundaries to achieving the only goal, winning. The double brandies, so enthusiastically consumed by Ambrose and Saffron, contained liberal quantities of laudanum. As the game progressed, so too the effects of the narcotic began to take hold. But what Ashfield could never know, Saffron had a secret ally.

Seven felt the touch to her legs, but she was already aware there was a problem. She could sense Saffron's mind drifting from consciousness. Seven spoke direct to Saffron's thoughts. "Saffron, please do not be alarmed, but I believe there is something wrong. I sense you are not well. I can help, but we need to establish physical contact."

"Sami darling, would you mind most awfully holding my hand for a moment. I'm feeling a little squiffy." Saffron declared, immediately proffering her left hand. It dangled in the air waiting to be held. Ashfield and his band of 'regulars' joined together in a communal frown as Seven took Sami's hand in hers, but they said nothing.

Seven's diagnosis quickly revealed the culprit, *Papaver Somniferum*. Seven communicated the implications, but without sound. "Saffron, the problem is something I can control. The brandy you consumed contained high levels of opioids. You will feel increasingly tired and out of touch. You may even experience mild hallucinations. I can help counteract the symptoms, but I cannot fully eradicate the chemical properties in these circumstances. However, you will soon start to feel the benefits of a tropane alkaloid, from the leaves of the plant Erythroxylum Novogranatense. The compound is now in your bloodstream. It will help to nullify the opioids and soon you will recover your *joie de vivre*. Have no fear Saffron, I am here for you. You will be fine. And you have games to win."

The stud poker continued. A simple game that began life in the snatched moments of respite within a terrible war of attrition, the American Civil War. Saffron too endured, and she continued to win. Seven made sure. Seven didn't need to look into their minds, it was enough to keep Saffron fully conscious, the girl was on a winning streak, and she deserved a little retribution after Ashfield's shameful attempt to disable the opposition. When the table reached game number seven every financial reserve had been drained for an ultimate concerted assault. The desperate holy grail of the final pot. It weighed in at thirteen pounds and ten shillings. A handsome amount helping fuel the increasingly intense, war of nerves. It was a similar scenario to before, only three players were left standing: a 'regular', Ashfield, and Saffron. The betting had taken on an air of desperation. The pressured atmosphere stemmed from many things, but ultimately the root was — so-called — male pride. None of the men liked being beaten by a woman. That's what they believed anyway. A deeper truth, they just didn't like being beaten. And blaming it on a woman, an outsider, was satisfying to their meagre minds, as well as convenient.

This final game had been a constant challenge. Ashfield and the 'regular' each had high pairs on the table, jacks, and aces. There were no other aces or jacks on display, so it was quite possible they had a third as their hole card. Throughout the game, they controlled the betting and they were confident. They believed in their own hubris, they bet high. Saffron started with a pair of 7s. She picked up a third with her penultimate hand and a fourth in the final. With the last hand, she knew she would win. Even as the pair opposite her, wrapped themselves in their conceit of omnipotence. The men went *all-in*. Saffron played their game. She appeared nervous, indecisive as the betting increased until they were able to bet no more. The pot had taken their every penny.

"Three jacks". Declared the 'regular'.

"Three aces." Exulted Ashfield.

"I have but three 7s on the table." Stated Saffron, "and a fourth here." She overturned her card with a flourish. There was total silence, only the sound of a fire crackling into embers. "Well. There we have it. I would like to wish you all good night. Shall we go up together Sami?" Declared Saffron with her familiar light touch.

Ambrose staggered from the table, he too had lost, but he really didn't care, Saffron had beaten Ashfield and that was enough, plus he was totally under the influence of the narcotic. Ambrose felt unbelievably tired. Leaden tired. It must have been the driving? And the brandy? He needed to sleep. And take a bath? No just sleep. He fought the fatigue and managed a "good night" to the table before stumbling after Saffron and Seven to the stairs. None of the players uttered a word as the trio left carrying the final pot of the night. Thirteen pounds and ten shillings.

59

THE BACK OF HER NECK

Betts sank back into the bath sipping hot milk. Possibly her most inspired idea of the day, the hot milk, followed by the bath. Exactly what body and mind needed. She sometimes had her best notions in the bath. Hadleigh was still asleep. She would wake him once she'd worked it out? How all the pieces fit together? And somehow they did. Her intuition to work undercover had certainly paid off, and with the arrival of the Hispano Suiza, it might have even saved their bacon, so to speak. The location was clearly significant. A meeting place? But who was meeting? Betts finished the milk and lingered in the water for a further few moments, her mind a-spin with possibility. The dial stopped at Hadleigh. She stood from the bath, quickly dried herself and dressed in a pair of striped pyjamas. She switched off the standard lamp and crept into the bed.

Betts lay still for a moment listening to the silence, and Hadleigh's breathing. "Are you awake Sir?" She whispered.

"I am indeed Betts. How was your bath?" Hadleigh had his back to her. They shared the same bed, but he was honourably facing the other way.

"It was delightful Sir. I didn't disturb you did I?"

"You never fail to disturb me Betts."

She was silent for a moment absorbing his words. "How do I disturb you Sir?"

"I can't stop thinking about you Betts. You never cease to amaze me, impress me, fascinate me."

"That's very kind of you to say so. Thank you."

"That's quite all right, it's important you know." The silence briefly returned.

"Sir, there's been a development, the Hispano Suiza is parked outside and I observed at least one of the men from the New Inn downstairs in the bar. He was playing cards with a group of people, including two rather attractive females who appeared totally out of place. He's probably still there. There's definitely something going on in this establishment Sir."

"And you don't think they followed us? They're here because this hotel is somehow connected?" Hadleigh's mind span with possibility.

"Correct Sir. It's a good job we're in disguise, incognito, as it were." Betts quietly laughed.

They lapsed into a moment's silence. "Would you mind if I put my arm around you Sir. I can't stop shaking?"

"Of course," Hadleigh uttered.

Betts draped her arm around him and pressed her body tight against his. They shared in the warmth of the bed and the tremors coursing through her. Betts continued. "I was thinking of what the waitress said about the hotel Sir. She's right you know. There is something spooky and dark about the place. We should have brought my mother-in-law." They both laughed and without realising what she was doing, Betts ran her hand over Hadleigh's frame, from chest to hip. It was entirely unconscious, but it had an immediate physical effect on Hadleigh. He tried to pretend it wasn't happening.

"We'd better get some sleep," Hadleigh announced, embarrassed at the erection pushing tight against his underpants. He hoped she wasn't aware.

"Sir, if you recall that night back at the new Inn when we invented our little charade to effect a get-away? I heard myself saying — *'the night had been given to us'* — a part of our spontaneous improvisation. But as the words emerged, I knew it stemmed from something more than play-acting; it came from a kernel of truth that has not diminished. It lingers, constantly seeping into my reality. This night has been given to us John, and if there's one thing we should have learned from that stupid war, it is how precious every moment can be. We have no idea what the future will bring, the only matter of importance is right here, right now. I want you to make love to me John. I suspect we're in a very bad place, with some potentially very nasty people, but we have one another. As long as we're together we'll make it through." Hadleigh turned over to lie on his back. He ran his hand gently through her hair, touching her head, the back of her neck. Hadleigh and Betts shared their first real kiss.

60

BLOODY GLORIOUS

D ust was the only problem. He didn't mind the dark or the cobwebs, the promise of what he might witness made all the unpleasantness worthwhile, a thousand times over. But that bloody dust.

"Get up the loft Son, and see what they're up to. If Ma's right, reckon you should well enjoy yerself." Mr. Ashfield smirked at the teenager, seventeen by only a week. "Make sure as you saves some for later." Ashfield Snr. cackled a laugh.

Jimmy didn't have his father's piercing blue eyes, but he had certainly inherited his father's prodigious sexual proclivities. There were actually two lofts, each running the length of the property. One over the front, the other covering the rear. James was balancing across the dusty rafters in the front loft, directly above bedroom number 1. The master suite with a fine copper bath and Mr and Mrs Thompson. A beam of light pierced the empty attic space. Jimmy closed his left eye and peered down. Every inch of the crawl was worth that first glimpse. She lay stretched out naked before him — a candid view of the bath and its occupant. That was always the plan when they put the spy holes in. It was the plume of hair around her crotch that fascinated him the most. Hers was tidy. Trim. It had shape, formed in a neat triangle. Not like the sprawling forest he was more familiar with. Like his mother, Ma Ashfield. He could see the Thompson man asleep, the fool didn't know what he was missing. Jimmy almost laughed, but he held back. Abruptly she stood. Jimmy held his breath. In that moment he realised Mrs. Thompson was probably one of the most beautiful women in the world. Even comparing her to the girls in them magazines, she was better, smoother, softer. His erection was painful, he wanted to relieve himself, but he hoped for an even better opportunity. She crept into the bed with Mr. Thompson. There wasn't much moonlight, but it was enough. They were talking. Jimmy couldn't make out what they were saying, just a load of mumbles, but if they were gabbin' together, there was hope. He would give them five minutes that should be plenty. And sure as the sun is hot there was some wriggling around under the covers. And then the blanket just fell away. And she was sat on top of 'im. Ridin' 'im. It were bloody glorious to watch. Course, there was no time for relief, but he could still tell the others. What a tale. But first he had to get back down to Pa. Let 'im know the coast was clear.

61

THE SINGER STOPPED

T he first two were easy, like scrumping apples from an orchard. The brandies Ambrose and Saffron downed with such naive innocence, had finally achieved their purpose. The cloaked men comfortably picked the pair up, easy as a sack of potatoes, and carried them down to the cellar.

"Strip 'em and tie 'em tight to chairs." The man with the gravel in his voice instructed. Ambrose and Saffron were unaware of the rough hands, the ripped clothing, the coarse, abrasive twine of rope. They were still far away from consciousness relishing in opiate dreams.

LITTLE JIMMY CHECKED the spy hole above room number seven, he couldn't believe his luck; she was stretched out in the bath just like the other woman. Two naked beauties in the same night, and this one with no 'air at all. He gave the signal and they went in, six to hold her down and four more to inject the dope. Enough morphine to knock out an elephant. They'd been warned about the woman, she had killed two of their number, they were prepared, but none of them expected her to be totally bald. The bath became a battleground. Any strategist would have seen the impossibility of her situation. Seven was attacked while reclining, relaxing, relishing, in the luxuriant embrace of a fragrant bath. Six pairs of muscular hands forced her under water while simultaneously four needles pierced her flesh. The syringe bearers quickly had to join in the fray. Trying to hold down this woman was like trying to capture a storm in a paper bag. But all at once the resistance sapped and the female sank slowly back into the scant water left after the ravages of the struggle.

SEVEN HAD NEVER TAKEN a bath before, not without her suit anyway. It was recommended to remove the suit on occasion, but bathing in natural water wearing only naked flesh, would never appear on a list of suggested out-of-suit activities. But it should Seven mused. She felt a therapeutic lightness of being, a transcendent glow seeping into every muscle. This was new. A sensation never previously experienced. "*It's sad, so sad. It's a sad, sad, situation.*" Five singing her only song filled her mind. The music was truly exquisite, her thoughts drifted ever deeper until she noticed a strange sound. She opened her eyes. It had been her, Seven had made the sound. She found it again in the back of her throat, a trembling on her vocals chords, a vibration tuned at 440,000 cycles per second, the note A. Seven could hum a pitch. She closed her eyes and started the her song again, but this time she hummed along with Elton. The individual notes fell into place as the tune progressed, and soon the logic of music itself began to unfold; the intervals, the melodic line, each individual phrase and intonation. "*Sorry seems to be the hardest word.*" The falling melody matching the fading spirit. In that moment Seven also uncovered regret, Perkins should have been spared. But she had no time to dwell on the notion, an existential crisis of hands and needles gripped her by the throat and plunged her beneath the waters of consciousness.

SHE COULD HEAR VOICES. Singing? No, this was chanting, a monophonic drone, an incantation. The language was hard to place? Latin. Maybe she was dreaming. Her suit? The bath. The hands upon her.

Seven's neck, feet, and forearms were secured to a metal table with thick leather bands and heavy steel chain. Her captors were taking every precaution. The air was thick with smoke, a heady mix of incense, candles, and male sweat. With great difficulty Seven tilted her head. She was surrounded by figures, a congregation of black cloaks and hoods, they even carried lit black candles. Seven manoeuvred her head the other way and it was the same view. Twelve she counted. Seven squinted in the dim light — she struggled without the suit — tall, dressing-room mirrors marked each of the five points of a pentagram drawn in bold chalk strokes. There were two more figures slumped awkwardly in chairs. Of course, Saffron and her driver. They were naked and tied and unconscious. Seven tried to reach out with her mind, but there was too much fog. Seven understood she'd been poisoned by a chemical that devastated her mental and physical control. Probably more *Papaver Somniferum,* but without her suit, she couldn't tell. And without the suit she had little hope of quickly repairing the damage. Thankfully, parts of her mind seemed to exist somewhere beyond her unresponsive body.

"GET a bucket of water and wake them up." The gravel-voiced man instructed.

Four of the hooded figures dispatched themselves and returned carrying pails of water. At the count of three they emptied the contents over the slumped couple. The captives would both have cried out in shocked surprise were it not for the cloth ties around their mouths. The kitchen chairs rocked with their struggles, but after a few moments the futile resistance subsided. The pair shivered in their naked chill. A new black-cloaked figure entered the room, but his hood was red as blood, it was Mr. Ashfield. He carried a wooden box before him possessing it with both hands in reverence. He placed it on the table, close to the manacles that bound Seven's feet. Ashfield opened the box and removed a ceremonial blade. He brandished the dagger above his head.

"Do as thou whilst." Ashfield called out.

"Is the only law." The congregation replied. Ashfield stood before the first cloaked figure. He held the knife before the man's face.

"Is the only law." The figure proclaimed in a gravelly voice.

Ashfield worked his way around the twelve, repeating the ritual, each figure adding a new voice to the growing chant. And not just men, women too. Even a comparative child — Jimmy was the final apostle to add to the choir. Ashfield signalled a stop. A heavy silence shackled the room. Ashfield walked around the table bearing Seven, studying her body, her shape, her nakedness.

"Can you hear me, woman?" Ashfield demanded.

Seven blinked her eyes.

Ashfield approached and pressed the ceremonial knife tip tight to her throat. "I'm going to untie your mouth. Try anything, and I will push this blade through to the top of your skull. You'll end up looking like an apple on a stick." Ashfield laughed.

Seven blinked again and Ashfield undid the knot. She breathed in air, hungrily filling her lungs.

"Who sent you?" Ashfield questioned, brandishing the knife with menace.

"No one sent me, I am an individual."

"You don't work for anyone? Not some government?"

"No. I function entirely for my own benefit and the good of humanity."

"Aah. I see. Some kind of vengeful warrior, righting the wrongs of the world are you?"

"They are your words."

"Is that why you killed Dykes and Roberts?" Ashfield demanded.

"Yes, for the abominations they committed, the same reason I will kill you." Seven replied with an even tone.

Ashfield laughed again, the congregation slowly began to join in, the cellar walls began to resonate in a maelstrom of mounting histrionics when abruptly there was a colossal crash. The ever-resourceful Ambrose had propelled himself into the air deliberately crash-landing on the back legs of his chair. The wood shattered instantly and from out of the broken remnants, the naked Ambrose erupted like a human volcano, brandishing a chair leg for a weapon. He struck down two of the brotherhood instantly, before he was overpowered and brought to the ground. They tied him again with heavy rope.

"Ang 'im up. I don't want no more interruptions." Declared Ashfield with irritation and a trio of the brotherhood attached Ambrose to a pulley, suspending him wrists high above his head, hanging from one of the barrel hooks mounted in the ceiling. Ambrose dangled in air, his feet six inches above the ground, like a side of pork in a butchers'. "I think it is time," Ashfield observed, and moved back to the table and Seven. The congregation re-assembled to their original positions. Ashfield led a recitation. The congregation joined in.

Deep-mouthed from their thrones deep-seated, the choirs of the æeons declare

The last of the demons defeated, for Man is the Lord of the Air.

Arise, O Man, in thy strength! the kingdom is thine to inherit,

Till the high gods witness at length that Man is the Lord of his spirit.

"Do what thy wilt, shall be the whole of the Law." Declared Ashfield, brandishing the ceremonial dagger in the flickering candlelight.

"Love is the Law. Love under Will." Came the response and Ashfield abruptly slashed Seven's wrist with a deep incision. The blood began to flow, spilling along the channel forged into the tabletop for that exact purpose, the precious fluid collecting in a silver bowl at the end of its journey. Ashfield followed suit with Seven's other wrist and made his way to the bowl. He used a copper ladle and made a dramatic spectacle of pouring Seven's warm blood to his mouth. He beamed a florid grimace back at his flock, rivulets of blood creasing his beard.

"Drink my brothers and sisters, we have much work ahead of us, and the night is long." The congregation rushed to take their fill of Seven's vital fluid. They sated themselves, revelling in the gore dripping from their lips, hot with anticipation of the orgiastic rites soon to come. Ashfield turned his attention to Ambrose. "We was going to 'ave a good time with you and yer girlfriend. Before we killed ya like. But disappointingly, I find myself unable to fully trust in yer ability to simply join in with the fun. I suspect ya might present a problem? And 'oo needs problems after all? But I wouldn't want you to proper miss out. I want you to see us takin' turns on 'er. You understand what I'm sayin' don't ya? We're gonna fuck your beautiful lady every which way to Hell." And without further words, Ashfield plunged the bloody ceremonial knife into Ambrose's side. Saffron screamed through her cloth tie as Ambrose cried out in agony, to eventually slump, dripping blood, quivering on his rope.

"Is the only law." Seven heard as he slit her wrist. The pain was indescribable and yet another unique experience. Seven had rarely known pain and the suit had always been there to protect her, to offer succour at every level of support. But this was raw and without hope of mitigation. Her own personal twenty-third-century defences were not up to this level of injury, no staunching of the flow, no tourniquets, not enough pain relief. But she held onto consciousness. Seven understood she had only minutes, but it was time enough. Seven knew what she had to do. She began to hum, the melody, the lyric, the strings, and orchestration, they flowed through her senses like spring water to a desert. In this moment of total and absolute devastation, Seven was at peace. She listened. But it was the phrase: "*It's sad, so sad, it's a sad, sad situation. And it's gettin' more and more absurd.*" That was when something beyond strange happened. And quite without precedent. Seven sang. She couldn't help herself, the melody simply sprang from her lips and vocal chords. "*It's sad, so sad. Why can't we talk it over? Ohh, it seems to me. That sorry seems to be the hardest word.*" She continued to sing. She thought of Perkins and a flood of memories from these few, precious weeks, days and hours. It was beautiful.

He was making his way to Saffron when Ashfield realised something wasn't right. At first, he thought his flock was dancing.

Jumping around like crazy, demonic fools. But then he saw the spurts of blood bursting from eyes, ears, nose. The flesh literally falling away, revealing the white of bone beneath. The brotherhood were rapidly disintegrating into demented, living corpses. Ashfield stopped and studied his own frame. He looked himself up and down. He held his hands before him stretching his fingers. No problems. It must be the blood he reasoned. Truth was he couldn't abide the stuff. Could never get on with black pudding either, the very thought made him want to retch. He might well have put the ladle to his lips, but Ashfield would never be the one to sup. Not blood anyway. He just let enough of the stuff fall about his beard to create the right effect. No. Ashfield was fine. In fact, he was more than fine, he felt magnificent, like a stallion, he unbuttoned his flies. He was totally ready now, it was finally time for sex with the girl. Ashfield was eager to hear that squeal when he stuck it in her. He made an animal grunt and pulled his penis free from the confines of his trousers. Ashfield enjoyed taking himself in hand. He was ever proud of his cock, both the size and the eagerness with which it sprang to attention. Like a dedicated private on his own personal parade, hah. Wouldn't catch him in anyone's army. He had all the gore and violence he could handle right here. And the sex. Ashfield studied his penis. Hard as a beam. The girl was tied, trembling with terror before him. Naked and terrified, totally at his mercy, her eyes wide with fear. He laughed with pride when he realised she was looking at his cock. Ashfield returned his attention to his penis. It was still rock hard, and still in his grip, but his boastful manhood was no longer attached to his body. Seven's blood had indeed penetrated his system. Ashfield watched with horror as his testicles withered and fell to the ground. He screamed but there was no sound, only the hiss, and rattle of bones as Ashfield's flesh decomposed into dust and silence.

AND FROM OUT of this temple of destruction, there arose a voice, singing a sad and beautiful song. "*What do I do when lightning strikes me? What have I got to do? What have I got to do? When sorry seems to be the hardest word. Ooh, sorry seems to be the hardest word.*" And abruptly the singing stopped.

THE THIRTY-EIGHTH BAR

Saffron stared into the bleak silence, the uneasy hush only punctuated by Ambrose's heavy, wheezing breaths and agonised groans. The poor man, she had to find help. Saffron had observed his earlier move with the chair in silent admiration. Now it was her turn. She tilted the elm seat onto its back legs, trying to gauge just how wobbly they might be. Saffron felt far more the wobbly one, but after a brief moment to strengthen her resolve, she leapt with all her might into the air, landing back down to ground with a heavy crash. The chair tumbled to the side and they fell to the floor together still attached. Saffron hit the ground with a resounding thud, jolting her leg, arm, shoulder, and face on the unforgiving flagstones. Now she was worse off, but Saffron wouldn't let go. Her elbows and knees took the brunt of the damage as she choreographed the conjoined pair back to an upright position. Saffron performed the chair leap a second time. The back legs creaked precariously, but they held. They didn't, however survive the third attempt and the chair crumbled around her with the satisfying crack of splintering wood. The ropes loosened enough for Saffron to break free and rush to Ambrose. The first step was to lower him to the ground. Saffron gingerly dressed the knife wound with the remains of his shirt, trying to staunch the flow of blood. She covered him as best she could with his coat and jacket. The blouse and skirt she had worn earlier had been ripped to shreds in the rush to remove them. Along with her underwear. But her coat, hat, and shoes were intact. She quickly dressed. The only hope for Ambrose was to find medical assistance and it had to be immediate. Could there be a telephone in the hotel? She knelt beside him, he had slipped from consciousness, Saffron knew the signs, there was no time to waste. Saffron stood ready to leave when she saw a faint blue light in the darkness, she heard the creaking stairs, footsteps moving toward her. Saffron wasn't the sort of girl to panic, she reached down for the gun Ashfield had found in Ambrose's coat, a Webley fitted with a Parker-Maxim suppressor. She held it before her, pointing directly at the stairs with hands steady as sunbeams.

"You don't need the weapon. I mean you no harm." She heard the words with absolute clarity, but there was no sound?

"Step into the light, let me see you. I'm armed." Declared a defiant Saffron aloud.

"Please, lower your weapon. I am here only to assist my companion, the woman you know as Sami. She is injured and needs my help." The words once again appeared in Saffron's thoughts. They changed the trajectory of her mind to memories of Sami and her sacrifice on the altar of stainless steel. Frank had more to say. *"Saffron, I apologise for this intrusion into your thoughts, but we both know there is no time. I might still be able to help her, but I need to act now."*

"And what about Ambrose?" Saffron asked aloud.

"I will help him also." Saffron lowered the gun and Five stepped out of the shadows. "Thank you." He said briefly and moved quickly past Saffron to the steel table and Seven's blood-

less, lifeless, body. He carried her folded suit in his hand; this was the source of the blue glow Saffron had witnessed emanating from the stairs. The suit's cerulean light increased dramatically as it gained proximity to Seven. Frank unfolded the fabric and spread the garment over the entirety of her still form. The nanoparticles began to migrate as a stream, seamlessly melding to her body. Suits were not simply worn, they were connected to their wearers through discrete DNA weaving. Frank grasped the open wounds of Seven's slashed wrists with his two hands. He closed his eyes and tilted his head upward. The blue glow spread like a wave through their arms, pulsing out filling their entire form. The intensity of light increased to an uncomfortable peak before settling back to a steady glow. Frank released Seven's hands and folded them across her. He made his way to Ambrose. Frank removed the dressing and pressed his palm over the wound. The blue glow returned to Frank's hand and the area of damaged flesh beneath. Ambrose was still unconscious, but the wheezing as he drew breath quickly disappeared. Frank withdrew his hand. The vicious wound from Ashfield's blade had sealed, the flesh was already beginning to bind together and heal.

"Will he be alright?" Saffron asked in a subdued voice.

"Yes. There will be a complete recovery. The blade pierced a lung, but he will be fine."

"What about your companion, Sami?"

"I don't know. She will need time to mend, which means I must move her away from here to a safe location. This can be done, but it would be preferable if it were later reported Sami was among the dead? This would help deter further investigation."

"You understand that's the reason why we're here; Ambrose and I? We were looking for her, Sami."

"Yes, I am aware of your situation, and I am also aware of two more detectives in this very building who are in the process of searching for me. They occupy room number one, and thankfully they would seem to be enjoying a good night's sleep. We should tend to our patients Saffron." Frank switched his attention to Seven. He touched her shoulder and a glow lit between them. "Status report," Frank demanded, but there was no response. Saffron joined him at the steel table.

"Ambrose is sleeping peacefully. Thank you. How is Sami?"

"Her body is responding, but not her mind. Communication through our thoughts, using our minds, is the medium we would generally use, but there is no response, nothing."

"I, I really liked your colleague. She was very... direct, honest. She had style, such great taste in clothes. And of course, the singing."

"What did you say?" Demanded Frank.

"I said about her being direct, and..."

"Singing? Are you saying she could sing?" Frank's question was framed in complete surprise.

"Yes. It was the last thing Sami did. Her final breath was a song."

Frank stared at Seven's still frame. Singing? How could she possibly sing? Unless Five had sung to her, and a song from him had brought about *the change*? But what did he sing? That was part of Five's personal memory. And it was gone, the instant when he decided to share a particular song with Seven. Of all the millions of possibilities, which one? "Saffron, do you remember anything of the song? The melody? The lyric?"

Saffron struggled to enter the moment, a scene of gruesome carnage. Hooded, cloaked figures, screaming in agony, only to disintegrate into bones and dust before her eyes. And poor Sami, strapped to that hideous altar, her lifeblood dripping away. Such a lovely voice." And as she said the words, a fragment of melody and lyrics popped into her head. "*It's a sad, sad, situation.*" Saffron sang aloud.

"Ah, of course, Mr. John, thank you." Said Frank with renewed hope. He took Seven's hand in his own and began to sing. "*What have I gotta do to make you love me? What have I gotta do to make you care? What do I do when lightning strikes me? And I wake up and find that you're not there.*" Frank wove every quantum of musical magic he could muster into the song. Saffron was spellbound, but Seven failed to respond. That is, until the thirty-eighth bar, when a tiny muscle at the back of her throat began to resonate, and hum along.

63

THE SILVER GHOST

I t was the early hours of the night, 1:35 am. Frank knocked gently on Mr. Fairbrother's bedroom door.

"Hello?" Mr. Fairbrother called in question.

Frank carefully opened the door and stepped into the room. "It's Frank Mr. Fairbrother. I apologise for disturbing your sleep, but I have been summoned to an emergency and I must leave as quickly as possible."

"Emergency? What kind of emergency? Who has summoned you?"

"My companion, her suit sent out an automatic distress call when her vital signs became compromised. I must go to her with all possible haste. May I take the Silver Ghost Mr. Fairbrother?"

"Of course Frank, and we must also do our best to help. Perhaps a better option might be to ask Harper to drive? The four of us could go with you? Collectively we might be of assistance? Where is your companion?"

"Weston-super-Mare, a hotel in the centre of the town."

Mr. Fairbrother was already out of bed. He tugged a series of bell-pulls. "I'm rousing the household Frank they will be with us shortly. We will assemble blankets, water, and a couple of thermoses of tea for the journey. Time for the off my boy." Declared Mr. Fairbrother heartily.

THE 69.4 MILES from Dorchester to Weston-super-Mare passed without incident. Harper enjoyed the role of chauffeur and the Rolls proved an exceptional machine. The original and deeply uninspiring official designation for the vehicle was 40/50 h.p. Hardly the stuff of legend, but the Silver Ghost nickname stuck and eventually was adopted as the official title. The 7.5 litre, six-cylinder engine had been crafted by hand and was assiduously maintained by Harper himself. Accordingly, when Mr. Fairbrother made the pronouncement, '*Time is of the essence Harper*', the driver took Mr. Fairbrother at his word. The journey might reasonably have taken around two hours, depending on road conditions — the familiar sight of sheep and cattle on narrow country roads slowed things considerably — but at this time of the morning and with the twin electric beams of the Silver Ghost lighting the way, Harper completed the trip in one hour and thirteen minutes.

But it was one hour and thirteen minutes too late. Frank chose to enter the Three Queens alone. The distress call led him direct to Seven's suit; now he had to find Seven herself. The hotel was shrouded in silence. Frank scanned the other rooms on the upper floor and identified the couple asleep in the large bedroom. Frank, who was never comfortable to simply intrude, insinuated himself into their minds. Detectives, he quickly discovered, and searching for him as well as Seven. He didn't need to see more. Frank quickly descended the stairs scanning for life forms. There were two in the cellar, but neither was Seven. Frank made his way down the final set of steps to the basement. He was aware of the girl, and the gun, but he was confident there was no serious threat. Like the detective pair cosy and warm upstairs, the young lady pointing a gun at him was imbued with a fierce streak of integrity.

IT WAS ONLY when Seven began to hum that Frank allowed himself to believe there was hope. He carried Seven's unconscious body to the Silver Ghost and placed her gently on the sprung leather backseat of the automobile. Clara understood how to care for Seven, her second twenty-third-century patient. Clara had already successfully nursed Frank through a similar, existential ordeal.

"My companion is alive, but barely. Clara, I need you to take her swiftly back to Princes Street and continue nursing her there until it is time for us to leave for America."

"Of course, but are you not coming with us Frank?" Asked a shocked Clara.

"No. It is too soon for me to leave. The detectives who have been searching for us are in the hotel. I want to ensure the three of you and Seven are far away from here before they stir. There is also an emergency device buried on Swanage Moor I need to recover before our journey to America. Do not concern yourselves, I will see you back in Princes Street."

Frank watched the Silver Ghost disappear back into the night before he returned to the hotel and his next mission; to unveil himself to the two detectives, the pair who had been doggedly on his trail from the beginning.

64

TWENTY YEARS

I t was Betts who woke first, she was aware of a blue glow lighting the room. She blinked and raised her head above the covers to see what it might be? A tall man, surrounded in cerulean luminescence stood at the foot of the bed.

"There is nothing to fear Miss Betts, my name is Frank. You and the Detective Inspector have been pursuing me and my companion over the past few weeks. It is time for us to talk."

Betts put her hand on Hadleigh's shoulder and gently shook him. "John, you need to wake up. Don't be alarmed, there's someone in the room and he wants to talk."

Hadleigh sat up abruptly. He squinted at the figure wrapped in blue light. "Who the devil are you? And what do you want?" Demanded the Detective Inspector.

"I am the man you have been searching for Inspector Hadleigh. My name is Frank. I assure you, I mean you no harm, I simply want you to understand what has taken place here tonight, and over recent weeks."

"Tonight? What happened tonight?" Hadleigh blustered, stumbling in his attempt to grasp reality.

"Fourteen people have died in the cellar of this hotel over

the past few hours. They were participating in a sacrificial cere-
mony that didn't go to plan."

Hadleigh and Betts stared at him trying to make sense of the
words and the situation. "Would you mind if we got out of the
bed and dressed?" Asked the Inspector.

"I would prefer you to stay where you are for the moment. I
want you to listen to what I have to say, and while you're still in
the bed, you are less likely to try anything foolish." Frank's logic
was indisputable.

The pair sat upright. Betts took some of the bed covers and
pulled them around her while Hadleigh wore his pyjamas with
pride. Frank maintained his position at the foot of the bed.

"Perhaps you might start by telling us where you are from?"
Suggested Hadleigh, firmly wrapped in a bubble of irritation.

"We come from the same place, Inspector Hadleigh. I am
born of this Earth as much as you, but three hundred years in
the future. My colleague and I were travelling to Europa, one
of Jupiter's moons when there was a cataclysm, an explosion
of some sort. I have no idea what might have been the cause,
but somehow we were catapulted back into the past, your
present. I was badly injured in the crash, my companion and I
became separated. Since we arrived in your time numerous
people have tried to murder us, and for a variety of reasons.
Tonight they succeeded in killing my companion, but in doing
so they also killed themselves. I will explain. The Three
Queens Hotel is associated with a cult. The basement has
been consecrated to Satanic worship and a temple established,
one of at least three in this nation where sacrificial rites are
practiced. Their preference is the murder of children. The cult
uses sweet shops in strategic seaside locations - they act as
hubs to attract, abduct and supply the required victims to the
temples. There were to be three killings tonight, adults in this
instance, and as I said, things didn't quite go to plan. When

they killed my companion they opened her veins and drank her blood. This formed the climax of the first ritual. What the thirteen cult members failed to understand was the nature of the liquid they had consumed. Our blood is not the same as yours, it is the result of three hundred years of evolution, a span of time that will see the extensive use of biological weapons on humanity; diseases that are truly terrifying in their destructive virulence. Mankind endured, but our blood still hosts a meta-culture of live viruses kept in check by our immune system. The people of your time have no such immunity. Accordingly, the thirteen who ingested the blood of my companion died of a particularly deadly disease within minutes."

"Are the bodies still in the cellar?" Questioned Hadleigh.

"Yes and no. Only bones remain, the flesh literally disintegrated. The cult members contracted a weaponised form of Ebola, a disease that consumes human flesh and organs. It would be wise not to touch what remains, in fact, you should really burn the entire building to the ground as a precaution."

The pair in the bed lapsed into a brief silence. "You said there were to be other victims?" Questioned Betts.

"Yes, two more investigators, working for your secret services. The second ritual would have climaxed with a series of sex acts, due to be performed on the two captives, male and female, before they too were put to death as sacrifice. I am confident they will validate everything I have revealed to you about tonight. The female, Saffron, suffered no significant damage, however the male was badly wounded with a dagger. I have repaired the injuries and both should make a full recovery. They are in the cellar now. Do you have any questions?" Frank paused with an impassive, but pleasant expression.

Betts wondered what he might look like with hair and eyebrows?

"Questions?" Exploded Hadleigh. "Good lord man, where do I start? What do you know about the killings in Swanage?"

"Nothing." Replied Frank with complete honesty.

"And you say your companion was killed as part of a sacrifice?" Hadleigh continued like a bloodhound on the trail.

"Yes."

"Four policemen were murdered in bizarre and cruel circumstances in Swanage. Could she have been responsible for the killings?"

"As I said, there have been numerous attempts to kill us both. My companion would have no qualms about killing any would-be attackers. She might even perceive herself as a vengeful agent. She would have seen what rests in their hearts, as have I. We have witnessed the evil and malice within, their thoughts and actions so depraved, it was a struggle for my colleague and I to conceive such acts could exist, especially in a society so apparently advanced. And the crimes so openly conducted. The thirteen members of the cult ultimately died by their own hands, hands awash with the blood of innocents. Was their terrible demise, not a fitting judgement for ritualistic murder? Would you choose to stand beside these people and call them Brother? Sister?"

Hadleigh could find no words. He was deeply confused and horribly conflicted, but mostly he felt consumed with righteous anger. The blue-tinged man should stand for his crimes, rallied through his brain, but beneath the rhetorical bluster lurked a dim light of empathy.

"What are your intentions Frank?" Asked Betts, who experienced significantly more than Hadleigh's faint ray of belief. She could see something considerable in this man.

"I intend to disappear. You will not hear of me again after tonight."

"You don't seriously think you can just walk away from all

this... mayhem. A bloodbath of fourteen victims." Declared Hadleigh.

"Hence the reason I am here and we are talking. I want you to understand the truth. I have no desire to inflict harm, the impulse is not within me. I was born to bring light into the world not darkness. And I was 97.4 miles away when all of this *mayhem* occurred. You are detectives. You seek the truth, I stand here as living proof to everything I have revealed to you. It would benefit you to hear and accept my words as an honest representation of the facts, I have given you nothing less. And something I suspect you are already beginning to understand; mine is a deeper truth and reality than you will find outside these four walls."

The room briefly rested into silence. "What would you have us tell our superiors?" Asked Hadleigh.

"It depends on their integrity," Frank observed with acute honesty.

"What on Earth do you mean by that?" Hadleigh blustered.

"The two secret service agents dispatched to this location were under orders from the same hierarchy as your own. I believe their immediate superiors are corrupt and directly implicated in the sadistic, ritual crimes committed here and at other locations around the Country. The two agents were not themselves implicated in the activities of the Cult, but knowledge of it made them expendable. They were both marked to die tonight. If you report all you know, do you honestly believe, they, your superiors, will allow you to continue to investigate? To live? Your knowledge is their greatest threat. You are a threat." Frank paused to allow his words to seep in. The two detectives said nothing. "You asked the question Detective Inspector, what should you tell these superiors? The answer lies in what you choose to do next. In the next ten minutes I intend to leave these premises and soon I will be gone from this land. You must understand the urgency of your situation here, in this hotel. The bodies in the cellar need to be destroyed. This is an imperative. They are a severe risk to the public in general. And in addition, the existence of a consecrated Satanic temple dwelling in the basement of these premises might also be best kept secret, along with the true fate of its followers. If a fire were to totally consume this building and the bodies, you might arrive at a more reasonable and plausible conclusion to the case you were tasked to investigate and solve. Every avenue of inquiry would be concluded with an unfortunate conflagration and the dead can be safely put to rest with whatever explanation you care to attach. They have established their own guilt, make them pay for the crime." Frank paused, waiting for a response, but it never came, there was only silence. "I will say good night then. Please do not try to follow me, you have matters here far more urgent to attend. Goodbye."

"Wait." Called Betts. "Frank, please, I have just one question?"

Frank paused. "Yes?"

"We have endured the most terrible suffering these last few years, but we kept our faith with the promise: 'A War to end all wars'. I would like to know if we will see another?"

Frank hesitated before he made his reply. "I am sorry Miss Betts. You will have the next twenty years in peace. This is your time, do not prevaricate." And without further words Frank turned and left the room.

65

THE PHOTOGRAPH

Hadleigh knocked before entering the room. "Good to see you Hadleigh, take a seat man." Hadleigh made himself comfortable in the creaking leather. "Drink?" Enquired Commander Thompson.

"Thank you Sir, I'll take a brandy."

The commander passed Hadleigh a glass filled with several measures of the fiery liquid before pouring himself an equally generous amount. They sat across from one another, warming the alcohol in the palm of hands before taking brief sips. The commander leaned forward and proffered Hadleigh a cigarette from an ivory and silver cigarette box. The nicotine and brandy brought the pair ever closer, blowing high plumes of smoke into the air like gushing volcanic geysers. A halo of blue tinged cigarette fog quickly encircled the room. "How do you feel?" Asked the Commander rather ambiguously.

"I'm doing very well thank you, Sir. Glad to see it all concluded." Hadleigh's response was brisk and precise.

Commander Thompson scrutinised his subordinate, the celebrated multi-faceted athlete, musician, and mountaineer. "I've read your report and like you Hadleigh, I am very gratified it would seem to be over." The Commander paused. He was hoping the inclusion of the word 'seem' might spur a response from his colleague. But no. The commander continued. "It is clear there was some manner of huge black market-come-smuggling and distribution operation taking place, significant without doubt and running across several counties, if not the entire country. And I agree with your conclusion, Hadleigh: rival gangs and in-fighting lead to their own fiery demise. Good riddance I say. There is little room for conjecture they were the most likely candidates in bringing about their own mutual extermination. But there's something odd about the whole business? That call from Whitehall only adds to the mystery, and we still don't know what their damned game was. Or do we Hadleigh?" The Commander's question was at the root of the entire conversation. The case might be closed, but it was still shrouded in unanswered questions. The forest of the commander's eyebrows remained high in expectation.

It was a shame, Hadleigh mused, he particularly liked the Commander. They shared that instinctive comrades' bond, a kinship of pain and suffering. But he also knew the strange man in the blue costume, Frank — how appropriate — was absolutely correct in his suggestion for caution. "I'm afraid not Sir. The fire brought an end to whatever and whoever was behind it all. Possibly we'll never know, but I have confidence the mysterious killings and illegal activities, whatever they might have been, are at an end."

The Commander nodded, but without conviction. He was still unsure if Hadleigh knew more.

"How did it go?" Despite the fact they were sat in the Wolseley on Police time and official business, Betts had neglected to add Sir. It was of course, deliberate.

Hadleigh relaxed into the leather and smiled. "I'm not sure he totally believed me, but Commander Thompson has signed off the report. We're in the clear, so to speak Betts, and with a week's paid holiday to boot."

She frowned. He probably didn't notice, but it was there. The stark emptiness of a surname. Betts realised she had moved beyond this, but for Hadleigh it wasn't yet time. "Where would you like to go next Sir?"

"Well, here's a thing Betts. I know the trail has gone cold as it were, but there was a lead I was hoping we might follow before the business at the Three Queens erupted. It will probably amount to nothing, but I'd like us to go back to Dorchester."

BETTS PARKED the Wolseley outside the house in Princes Street. Hadleigh reminded her of the day they had stopped and listened to a wonderful pianist perform a piece by Debussy.

"You asked me just how good the playing actually was? I described the performance as the best I ever heard. But it wasn't only me Betts who coined that phrase. The waitress at the Inn opposite the clocktower, located literally around the corner, less than a hundred yards from Princes Street described our mysterious busker, whom we now know was Frank, with exactly the same description. *'Best she ever heard'* formed her summary. I have a hunch there might be a connection Betts."

Betts tugged the bell-pull. A maid in a blue and white uniform answered the door. Hadleigh spoke.

"Oh, good afternoon. There is no reason to be concerned, I am Detective Inspector Hadleigh, this is my assistant Betts. Would it be convenient to speak with the owner of the house?"

"Would you like to come in out of the cold Sir, Miss?" The maid led the pair into a sitting room. Hadleigh noticed a beautiful Steinway piano, statuesque in the spotlight of the tall picture windows. "If you'd care to take a seat, I will fetch Mr. Fairbrother."

They thanked the maid. Betts prepared to sit, but Hadleigh was drawn as if mesmerised. The detective couldn't resist inspecting the piano up close. He lifted the lid to the keyboard and studied the black and white ivory keys, reflected, along with the famous Steinway name in the highly polished rosewood. Hadleigh's gaze followed the long frame, a baby grand he noted and looked up from the piano. A photograph caught his eye, an old man and a young boy smiling together outside a concert hall. In a rush Hadleigh recognised the face, it was George. He grasped the frame from the mantlepiece and feverishly held it before him. Hadleigh found himself shaking uncontrollably. He stumbled and sat heavily on the leather piano stool, but immediately he slid to the floor, shaking as if in the grips of epilepsy. Betts rushed to his side and put her arm around him, the trembling was getting worse. In the same moment Mr Fairbrother entered the room.

"What on Earth?" He demanded.

"I'm so sorry, Mr. Fairbrother is it?" Asked Betts.

"It is, but I fail to understand? What on earth is going on? Is the man ill?"

"In a manner of speaking, it's to do with the war Sir. Seeing the photograph triggered a reaction. It is a condition known as delayed trauma. Could I trouble you for a cup of sweet tea? Perhaps a spoon of laudanum if you have it, and a blanket?"

"Yes of course." Mr. Fairbrother rang a bell.

〜

IN THE END the best remedy was sleep. They managed Hadleigh to a guest room, closed the curtains and left him to slumber, allowing rest and the laudanum to restore some peace to his tortured mind.

"I would be grateful if you could enlighten me of what just happened?" Requested a confused Mr. Fairbrother. They had returned to the sitting room where Hadleigh's trauma had first begun.

Betts retrieved the photograph from the mantlepiece. "May I ask you who George was Sir?"

"He was my nephew. I note you use the past tense?"

Betts sighed. She replaced the photograph to the mantle-piece and sat with Mr. Fairbrother on the sofa. "May I speak openly Mr. Fairbrother?"

"Of course. It is the only option."

"I am truly sorry to speak of such things, but Hadleigh was there, at the moment of your nephew's death. They shared in the tragedy, it was the same mortar bomb that took Detective Inspector Hadleigh's arm. George and Hadleigh met on the day of the battle of Bazentin le Petit. During the lull in fighting, after the success of the initial assault they found time to play piano and perform together. They took full advantage of the moment's brief respite in the village. George had discovered a grand piano and a library of music abandoned in a chateau. Hadleigh heard George playing and together they performed a suite written to be played by four hands on a single keyboard, composed by Gabriel Faure. And they performed to an enthusiastic audience, their comrades. A company of men and soldier-boys waiting for battle. George and Hadleigh brought the gift of music to them. For many it would be the final melodies they would ever hear, but, at least in the short hours before the inevitable battle, they had the chance to witness something beautiful. I know for John, playing the piano with George that day, especially in the dreadful circumstances, was one of the most wonderful and profound experiences of his life. But the war had only paused, the fighting, the futile loss of life carried on; George died, but Hadleigh survived. John has carried the guilt since the day. He suffers for the fact it wasn't he who was killed. Hadleigh had encouraged George to stay close, he thought he could protect him. Hadleigh has never forgiven himself."

"Is that why you came here, to this house?"

"No, not at all. We were following quite a separate trail. Strange as it might sound, we happened to hear a pianist while we were passing your house. It was two weeks previous. The playing was absolutely exceptional. Hadleigh described the performance as the best he had ever heard. We simply came here to ask the question Mr. Fairbrother, who was the pianist?" Mr. Fairbrother abruptly stood and returned the picture frame to the mantlepiece. Betts couldn't fail to notice he comported himself with the vigour and sprite of a man considerably younger. The detective in her never tired, her mind began to stitch the emerging pieces into a design that was both radical, and plausible. Mr. Fairbrother remained at the mantlepiece.

"I often marvel at the complex web of life that interweaves, intersects, and unites so many of us. I am both horrified and heartened by what you have revealed to me Miss Betts, and for your candour I am most grateful. I thank you most sincerely. My heart soars at the thought of George finding moments of musical solace, despite the confusion and futility of battle. To have uncovered kinship with another soul in those final hours was a divine gift. I have absolute faith Miss Betts. I believe. As I also understand the terrible tragedy that befell my George and so many others was already written. It was a grievous sin against Man that was destined to take place, and we cannot hold ourselves nor certainly any other victim to blame. There are those I would accuse. Many were attached to a notion of war, without ever truly understanding the reality. Others sought nothing else than to profit, but that is another matter. You seek the pianist?" Mr Fairbrother questioned and completed another of his age-defying moves, walking briskly, almost skipping over to the piano. He pulled out the leather piano stool and sat. He placed his thumb on the Bb key and followed the note with the G above. The two pitches of the major 6 lit the room like a sparkling ray of sunlight. "He sings as well you know." Mr. Fairbrother declared, smiling at the detective with the serenity of the blessed. "There has been but one light in my life in the weeks, months, and years since George died. Nothing would shake me from my despondency. The desolate, wretched void of living. My life was already over. I awaited death's embrace with eager arms. But all changed when I heard a young man sing. He reminded me of that most precious gift we so absently possess, life. The young man gave me reason to live again, and remarkably, he achieved this minor miracle through music. And I have witnessed others' to be equally moved. Miss Betts, this young man has a gift beyond anything you might reasonably imagine. He is absolutely the person you seek, but I promise you, he is gone. My only hope is that one day I might see him again."

"What is his name Mr. Fairbrother?"

"But you already know his name Miss Betts, it is Frank, and they are both long gone. Far, far away from here. My deepest, most earnest wish is that we will hear from Frank again. When things have changed, altered into something new. And who knows Miss Betts, it might even happen in our lifetimes?"

"There's no point in asking you where he's gone I suppose?"

"No. But he will return, I told you, I have faith. And on that tumultuous day for mankind, whether in the near or distant future, we will need to listen, for in his words reside answers mankind should heed."

66

FALLEN ANGEL

Seven had taken to leaving the curtain of her bedroom window open. Practicality was not her intention. Admittedly the moon glow was yet another medium for charging her suit, almost any form of transmutable energy would suffice, but aside from such fleeting necessities, the glow when sleeping under moonlight was particularly soft, our satellite shares only reflected beams. The hour was a little after 6 in the morning and the last legions of light particles cast themselves across the lunar surface, making the dust dazzle like a silver beacon. Seven thrilled at the spectrum of the Heavens. The astral bodies never failed to excite her senses, she had a personal stake in the bigger picture. Seven wrapped a heavy cotton dressing gown around herself and left the room, an easy costume to wear, she was on her way to the garden. It would be another half an hour before sunrise and she was eager to inspect her former home, beyond the earthly confines of gravity and atmosphere. She was aware it was bitterly cold, the consequence of a cloud-free vista, but the cold would never matter as long as the suit and she were entwined. Seven wondered if she'd ever remove it again? Especially after what happened last time. She shuddered at the memory. The house in Princes Street had provided refuge for her just as it had for Five. It had been a total of four days before Seven regained consciousness. Clara drew on her experience of tending Frank at the beginning, but it was only when he returned with the *porta-med* from the utility pack that Seven's recovery was assured. By the time she was fully conscious, Five, or Frank as the household called him, together with Clara and George's former comrade, the chauffeur Harper, had taken a Cunard liner from Southhampton, England. They were bound for New York and the promise of a new beginning in America. The arrival of the two detectives on the marble doorstep just a few days later had sent shockwaves throughout the household. The investigators had no idea Seven was upstairs the whole time, the bedroom adjoining the guest room where Hadleigh later slept. It was clearly time for her to leave. And she was ready. An easy relationship with Mr. Fairbrother had flourished quite spontaneously. He had been there when she woke to hold her hand and tell her she was safe. His kindness and that of the whole household became yet another new and rewarding experience. Even before she opened her eyes, Mr Fairbrother was captivated by this enigmatic, future version of woman-kind. Each day his anticipation grew for the thrill of her presence. They spent hours in frequent and fascinating conversation, and playing cards, every type of game he knew. They would walk together, sharing a love and admiration for the wonder of nature. Mr Fairbrother spent every hour he could with the beguiling female, he treated her with heavy helpings of awe and respect. Seven was conscious of his growing admiration, or was it infatuation? Frank had inadvertently created a problem. His nano-particles had performed a superb job of rejuvenation on Mr. Fairbrother. Possibly too good a job. Seven smiled to herself. The grass crunched with a light frosting of spindly ice. Seven scrunched her toes, enjoying the glow spreading through her feet. Life was exhilarating. The dawn must be close, the morning star crept above the horizon. Actually not a star at all, this was the planet Venus, an old friend. Those pathetic, disgusting abominations, the ones who spread her across their steel altar, surrounding themselves for protection with a chalk pentangle. Not a single one of those cloaked figures had any real notion, not a faint glimmer of understanding as to the meaning or symbolism of their actions. They would never have known each prayer and every utterance was a dedication to this beautiful heavenly body. Venus, the *light-bringer*. The *Fallen Angel*. The Biblical Lucifer went by the same descriptions. The orbit of the planet Venus creates a natural pentagram in the cosmos as it circles the Sun. This is called the *Rose of Venus*. The pentagram as a form features a list of mystical credentials inherent in the design. The structure emerges from the calculations of the Fibonacci sequence, these foundations are also rooted in the *Golden Ratio*. The *Golden Rectangle*, one of the divine shapes, can be extrapolated *ad infinitum*. The Golden Rectangle is a critical factor in architecture and art, the rule of thirds, the foundation of the portrait perspective. The pentagram also functioned as the secret symbol used to identify Pythagoreans. A case-load of *prima facie* evidence all present and correct to further under-score the mystery. What did any of it mean? Seven frowned. She had no answer, but she was keen to find one. Those cultish fools with their naive fixation on the planets and cosmos had threat-ened her life and garnered her interest. Her thirst to find those responsible for the abominations had not in the least dimin-ished, on the contrary, she was eager to carry on her quest. Her mission of good works — with a subtext of righting the evils of the planet. Seven could easily cast herself into the role of *fallen angel*. An agent of righteous vengeance. Exactly. She had arranged to travel later that day to Weston-super-Mare with Mr. Fairbrother in the Silver Ghost. They were going to recover

Seven's repaired motorcycle. By day's end, she would be back on the road, the wind in her face and the memory of that fateful night far, far behind. There was just one final score to settle before she could truly move on. "Hmm."

THE SILVER GHOST felt like another world after the bump and grind of the Commer. This was a domain where comfort and design could co-exist with technical practicality. Seven sat beside Mr. Fairbrother. The seating was leather and expansive, easily room enough for three, but there were only two. Seven liked old technology, it made her smile. With certain exceptions. Definitely not the lorry. That made her bones ache, but this automobile, and her beloved Brough, they seemed to possess something inexplicably individual. Seven experienced a warm glow. She found herself anticipating, looking forward to the sight of an inanimate object. She frowned. But it didn't matter. Seven admired the polished wood and dashboard equipment arrayed before her. She especially liked the dials. The simple, direct functionality, wrapped in brass and glass. Even the oil gauge, which hardly ever moved. It was all delightful, resulting in a wonderful mix along with the resonant thunder of tumbling pistons. The roads on the other hand were still painful. Or maybe it was the suspension responsible for crimes against back and bone? More likely both. If she were around for a greater length of time she could have built a modification, something better suspension-wise. A gesture to repay the kindly man, Mr. Fairbrother, a present. She quivered at the thought of Frank's gift, his present to her. It rang at the back of her mind like a nagging bell, tempting, tantalising, but she was making herself wait. It had to be right because one day Seven hoped she would see Frank again. And she would thank him for saving her life, and for the gift. And with the greatest pleasure she would reveal her ultimate choice. But it was an almost impossible decision. Frank had gifted her a copy of the entire archive: *Songs of the Twentieth Century, the Complete, Collected Libraries of Recordings and Performances.* How could she possibly know where to start?

"Do you know where you might travel next Seven? You have papers now, you can go most anywhere you choose, certainly within the British Empire?" Mr. Fairbrother called out above the revolutions of the engine.

"I plan to visit London briefly, and then? I feel the need to explore Mr. Fairbrother, I will travel. I intend to witness the wonder of this planet before it disappears. And when the time comes to assist her, I will be the instrument in making things right."

"Good for you." Mr. Fairbrother declared. "What are your thoughts about La Scala in 1926? I anticipate it will be a most wonderful occasion."

"I agree. It's a splendid idea Mr. Fairbrother, it is already written into my future. I hope nothing will derail our purpose."

"We must endure and believe." He paused. "I wish you would call me Edmund my dear? It is my Christian name after all."

"If you wish. Edmund, I want you to understand how grateful I am for your kindness, I would like to say thank you."

"It has been my pleasure my dear. I am forever grateful to have met you, and Frank, and Clara. You appeared as an almost divine trinity, and you have most successfully resurrected my life." He laughed at his good fortune and superb health. "Good Lord Seven, you really have no idea what chronic pain feels like. We take our health far too lightly. But when the burden of suffering is gone appreciation soars, and the release is just, astonishing." Mr. Fairbrother paused to exhilarate in the wind rushing through his hair. The roof canopy was down and the chill winter temperatures added to the visceral sense of moment. "If I could have one wish it would be to hear that piece of Puccini Frank introduced to me, *Nessum Dorma.* A whole seven years seems a long time to wait before I am able to again listen to the Maestro's most famous song. I have only scant memory, but I will remember the thrill of his music always."

And at last Seven had an answer, one of which she knew Frank would approve. "Edmund, if you would allow me to drive the Rolls Royce over the last few miles, I believe I have the solution to your request. You only have to touch my arm, relax, and close your eyes. I can promise you *Nessum Dorma,* and a performance by Signor Luciano Pavarotti."

67

DAMOCLES AND DAUGHTERS

"What shall we do next?" Hadleigh declared. It was one of those ambiguous, cryptic comments she so hated.

"It occurs to me the familiar post-coital response is generally a cigarette. Sir. Would you like me to light one for you?" Betts propped herself onto an arm and looked down on the miscreant, guilty of carelessly throwing ambiguities into the air.

Hadleigh lay on his back staring at the elaborate plaster ceiling rose. A huge and intricate Victorian design, it reminded him of writhing snakes. Hardly conducive to a good night's sleep, but every other aspect of the elegant Grand hotel room was luxurious and quite perfect. Hadleigh had been tempted to say yes to the cigarette, just for fun, to witness her righteous outrage. But he knew he would be playing with fire, Betts-fire, and that was something best avoided.

"I'm so sorry Betts, my utterance was somewhat random I must admit, but the fact is, without the daily dynamic of murder and mayhem to focus our energies, the prospect of returning to institutional rigidity doesn't appeal in the least. I don't want this to end Betts, in any respect. I fervently believe in *Us*. In addition to... well you know, the other aspect of *us*... I am fiercely proud of our superb, professional partnership. We are a fantastic investigative team Betts, a top team. But we both know how the constabulary sees things and the reality is, as a female you will never be given the opportunities you deserve. You are an outstanding detective Betts. And, returning to the other... you know... *Us*. You and me. The last few weeks in your company have left me only wanting more. I was thinking we might try something new? Job-wise. Together."

"That sounds intriguing Sir? Don't stop."

"I made a start with what we do best and most enjoy, and I determined we might try and set up a small detective agency, specialising in investigations on behalf of female clients."

"Oh, that's a brilliant concept Sir. Well done. And yes, I'd love to play a part." Betts paused in her positivity to reposition herself, moulding her form tight against his. "Do you have any ideas for a name?"

His left arm found a path to her naked shoulder. "I was thinking: *Hadleigh and Betts Detective Agency*?" Hadleigh almost held his breath in expectation of her response.

"Hadleigh and Betts, Betts and Hadleigh? No, you're right, Hadleigh should come first. I like it, everything about it. What role would you have me take Sir?" Betts asked playfully.

"Partner. Equal and absolute. We work together, we are the team. We assess each case together, devise a strategy together, we do the detecting together. I hope my intentions are clear Betts?" Hadleigh enquired.

"Absolutely crystal Sir, like a champagne glass." So that was it. Maybe not exactly what she might have anticipated, but nevertheless, her most pressing desires had been assuaged. One by one they fell into line, like a paddling of ducks on a pond. Her mind began the drift towards sleep, just in time she remembered the note. "There's something I've been meaning to tell you John.

I think they have a plan to meet, Mr Fairbrother and Frank. A date in the not too distant future, six years and five months to be exact; at a concert in Italy."

"How do you know of this?" Hadleigh responded with surprise.

"There was a handwritten note on the mantelpiece. When I saw the date, I thought it prudent to commit the details to memory: 25/04/26. Sunday, La Scala, Milan. *Turandot*, Puccini. I'm sure I remember your saying you have a fondness for Puccini?"

"Absolutely, he is without doubt my favourite opera composer. It would give me the greatest pleasure to take you to see Madame Butterfly as soon as we have the opportunity. Puccini in a prestigious opera venue is a momentous experience and one I would love to share with you Betts." He paused as if he might say more, but there were no additional words of romance. "Interestingly, even as a devotee I have no knowledge of any work by the name of *Turandot*? What a prospect. I can only repeat *outstanding* many times over, you really are a wonderful detective Betts. It will be my absolute honour to work with you."

"Thank you Sir. I appreciate your confidence and I wholly share your enthusiasm for our professional partnership. Madame Butterfly sounds divine. What shall we do about La Scala?"

"Put it in the diary Betts and one way or another, we will find time to make our way over there. If *Turandot* is to be Puccini's next opus the date might mark the premiere? La Scala would certainly be the right setting. What a night that will be Betts, we should dress in our finest clothes." Hadleigh paused in his imagining. "But that is some few years off, at this moment we need to attend the business of the here and now. Any thoughts on a strap-line to our new business venture?"

"How about *Diligent and discrete, the Agency that listens.*" Suggested Betts.

"Wonderful Betts, a clear mission statement. So what's the verdict? Are we setting our sails to the wind? Under our own banner so to speak?"

"There's no question. I absolutely believe we should Sir, especially in view of Frank's answer to my question. *Twenty years.*" Betts paused. "I don't regret the asking I would always rather know, but there is undoubtedly something of the sword of Damocles hanging over us. When Daniel and I married, I always imagined I would have children. What if I were to have sons? I can't bear the thought of my child, or even worse, children going off to die on some nameless, foreign field. It's just the right number of years to take sons away."

"Then we should start with daughters Betts, the sons can come along later," Hadleigh said softly and they kissed again.

68

A NEW BEGINNING

S even had only a vague map to guide her, a sketch conceived from a mist of scant memory, but it helped make sense of the warren of tunnels and corridors and grand spaces in Admiralty Arch. With a little VR to smooth out the unseen edges Seven crept her way through the core of the Establishment. Even within the secretive focus of her stealth, it was impossible not to admire the commanding marble stair-cases, statues, pillars, fine woods, rugs, and portraits. These people certainly enjoyed surrounding themselves with the trap-pings of luxury. Seven easily made her way past the terminal two doors and four locks that protected the sanctity of her desti-nation — a most prestigious office with a spectacular view. Walnut panels and animal heads adorned the walls, grand indeed. The fireplace was an extravagance in red marble with a gold-leaf French mirror positioned proudly above. No doubt a trophy acquired from Napoleon himself, the mercury-backed glass had all the credentials. But there were two further, more extravagant pieces of furniture occupying the splendid domain. Firstly, a monumental desk, constructed from an elaborate combination of ivory and walnut, a vainglorious concoction of

Empire-elegance. The expansive surface accommodated a pair of telephones in contrasting colours resting on black onyx plinths. But the object commanding every gaze was a giant globe standing one metre tall, enclosed in a finely wrought circular frame of light oak. It took its rightful place, centre-stage in the light-beams of the picture window. A proud and noble piece with an open invitation to reach out and make the world spin. Seven locked the doors behind her and stepped into the chamber. The safe was easily located concealed behind a portrait of Edward VII, the monarch who commissioned the building. It was a *Chubb* and promised resistance to both fire and thieves, but it had little, actually no chance with Seven. It gave up its secrets and Seven sat down to read. It was still only 1:40 am. Time as always was on her side.

WHEN SHE HEARD keys jangling in the locks at 6:24 am Seven anticipated cleaners to be on their way in. But no, it was a man, not especially tall, but hunched forward with the weight of invisible burdens. The overcoat was cashmere, long, black, and elegant, his head topped with a bowler hat. In gloved hands he carried a Times newspaper and a silver-handled cane. The man switched on the electric light and left the coat, hat, gloves and cane on the stand by the door. Beneath the cashmere he was wearing a suit, beautifully tailored no doubt, but the style was distinctly pre-war, it featured an extravagant excess of material. A high shirt collar was also in evidence. This was a man comfortable with life in the manner of how things used to be. He crossed the expansive rug clutching the Times and sat at his desk. The office was pleasantly warm, 16° according to her suit. The radiators had begun to rumble and rattle around 5:30 helping set the stage for another busy day in the ministry, a furtive world of murmurs and secrets. He made himself comfortable, switched on a desk lamp and poured a double shot from a bottle located in the bottom desk drawer. He downed the liquor, dispensed with the glass, and opened the paper in one fluid movement. The man was clearly performing a small, but well-oiled ritual. Seven watched him read. She was in no hurry and she enjoyed eavesdropping on his thoughts. In this moment of brief respite Seven was happy to enjoy the peace and comfort of quiet repose, before the breaking of the inevitable storm. The telephone rang, not the black one, this was the red phone. The bell sounded three times and ceased. It quickly began again and on the third peel the man picked up.

"Speak." He insisted. The voice at the other end spoke. "I'm not sure if I care for your tone either," came the first man's terse reply, he was clearly irritated. Seven boosted her audio sensitivity, now she heard both voices.

"Get a grip Gerald this is no game." Insisted the telephone voice. "The situation is evolving fast in Germany and we need to keep a steady hand on things here. What news from the two chaps in the field?"

"One of them is a woman." Observed the man sat at the desk, holding the red telephone, Gerald.

"I don't give a God-damn if one of them's a monkey, answer the question." Insisted the caller.

"I haven't heard from Ambrose since the night of the fire. I presumed he and the girl were among the casualties."

"Is that really the best you can do Gerald? *Presumed...* What sort of a department are you running there? I hope this is just a momentary blip Gerald? And your presumption is wrong. Your agents survived and finished up being interviewed by that intrepid nuisance, Hadleigh. He has a bad habit of turning up at the wrong time. The man's either born lucky, or there's some actual detective work going on for once. Bloody annoying though. Get rid of them Gerald."

"What? Hadleigh?" Asked an unsettled Gerald.

"No, you bloody fool, Ambrose and the girl — the translator. Loose ends Gerald. Tidy them up like a good chap and we'll talk again tomorrow." The line clicked dead. Gerald replaced the receiver and retrieved a handkerchief from his breast pocket. He mopped his feverish brow. Gerald lit a cigarette taken from the silver caddy on his desk and inhaled deep. He closed his tired eyes for a brief moment before he wearily levered himself up from the chair and began the familiar path to the tall elegant window. The view everyone envied. His favoured thinking position. The office faced directly down the Mall straight to the noble residence, Buckingham Palace. But Gerald didn't achieve the favoured thinking destination, not on this occasion. The red phone trilled again. He froze. It rang the prescribed three times and stopped. Gerald rushed back to his seat at the desk and waited. Nervous. Anxious. The handkerchief was back in his hand. He absently mopped his brow. The bell on the red phone began to ring. Tiny rivulets of perspiration sprang free from his hairline, Gerald felt the damp patches forming beneath his Saville Row pinstripe. He picked up the receiver on the third toll.

"Speak." Gerald uttered, but failed to achieve his usual gusto.

"It's me Sir, Ambrose Sir. She got away Sir. She'll be coming after you next. Sir."

"Where are you Ambrose? I need you here man, urgently. And what on Earth are you blathering about? What woman?" Gerald demanded, happily reviving his virulently pernicious mode.

"The woman who killed the others. We told her Sir, and we drew a picture of how to find you Sir. We told her what a two-faced, lying scum-bag you are Sir. And she's going to kill you Sir. Soon."

The line went abruptly dead. Gerald was trembling. He replaced the receiver in a daze shaking his head in disbelief. On unsteady legs Gerald set a choppy course for the Edward VII portrait and with fingers he could barely control, he eventually opened the *Chubb*. He stared in disbelief at the empty shelves. Gerald felt himself stagger as his world tilted. He reached out and held onto the safe door, steadying himself. Gerald felt consciousness ebbing. He thought of calling for help, but immediately realised no one would hear. The room was totally sound-proof, floors, ceiling, everything. Slowly, Gerald made his way back to the desk. He sat heavily and poured another generous Napoleon. Gerald stared across the room. He found himself squinting, his brain trying to make sense of the electricity dancing before his eyes. The waiting was finally over. The leather armchair by the window shimmered with light, a form quickly coalescing, inexplicably materialising from out of the chair. A woman in a blue haze abruptly stood before him.

Instinct took over. Gerald had a firearm mounted just below the desk-top. All he need do was reach forward, grab the Webley and... The MkVI revolver appeared above the leather pad in a flash of surprising dexterity. Without the least hint of hesitation Gerald emptied the first five rounds into the belly of the woman-assailant. Or at least that was the intention. The quintet of antic-ipated gunpowder explosions issued forth as empty metallic clicks. Considerably underwhelming in both volume and effect. Seven snatched the gun from his grasp and hit him across the face with the barrel. A *pistol-whipping* as the Americans would describe Seven's savage response. The blow catapulted Gerald from his chair to the floor, a bloody gash striping his face. He squirmed away from Seven, clinging to the floor like a wounded animal, finally stopping to cower, fearful and whimpering on a sumptuous red rug.

Seven presented six bullets in her palm. "You would have

shot me five times without even asking my name Gerald. That doesn't bode well, certainly not in terms of our unfolding relationship. And I do feel in a sense already acquainted with you Gerald. I know exactly who you are and what you do. I read everything you hold secret in the safe, all 10,019 pages. I suspect I have already seen far too much, but I have to ask, is there anything you would care to add in mitigation?"

"If you have read the documents you will understand my role to be relatively minor. I simply co-ordinate. My job is organisation, logistics, moving..." Gerald hesitated, "items from one location to another. That is all."

Seven stepped over his torso and pistol-whipped him again. Gerald screamed with pain.

"Please don't underestimate me Gerald. I am not in any particular hurry with my questions. The doors are securely locked and we both know this room to be highly soundproofed. It was always designed for use by the security services and you are a lot more than a mere coordinator to occupy an office such as this. King and Country have done you proud Gerald, but I'm not interested in any of that. Tell me about your role within the other organisation. The one with sweet shops at the seaside. Would you care to try a little harder this time? Or do you require more pain?"

Despite the blood and discomfort Gerald summoned a sneer. "You have no conception of who we are. This has been in the planning for generations, my Father, his Father before him. We are committed. The families are united in blood. The *Left Hand Path* will triumph just as before. History will mark this time as a new beginning. The moment is ours. For you and your kind it is already too late. We have broken Europe and Russia. Very soon we will have the world."

Seven frowned. "Grandiose plans for world domination are

hardly anything new Gerald, but why do you need to make children suffer?"

Gerald adopted an expression of deep disdain. "You clearly have no understanding. This is no idle fancy. We follow a line that traces back across the aeons. We strive to bring about what needs to be. We will invert your frail, moral perspective. We will commit the most egregious sins, indulge in the most heinous acts and crimes. We will undermine everything you perceive to be good. And believe me, it will be wonderfully easy to recruit as much fresh blood as we need. Once the plebs understand what we have to offer, a maelstrom of sex and violence and power. We will make armies from our legions of followers, the initiates. Through degradation and perversion we will teach redemption. A new age of glory will descend upon the Earth. This is what has been foretold." Gerald paused to sniff contemptuously. "You seem not to know as much as you think you know. *'Blessed be he that permits the forbidden.'* 1666 would be a good place to start if you really seek the truth." Gerald's face twitched with a painful grimace of satisfaction.

"1666. Hmm. You are actually the second person to recommend that year as a point of interest, I will certainly investigate, but on a different note Gerald, there would seem to be some obfuscation on your part. My kind? Who are my kind?"

"The populace. The proletariat. The sheep who follow the rules. Our rules." Gerald replied with a note of triumph.

Seven laughed. "Thank you Gerald. Really, I mean it. You accept me as a member of the populace without question. You have no idea how much that gratifies me. However, I do take exception to being labelled as being part of any herd. I am an individual Gerald and this is something I have only recently come to appreciate. We can all be individuals, that is our right. But I suspect you and your organisation pay little heed to individuality, to our human rights, quite the opposite." In a flourish

Seven snatched at the grand curtains and brought the entire rail crashing down in an avalanche of fabric, plaster, and metal. Gerald saw his moment, but Seven was faster and his scramble to the door ended with a blow to the back of the neck. He crumpled in a heap on the polished oak parquet. With binding from the curtain, Seven bound Gerald's hands and feet, and by securing together two tasseled curtain pull-chords, she created a secure thirty-foot hangman's noose. The buzzer on the inner door began to sound repeatedly along with a red light flashing with urgency above the doorframe. Seven listened to the concern of the staff gathering on the other side of the inner sanctum. Gerald was beginning to stir. "Why is Frank so important Gerald?" Seven asked lightly.

He frowned a bloody creased frown. "Frank? Jacob Frank?" He uttered, and that was enough. Seven tied one end of the rope to the foot of the giant atlas and with the noose wrapped tight around Gerald's neck she lifted and flung his flailing body feet first through the picture window with the stunningly patriotic view. Glass and wood shattered in a glorious eruption of translucent crystal shards and splintered frame. A fittingly dramatic fanfare to celebrate Gerald's maiden flight. His rapid descent on the end of a rope abruptly stopped as the globe crunched solid to the window frame, stretching and snapping his neck in a blink. A twisted image of the palace at the end of the Mall was the last thing Gerald ever saw. Within seconds the inner doors to Gerald's office burst open and a throng of ministry personnel poured in. Seven observed the shock and disbelief in their expressions with some satisfaction. An almost imperceptible "hmm," spilled from her concealed form as Seven walked from Gerald's office, unseen in her suit's stealth mode. No one noticed. All attention was on the twitching curtain rope anchored to a trapped globe suspending the body of the Director of Secret Operations, Sir Anthony G. Hawksley.

Dangling in space from a shattered window in Admiralty
Arch.

SEVEN HAD no need to travel far in the energy-draining stealth
mode. The carpet bag was exactly where she had left it several
hours earlier in the lady's cloakroom. Seven dressed quickly and
made sure her makeup was up to close inspection. With her wig
and stylish *Parisian Lady* outfit in place, she rejoined the throngs
of alarmed and animated staff. The corridor buzzed with whispers and rumours.

"They say it was murder?"

"I heard it was a suicide?"

"Have you tried leaving the building at all?"

"Not a chance, every exit and entrance is sealed tight."

Seven hadn't anticipated this level of commotion, certainly
not sealed exits. She considered the incriminating contents of
the safe in her bag. The basement was the only option for a
discrete exit. She made her way to the bottom of the service
stairs and found herself in a long corridor 210 meters in length.
There were many rooms leading off, but on Ambrose's sketch, x
marked an emergency exit at the far end of the corridor. But the
corridor itself was otherwise a dead end and she could easily be
trapped. Seven made haste, time was of the imperative. She tried
to move at pace, but her clothes, the skirt, the shoes, the stock-
ings — argh — they all conspired against her. Every garment
was designed to impede rapid motion. She reached a halfway
point in the tunnel when a voice shouted an instruction. It
echoed with the insistence of authority down the shiny walls.

"Hey there! Miss. Excuse me. You shouldn't be down here.
Stop!" And the owner of the voice began to run after her.

There was no option, Seven lifted up her skirt and ran.

Within seconds the door at the end of the corridor stood before her, the nanoparticles did their job and sprang the lock. She stepped through and quickly refastened the door. Seven stood in a goods reception area, there was no outer door, but there was an exit, a padlocked loading hatch opening to the street above. It took just minutes for Seven to make her way from the basement to the road overhead, and only seconds more for the bots to dutifully reconfigure the padlock to the outside. Seven heard the agent pounding his fists in frustration on the hatch. She allowed herself to smile, but she couldn't be complacent. Seven moved swiftly through the rapidly assembling and excited crowd filling the area. They gathered to witness the sensational spectacle of a hanging man. Apparently a toff. Photographers were busy lining up their shots and rickety tripods, this was a sight Londoners and the world were keen not to miss. Perfect. Seven made her way down the Mall walking against the flow of public tide. Seven cautiously looked back. She saw the agent, the one who chased her, but now with another man. They were talking to members of the public and clearly searching. Seven was in no doubt she had become the object of their quest. She moved deeper into the park seeking the cover of trees and shrubs, and once clear, Seven hoisted up her skirt again and made haste. By the time she reached her destination, the drinking fountain in St James Park, she was quite breathless.

"Hello Cherie. Everything you requested is waiting for you in the green Harrods bag on the other side of that wonderfully grandiose bush. The shrubs here are quite private, I did check, but I wouldn't dally darling. You would seem to have stirred something of a hornet's nest." Saffron winked knowingly at Seven.

When she emerged some moments later Seven had returned to the taut comfort of her beloved leathers. The elegant French lady went into the carpet bag to be duly packed away.

"Are we ready for the off Cherie?" Asked Saffron, pulling a pair of leather goggles over her eyes.

"There's no point in hanging around." Observed Seven returning the wink. She wondered if her comment was humorous? Saffron laughed and put her thumbs up. The two ladies in tight black leather fired up their twin Brough Superiors with a defiant roar and headed at a steady pace down the Mall, away from the clamour of Admiralty Arch. Far too many folks hanging around.

"Where are we going?" Saffron shouted above the noise of the engines.

"Paris Saffron. Paris will be the start. Nous allons vivre *les Années folles*."

EVERY JOURNEY DOES INDEED HAVE a beginning and Seven had a hundred years of song to explore as she traversed the splendid, wide roads of France. She exulted in her first personal song selection, a recommendation from Frank, it had achieved five stars on his *play-list #1*. '*I'm Every Woman*' filled her mind, a glorious affirmation of the divine feminine, a concept that resonated through every fibre of her being. It started with simple humming, but soon Seven was singing, trading phrases with her first favourite vocalist, Whitney Houston. Life felt good in this twentieth year of the Twentieth Century, especially when you had an inside line to the tumultuous events of the road ahead.

EPILOGUE

There was no doubt Frank and the *porta-med* saved her. Frank uncovered the location of the two utility packs and transponder from her waking mind and with the assistance of Ashfield's Commer van, Frank retrieved the precious twenty-third century bundle from Swanage Moor. The rest is known.

Except for the transponder.

On the night before she left the house in Princes Street, Seven was preparing to bury the device in the Fairbrother garden when she noticed Frank had switched the beacon off. Seven frowned, but she quickly understood. Best leave it that way. There was work to do and they had no need of complications from the future. One of those spontaneous smiles formed. Time was still very much on their side.

Printed in Great Britain
by Amazon

82992322R00185